THE FLYING SQUADRON

By the same author

VOYAGE EAST: A CARGO SHIP IN THE 1960s

WAGER (a novel)

Nathaniel Drinkwater novels

AN EYE OF THE FLEET

A KING'S CUTTER

A BRIG OF WAR

THE BOMB VESSEL

THE CORVETTE

1805

BALTIC MISSION

IN DISTANT WATERS

A PRIVATE REVENGE

UNDER FALSE COLOURS

THE FLYING SQUADRON
Richard Woodman

JOHN MURRAY

For the crew of the cutter
Grace O'Malley
in gratitude

© Richard Woodman 1992

First published in 1992
by John Murray (Publishers) Ltd.,
50 Albemarle Street, London W1X 4BD

The moral right of the author has been asserted

A catalogue record for this book is available from the British Library

ISBN 0–7195–5074–2

Typeset in 12/13 pt Baskerville by Wearset, Boldon, Tyne and Wear
Printed in Great Britain by
The University Press, Cambridge

Contents

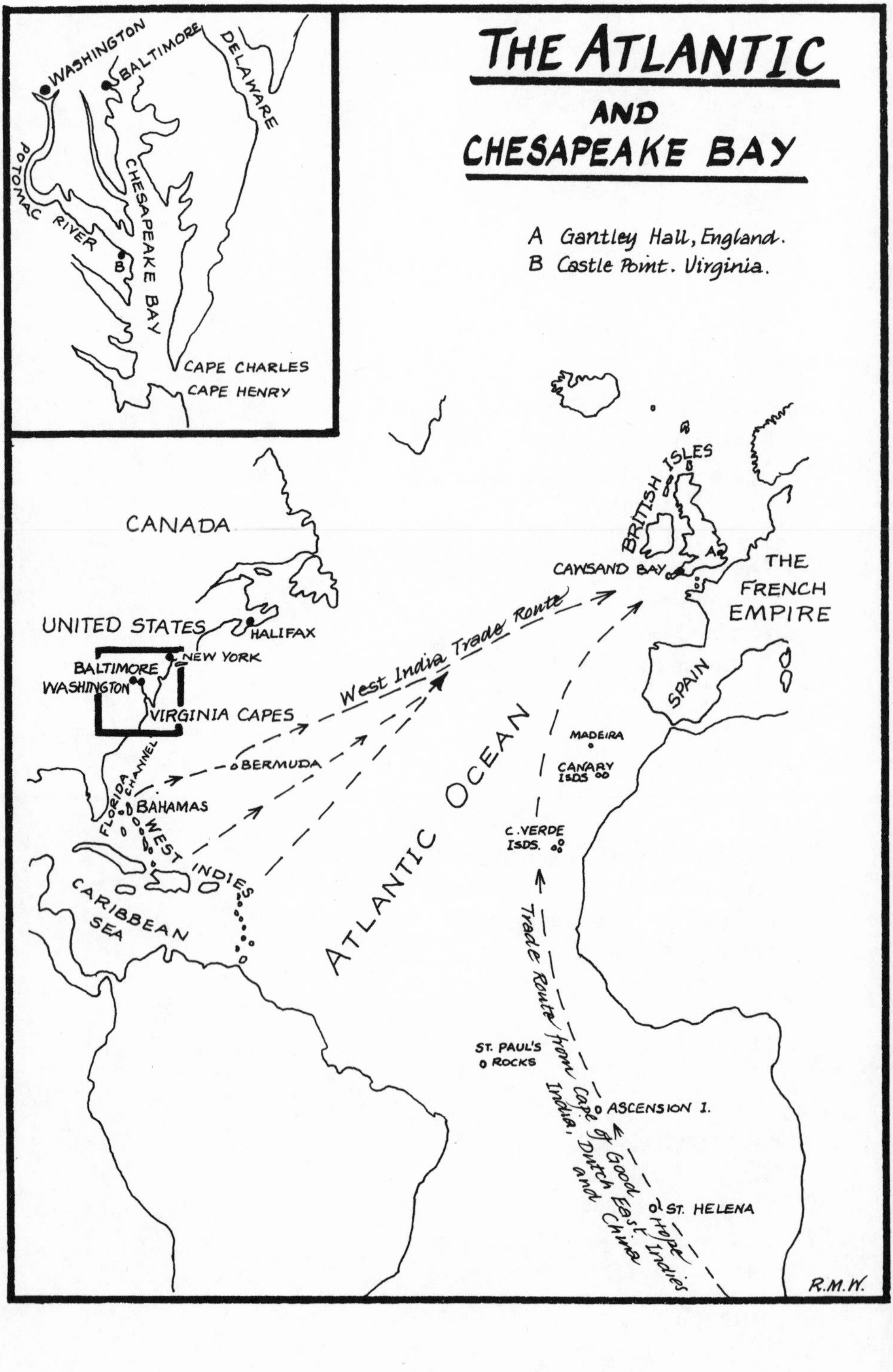
THE ATLANTIC
AND
CHESAPEAKE BAY
A Gantley Hall, England.
B Castle Point. Virginia.
WASHINGTON
BALTIMORE
DELAWARE
POTOMAC RIVER
CHESAPEAKE BAY
B
CAPE CHARLES
CAPE HENRY
CANADA
UNITED STATES
HALIFAX
NEW YORK
BALTIMORE
WASHINGTON
VIRGINIA CAPES
FLORIDA CHANNEL
BERMUDA
BAHAMAS
WEST INDIES
CARIBBEAN SEA
West India Trade Route
ATLANTIC OCEAN
BRITISH ISLES
A
CAWSAND BAY
THE FRENCH EMPIRE
SPAIN
MADEIRA
CANARY ISDS
C. VERDE ISDS.
Trade Route from Cape of Good Hope
India, Dutch East Indies
and China
ST. PAUL'S ROCKS
ASCENSION I.
ST. HELENA
R.M.W.

PART ONE

Hawks and Doves

'You will have to fight the English again . . .'
NAPOLEON

The knock at the door woke Lieutenant Frey with a start. His neglected book slid to the deck with a thud. The air in the wardroom was stiflingly soporific and he had dozed off, only to be woken moments later with a headache and a foul taste in his mouth.

'Yes?' Frey's tone was querulous; he was irritated by the indifference of his messmates, especially that of Mr Metcalfe.

'Beg pardon, sir.' Midshipman Belchambers peered into the candle-lit gloom and fixed his eyes on the copy of *The Times* behind which Mr Metcalfe, the first lieutenant, was presumed to be. He coughed to gain Mr Metcalfe's attention, but no flicker of life came from the newspaper, despite the two hands clearly holding it up before the senior officer's face.

Frey rubbed his eyes and sought vainly for a drop of wine in his glass to rinse his mouth.

'Sir . . .', Belchambers persisted urgently, continuing to address the impassive presence of Mr Metcalfe.

'What the devil is it?' snapped Frey, running a finger round the inside of his stock.

Relieved, Belchambers shifted his attention to the third lieutenant. 'Cap'n's gig's approaching, sir.'

Glaring at the newspaper, Frey rose, his fingers settling his neck linen. He kicked back his chair so that it scraped the deck with an intrusive noise, though it failed to stir the indifference of his colleagues. Piqued, he reached for coat and hat.

'Very well,' he said, dismissing Belchambers, 'I'll be up directly.'

From the doorway, as he drew on his coat, Frey regarded his colleagues in their post-prandial disorder.

Despite the bull's eyes, the skylight shaft and the yellow glow of the table candelabra, the wardroom was as ill-lit as it was stuffy. At the head of the long table, leaning back against the rudder trunking, Mr Metcalfe remained inscrutable behind his newspaper. Mr Moncrieff, the marine officer, was slumped in his chair, his pomaded head thrown back, his mouth open and his eyes shut in an uncharacteristically inelegant posture.

Ignoring the midshipman's intrusion, the master, his clay pipe adding to the foul air, continued playing cards with the surgeon. He laid a card with a snap and scooped the trick.

'Trumps, by God,' grumbled Mr Pym, staring down at his own meagre hand.

Wyatt, the master, grinned diabolically through wreaths of puffed smoke.

Frey looked in vain for Mr Gordon, but the second lieutenant had retired to his cabin and only Wagstaff, the mess-servant, reacted to Frey's exasperated surveillance, pausing expectantly in his slovenly shuffling as though awaiting rebuke or instruction. Frey noticed that there was little to choose between his filthy apron and the stained drapery which adorned the table. With an expression of mild disgust Mr Frey abandoned this scene of genteel squalor with something like relief, and retreated to the deck, acknowledging the perfunctory salutes of the marine sentries *en route*.

Emerging into the fresh air he cast a quick look about him. His Britannic Majesty's frigate *Patrician* lay at anchor in Cawsand Bay. The high blue arch of the sky was gradually darkening in the east behind the jagged, listing outline of the Mewstone. The last rays of the setting sun fanned out over the high land behind Cawsand village. Already the stone houses and the fish-drying sheds were indistinct as the shadow of the land crept out across the

4

water. The still depths of the bay turned a mysterious green, disturbed only by the occasional plop of a jumping mullet and a low swell which rolled round Penlee Point, forming an eddy about the Draystone.

In contrast to the stifling air below, the deck was already touched with the chill of the coming night and Frey paused a moment, drinking in the pure tranquillity of the evening.

'Boat 'hoy!'

The bellow of the quarterdeck sentry recalled him to his duty. He settled his hat on his head and walked to the ship's side.

'Patrician!'

The answering hail brought some measure of satisfaction to Mr Frey. The stark, shouted syllables of the ship's name meant the captain was aboard the gig and, in Frey's opinion, the captain's presence could not occur soon enough.

More marines, the side-boys and duty bosun's mates were running aft to take their stations. Tweaking the sennit-covered man-ropes so they hung handily down the frigate's ample tumble-home on either side of the steps, Belchambers raised two fingers to his hat-brim.

'Ship's side manned, sir; Cap'n coming aboard.'

'Very well, Mr Belchambers.'

Frey watched the distinctive blue and white paintwork of the gig; the oars rose and fell in perfect unison. As the oarsmen leaned back, the bow of the boat lifted a trifle and Frey caught sight of Captain Drinkwater alongside the coxswain. There was another figure too, a civilian by the look of his garb. Was this the mysterious passenger for whom, it had been intimated, they were waiting?

A second boat crabbed out in the gig's wake. She was larger, with an untidy clutter of gear in her waist and a consequently less synchronous movement of her oars. Midshipman Porter had a less sure hand upon the tiller of the overloaded launch as it visibly struggled towards them. Frey rightly concluded it had left Dock Town hard well in advance of the gig and had been overtaken.

He stood back in his place as the gig ran alongside and a moment later, as the shrilling of the pipes pierced the peaceful stillness, Frey touched the fore-cock of his hat and Captain Drinkwater hove himself to the deck.

For a moment, as the pipes completed their ritual shrieking, Drinkwater stood at the salute, his eyes swiftly taking in the details of the deck. At last the tremulous echoes waned and faded.

'Evenin', Mr Frey.'

'Evening, sir.'

Drinkwater stood aside and put out a hand.

'Come, sir,' he called back to the civilian in the boat who stared apprehensively upwards. 'Clasp the ropes and walk up the ship's side. 'Tis quite simple.'

Frey suppressed a smile as Drinkwater raised his left eyebrow a trifle. The side party waited patiently while the man-ropes jerked and a young man, elegantly dressed in grey, finally hauled himself breathlessly on to the deck. Frey regarded the stranger with interest and a little wonder. The cut of the coat was so obviously fashionable that it was difficult not to assume the newcomer was a fop. Aware of the curiosity aroused by the contrast between the somewhat grubby informality of Frey's undress uniform coat and the attire of his companion, Drinkwater gave his guest a moment to recover his wind and gape about. Turning to the third lieutenant, Drinkwater asked, 'First Lieutenant aboard, Mr Frey?'

'Here, sir.'

Metcalfe materialized by magic, as if he had been there all along but chose that precise moment to forsake invisibility.

'We'll get under weigh the moment the wind serves.'

Metcalfe cast his eyes aloft and turned nonchalantly on his heels, his whole demeanour indicating the fact that it was a flat calm. 'Aye, aye, sir . . . when the wind serves.'

Frey, already irritated by the first lieutenant's idiosyncratic detachment, watched Captain Drinkwater's reaction to this piece of studied insolence with interest and anxiety.

'You take my meaning, Mr Metcalfe?' There was the hint of an edge to Drinkwater's voice.

Metcalfe completed his slow gyration and met the cool appraisal of his new commander with an inclination of his head.

6

'Perfectly, sir. May I remind you the ship still wants thirty-seven men to complete her establishment. The watch-bill . . .'

'Then, sir,' snapped Drinkwater with a false formality, 'you may take a party ashore when the launch is discharged and see what the stews of Dock Town will yield up.'

Frey noted the irritation in Drinkwater's tone as he turned back to the young man in grey.

'Mr Vansittart, please allow me to conduct you below, your dunnage and servants will come aboard from the launch directly . . .'

Frey nodded dismissal to the side party and exchanged glances with Midshipman Belchambers. They were, with Mr Comley the boatswain and Mr Maggs the gunner, the only officers remaining from *Patrician*'s last commission. Despite the drafts from the guardships at Plymouth and Portsmouth, the pickings of the Impress Service sent them by the Regulating Officers in the West Country and the sweepings of their own hot-press, they remained short of men.

Patrician had been swinging at a buoy in the Hamoaze when Captain Drinkwater had first come aboard and read his commission to the assembled ship's company. Her officers had regarded with distaste the mixture of hedge-sleeping vagrants, pallid gaolbirds, lumpish yokels and under-nourished quota-men who formed too large a proportion of the people. Afterwards Lieutenant Gordon had spoken for them all: ''Tis hands of ability we want, seamen, for God's sake,' Gordon had continued despairingly, 'not mere numbers to fill slots in a watch-bill.'

'That's all you're going to get,' said Pym the surgeon, having inspected them for lice, the lues, ruptures and lesser horrors, adding with some relish, 'a first lieutenant who slept in the ship would be an advantage . . .'

It was not, Frey thought, as Drinkwater and the grey-coated gentleman disappeared below, a very propitious start to the new commission. An absentee first luff, a crew of farm hands and footpads, with what looked like a diplomatic mission, did not augur well for the future. Mr Metcalfe had appeared eventually, in time to throw his weight about while they had completed rigging, warped alongside the hulk and taken in powder and shot. He had a talent, Frey had observed as they dropped down to the anchorage at Cawsand, for a dangerous inconsistency which threatened to set the ship on its ears and kept its unsettled, ignorant and inexpert company in a constant state of nerves.

Mr Metcalfe was of the opinion efficiency manifested itself in proportion to the number of officers disposed about the deck and the orders given. He believed any transgression or failure should be corrected, not by instruction, but by abuse and punishment. Tactful attempts by the mild and sensitive David Gordon to point out the folly of this procedure brought down the wrath of Mr Metcalfe on the unfortunate head of the second lieutenant.

Out of Metcalfe's hearing Moncrieff had shrewdly observed it a matter of prudence to 'keep the weather gauge of Mr Metcalfe. He wants at least one of you Johnnies betwixt himself and trouble.' And failing to see the light of any comprehension in his messmates' eyes in the aftermath of Metcalfe's humiliation of Gordon, he had added, 'to keep his own yard-arm clear, d'you see, and the smell of himself sweet in his own nostrils.'

The quaintness of Moncrieff's assertion had imprinted itself on the minds of his listeners and Mr Wyatt had affirmed the opinion as sound by a loud and conspicuous hawking into the cuspidor.

Sadly, the first lieutenant had had his way, for the mysteries of 'official business' had kept Captain Drinkwater ashore almost continuously until this evening and Frey had not enjoyed his commander's absence.

'Frey?' The peremptory and haughty tone of Metcalfe's voice cut aptly into Frey's train of thought.

'Sir?' He looked round.

'You heard the Captain, Frey. You and Belchambers are to take the launch and scour the town for seamen. Try the village there,' Metcalfe said, in his arch tone, nodding at Cawsand where the first faint lights were beginning to show in the cottage windows.

'Aye, aye, sir.' Frey's acknowledgement was flat, formal

and expressionless. There were no seamen to be had in Cawsand, nor within a night's march into Cornwall. They might pick up a few drink-sodden wretches in the dens of Dock Town, but he was not optimistic and was disappointed in Drinkwater's suggestion that anything practical might be achieved. He was about to walk away when Metcalfe spoke again.

'And Frey . . .'

'Sir?'

'Let me know', Metcalfe said with a pained and put-upon look, 'when the Captain is coming aboard next time.'

'The midshipman reported the boat's approach to you in the wardroom.'

'Don't be insolent, Frey, you don't have the charm for it and it ill befits you.'

Frey bit off a hot retort and held his tongue, though he was quite unable to stop the colour mounting to his cheeks. Beyond Metcalfe's shoulder he could see Captain Drinkwater had returned to the quarterdeck.

'I know you served in the ship's last commission,' Metcalfe went on, oblivious of the captain's approach, 'but it don't signify with me, d'you see?'

'Mr Frey.' Drinkwater's curt voice came as a relief to Frey.

'Sir?'

Metcalfe swung round and saw Drinkwater. 'Ah, sir, I was just directing Mr Frey to take command of the press . . .'

'I told you to deal with that, Mr Metcalfe. Mr Frey has another duty to perform.'

'Indeed, sir, may I ask what?'

Drinkwater ignored Metcalfe, addressing Frey directly, over the head of his first lieutenant. 'The launch has, in addition to Mr Vansittart's personal effects and two servants, a large quantity of cabbages, Mr Frey. See they are got aboard and stowed carefully in nets. I want them exposed to the air.'

'Cabbages, sir?' said the first lieutenant, his face registering exaggerated astonishment, 'Are they your personal stores?'

'No, Mister,' Drinkwater said, a note of asperity creeping into his voice, 'they are for the ship's company.'

The captain swung on his heel; Metcalfe stared after him until he was out of earshot.

'Rum old devil, ain't he, Mr Frey?' and the remark shocked Frey for its shift of ground, betraying the inconsistency he had already noted in Metcalfe, but striking him now as deeper than mere pig-headedness.

Frey did his best to keep his voice non-committal. 'Excuse me, sir, I've my duty to attend to.'

'Ah, yes, the cabbages,' Metcalfe said, as though the earlier invitation to complicity had never passed his lips. Lapsing into an almost absent tone he muttered, '*Two* servants, damme,' then, raising his voice he bellowed, 'Mr Belchambers! Lay aft here at the double!'

The King's Messenger

Captain Nathaniel Drinkwater hauled himself up the companionway against the heel of the ship and stepped on to the quarterdeck. Clapping one hand to his hat he took a quick reef in his billowing cloak with the other and made his way into the partial shelter of the mizen rigging.

'Morning, sir.' The third lieutenant approached, touched the fore-cock of his hat and added, quite unnecessarily, 'A stiff breeze, sir.'

'Indeed, Mr Frey.' Drinkwater stared aloft, at the whip of the topgallant masts and the flexing of the yards. The wind had veered a touch during the night and had hauled round into the north-west quarter. He knew from the tell-tale compass in his cabin that they were making a good course, but he knew also that the shift of wind would bring bright, squally weather. The first rays of the sun breaking above the cloud banks astern of them promised just such a day.

'Let's hope we've seen the last of that damned rain and sea fret,' Drinkwater said, turning his attention forward again, where the bow swooped, curtseying to the oncoming grey seas.

Two days west of the Scillies, clear of soundings and with a fine easterly wind giving them the prospect of a quick passage, the weather had turned sour on them, closed in and assailed them with a head wind and sleeting rain.

'Treacherous month, August,' Mr Wyatt the master had

said obscurely. In the breaks between the rain, a thick mist permeated the ship, filling the gun and berth decks with the unmistakable stink of damp timber, bilge, fungus and human misery. The landsmen, yokels and town labourers, petty felons and vagrants swept up by either the press or the corruption of the quota system which allowed substitutes to be bought and sold like slaves, spewed up their guts and were bullied and beaten into the stations where even their puny weight was necessary to work the heavy frigate to windward.

In his desperation to man the ship, Drinkwater had written to his old friend, Vice-Admiral Sir Richard White, bemoaning his situation. *You have no idea the Extremities to which we are driven in Manning the Fleet Nowadays. It matches the worst Excesses of the American War. We have every Class of Person, with hardly a Seaman amongst them and a large proportion of Men straight from Gaol . . .*

Sir Richard, quietly farming his Norfolk acres and making the occasional appearance in the House of Commons on behalf of a pocket borough, had written in reply, *My Dear Nathaniel, I send you Two Men whom you may find useful. Though both should be in Gaol, the one for Poaching, the other for Something Worse. I received your Letter the Morning they came before the Bench. Knowing you to be a confirmed Democrat you can attempt their Reformation. I thus console my Guilt and Dereliction of Duty in not having them Punished Properly according to the due forms, &c, &c, in sending them to Serve their King and Country . . .*

Drinkwater grinned at the recollection. One of the men, Thurston, a former cobbler and of whom White had insinuated guilt of a great crime, was just then helping to hang a heavy coil of rope on a fife-rail pin at the base of the main mast. About thirty, the man had a lively and intelligent face. He must have felt Drinkwater's scrutiny, for he looked up, regarding Drinkwater unobsequiously but without a trace of boldness. He smiled, and Drinkwater felt a compulsion to smile back. Thurston touched his forelock respectfully and moved away. Drinkwater was left with the clear conviction that, in other circumstances, they might have been friends.

As to the crime for which Thurston had been condemned, it was said to be sedition. Drinkwater's enquiries had elicited no more information beyond the fact that Thurston had been taken in a tavern in Fakenham, reading aloud from a Paineite broadsheet.

Sir Richard, not otherwise noted for his leniency, had not regarded the offence as meriting a prison sentence, though conditions in the berth deck were, Drinkwater knew, currently little better than those in a gaol house. Thurston's natural charm and the charge imputed to him would earn the man a certain esteem from his messmates. Prudence dictated Drinkwater keep a weather eye on him.

Drinkwater watched the bow of his ship rise and shrug aside a breaking wave. The impact made *Patrician* shudder and throw spray high into the air where the wind caught it and drove it across the deck to form a dark patch, drenching Thurston and the party of men with whom he went forward.

Frey crossed the deck to check the course at the binnacle then returned to Drinkwater's side.

'She's holding sou'west three-quarters west, sir, and I think another haul on the fore and main tacks will give us a further quarter point to the westward.'

'Very well, Mr Frey, see to it.'

Drinkwater left to Frey the mustering of the watch to hitch another fathom in the lee braces and haul down the leading tacks of the huge fore and mainsails. He looked over the ship and saw, despite eight months in dockyard hands, the ravages of time and long service. His Britannic Majesty's frigate *Patrician* was a cut-down sixty-four-gun ship, a class considered too weak to stand in the line of battle. Instead, she had been *razéed*, deprived of a deck, and turned into a heavy frigate.

A powerful cruiser when first modified, she had since completed an arduous circumnavigation under Drinkwater's command. During this voyage she had doubled Cape Horn to the westward, fought a Russian seventy-four to a standstill and survived a typhoon in the China Seas. A winter spent in home waters under another post-captain had further tested her when she had grounded in the Baie de la Seine. Refloated with some difficulty she had subsequently languished in dock at Plymouth until recommissioned for special service. Her prime qualification for this selection was her newly coppered bottom which, it was thought, would give her the fast passages Government desired.

'Well, we shall see,' Drinkwater thought, watching the sunlight break through the cloud bank astern and suddenly transform the scene with its radiance, for nothing could mar the beauty of the morning.

The grey waves sparkled, a rainbow danced in the shower of spray streaming away from the lee bow, the wave-crests shone with white and fleeting brilliance, and the details of the deck, the breeched guns, the racks of round shot, the halliards and clewlines coiled on the fife-rails, the standing rigging, all stood out with peculiar clarity, throwing their shadows across the planking.

The sails arched above them, patched and dulled from service, adding their own shadows to the play of light and shade swinging back and forth across the wet deck, which itself already steamed under the sun's influence.

Drinkwater felt the warmth of the sunshine reach him through the thickness of his cloak, and with it the sharp aroma of coffee floated up from below. A feeling of contentment filled him, a feeling he had thought he would not, *could* not, experience again after the months of family life. He wished Elizabeth could be with him at that moment, to experience something of its magic. All she knew was the potency of its lure, manifested in the frequent abstraction of her husband. He sighed at the mild sensation of guilt, and at the fact that it came to him now to mar the perfection of the day, then dismissed it. A great deal had happened, he reflected reasonably, since he had last paced this deck and been summoned so peremptorily to London, what, a year ago?

Then he had been in the spiritual doldrums, worn out with long service, seeing himself as the scapegoat of government secrecy and hag-ridden with guilt over the death of his old servant Tregembo in the mangrove swamps of Borneo. He had thought at the time that he could never surmount the guilt he had felt, and had accepted the mission to Helgoland in the autumn of 1809 with a grim, fatalistic resignation.

But fate, in all things capricious, had brought him through the ordeal and, quite providentially, made him if not wealthy, then at least a man of comfortable means. True, he had been ill for some months afterwards, so reduced in spirits that the doctors of Petersfield feared for him; but the care of his wife, Elizabeth, and the kindness of old Tregembo's widow Susan, their housekeeper, finally won their fight with the combination of the blue devils, exposure and old wounds.

With the onset of summer Drinkwater and Elizabeth left the children in the care of Susan Tregembo and travelled, spending Christmas at Sir Richard and Lady White's home in Norfolk where their children, Charlotte-Amelia and their own Richard, had joined them. It had been a memorable few months at the end of which Drinkwater's convalescence was complete. It was from the Whites' house that Drinkwater wrote to the Admiralty soliciting further employment. Nothing came of his application, however, and he was not much concerned. The short, cold winter days of walking or riding, of wildfowling along the frozen salt-marsh, were pleasant enough, but the luxury of the long, pleasurable evenings with Elizabeth and the Whites was not lightly to be forsaken for the dubious honour of a quarterdeck in winter.

'You'll only get some damned seventy-four blockading Brest with the Black Rocks under your lee, and some damn fool sending you signals all day,' White had mistakenly consoled him. For although Drinkwater did not have the means for an indefinite stay ashore, nor the inclination to consider his career over and to be superseded by the back-benches of the House of Commons, life was too pleasant not to submit, at least for the time being, to the whim of fate.

Games of bezique and whist, the sound of his daughter's voice singing to Elizabeth's accompaniment, the warmth of White's stable and the smell of fresh meat from the kitchen had served to keep him content. Elizabeth was happy, and that alone was reward enough. He had played with Richard, Montcalm to his son's Wolfe as they re-fought the capture of Quebec above a low clay cliff undercut by the River Glaven. Richard, a year senior to

White's boy Johnnie, died spectacularly in his young friend's arms with victory assured as Drinkwater himself expired uncomfortably among the crackling stalks of long-dead bracken.

He had led his daughter out at the New Year ball and seen her eyed by the local bloods, flinging her head up and laughing, sometimes catching her lower lip in her teeth as he had first seen Elizabeth do in an apple orchard in Cornwall thirty years earlier. And best of all, he had lain nightly beside his wife, moved to acts of deep affection, a poor acknowledgement of her gentle constancy.

Nor had this idyll been rudely terminated by the intrusion of duty. In the end it had been crowned with an unexpected event, a circumstance of the utmost felicity for them all.

Two days into the new year, as the spectre of reaction began to show its first signs with the planning of arrangements to return the children to their home in Hampshire, White received an unexpected letter from solicitors in Ipswich. Sir Richard had inherited a small estate betwixt the Deben and the Alde, a remote corner of Suffolk lying east of the main highway north from the county town, within sight of the desolate coast of Hollesley Bay and comprising one modest house and two farms. The estate had once formed part of the lands of a dispossessed priory, the ruins of which stood romantically in its north-west corner.

'It sounds delightful,' said Elizabeth over breakfast, as Catherine White explained the lie of the land and Sir Richard scratched his head and pulled a face.

'Too damned far, m'dear,' he explained, 'no good to me. Belonged to a cousin o' mine. Eccentric fellow; built the place but never married. House can't be more than three years old.' White picked up the letter again, searching for a fact. 'They found him dead in a coppice, frozen stiff, poor devil.'

They had fallen silent, sipping their chocolate with the spectre of untimely death haunting them.

Later, as Drinkwater and White drew rein atop a low rise that looked west to the Palladian pile of Holkham Hall gilded in the sunshine of the winter morning, Sir Richard had turned in his saddle.

'It's the place for you, Nat . . .'

'What is?' asked Drinkwater, staring about momentarily confused, his mind having been fully occupied with his mount and the need to keep up with his host.

'Gantley Hall. I can't keep the place, damn it; have to sell it. What d'you say? Make me an offer.' And he put spurs to his big hunter and cantered off, leaving Drinkwater staring open-mouthed after him.

And so, after a visit in perfect spring weather when the red-brick façade glowed in the afternoon sun and the young apple trees were dusted with the faint, lambent green of new buds, Elizabeth pronounced herself delighted with the house. Less easily satisfied, Drinkwater had interviewed the sitting tenants in the two farms and voiced his doubts.

'If I return to sea, my dear, how will you manage?'

'Well enough, Nathaniel,' Elizabeth had said, 'as I have always done in your absence.'

'But an estate . . .'

'It is a very modest estate, my dear.'

'But . . .'

His protests were brushed aside and they concluded the treaty of sale. By midsummer they had removed from Hampshire and brought with them Louise Quilhampton, Elizabeth's friend and companion; her son, Lieutenant James Quilhampton and his wife Catriona migrated with them, renting a house in Woodbridge, content to enjoy married life until, like Drinkwater himself, necessity drove James to petition the Admiralty for another posting.

For Drinkwater the summons had come too early, but the letter was a personal one, penned by John Barrow, their Lordships' Second Secretary, whose attitude to Captain Drinkwater had, hitherto, been cool.

It transpired that Drinkwater's success in Hamburg and Helgoland* had rehabilitated his reputation with Barrow. Behind the Second Secretary's phrasing Drink-

*See *Under False Colours*.

water perceived the shadow of Lord Dungarth, head of the Admiralty's Secret Department, and although his new posting did not derive from Dungarth but from the Foreign Office, he was not insensible to his Lordship's backstairs influence:

... To Conduct with all possible Dispatch the Bearer, Mr Henry St John Vansittart, to the shores of Chesapeake Bay, Providing Him with such Comforts and Necessities as may appear Desirable, to Land and Succour Him and Render Him all such as may, in the circumstances, be Appropriate ...

Thus ran his instructions and thus far his duty had been light, for poor Vansittart proved a miserable sailor and had yet to make a single appearance at Drinkwater's table. Perhaps, mused Drinkwater, stirring himself and beginning a slow promenade between the windward hance and the taffrail, the seductive aroma of coffee would finally tempt the unfortunate man from his cot.

Reaching the after end of his walk Drinkwater nodded at the stiffening marine sentry posted at the quarter to heave the emergency lifebuoy at any sailor unfortunate enough to fall overboard. For a moment he stood watching the sea birds quartering their wake.

Frey pegged the new course on the traverse board and met Drinkwater as he turned forward again.

'West sou'west, sir,' Frey announced with an air of triumph.

'Very well,' Drinkwater nodded, recalled to the present. He wanted a quick passage, not so much to conform to their Lordships' orders as to avoid the equinoctial gales blowing up from Cape Hatteras. After discharging his diplomatic duty he was under orders to return Mr Vansittart to London and had high hopes of seeing in the new year of 1812 with his family at Gantley Hall, even, perhaps, returning some of Sir Richard White's generous hospitality.

There was also the question of James Quilhampton, who looked to Drinkwater for interest and advancement. They had discussed the possibility of his serving under Drinkwater, but the matter had been compromised by the appointment of Metcalfe to the *Patrician*. Besides, Quilhampton had had independent command of a gun-brig and itched again for his own quarterdeck, no matter how small. The career of His Majesty's gun-brig *Tracker* had terminated suddenly in capture, and though cleared by a court-martial, Quilhampton wanted nothing more than to prove himself.*

Drinkwater could only support his friend's ambition and promise to do what he could, leaving Quilhampton to enjoy the favours of his bride for a little longer.

But there were more immediate and pressing matters to consider, matters upon which all these wild and selfish speculations depended. To these Drinkwater now gave his attention.

'How are the men shaping up in your opinion, Mr Frey?'

'You know how it is, sir. At the moment the old hands delight in showing the landsmen their superiority and in frightening them with their antics aloft.'

'Aye, I've seen the conceit of the t'gallant yard monkeys.'

'In a day or two they'll tire of that and begin to complain that all the labour falls on their shoulders.'

'Once we run out of fresh food, I expect,' Drinkwater added.

'Yes, sir,' Frey thought of the cabbages stowed in the boats on the booms and the rupture they had caused between himself and the first lieutenant. Relations between Mr Metcalfe and himself were not cordial.

'Happily this passage should settle most of them into the ship's routine and teach them their business,' Drinkwater went on, thinking of White's caution. 'Thank heavens we ain't keeping watch and ward off Ushant with the Black Rocks under our lee and the guns at St Matthew contestin' the point every time we stick our nose into Brest Road . . . Good Lord . . .'

Drinkwater broke off, excused himself and walked forward as the pale figure of Vansittart appeared, rising cautiously from the companionway.

'Good mornin', Vansittart. How d'you fare today?'

Vansittart drew a dank lock of hair back from his

*See *Under False Colours.*

19

forehead, looked upwards and caught sight of the swaying mastheads. Frey saw him swallow and seize the rail with white knuckles.

'Stare at the horizon, man,' Drinkwater snapped sharply, catching hold of him. 'Come, sir, walk to the rail. There, 'tis easy once you have the knack of it.'

Beneath their feet the deck bucked as *Patrician* slammed into a wave. Vansittart staggered, but kept his balance and reached the bulwark. Sweat stood in beads upon his face and he slowly shook his distressed head.

'Dear God, Captain, if I had known . . .'

'The horizon, sir, keep your eyes on the horizon.'

The four men at the frigate's double wheel wore broad grins. Two of them, landsmen manning the after wheel, had been in a similar condition a few days earlier. They chuckled with the relish of the relieved.

'Mind your steering there,' Frey growled, suppressing his own amusement. He regarded Vansittart's stained and unbuckled knee breeches, the rumpled stockings, loose stock and revolting shirt. The contrast with his first dandified appearance aboard *Patrician* was most marked, the more so since his ensemble was the same. Such disregard for his person indicated the extremity of his illness.

'You *will* become accustomed to the motion, I promise you,' Drinkwater was saying, 'but you must have some breakfast.'

'Zounds, sir, no breakfast, I beg you . . .'

Drinkwater turned, his eyes twinkling. 'Pass word for my steward,' he ordered, and when the man made his appearance, said, 'Mullender, bring some cushions on deck.'

Solicitous for his guest, Drinkwater had them placed on the inboard end of a quarterdeck gun-truck and helped Vansittart ease himself down on to them.

'An hour sitting in the sunshine and you'll have an appetite like a midshipman, Vansittart. Now heed what I say and keep your eyes on the horizon . . . good man.'

Vansittart mumbled his thanks and Drinkwater left him. One bell was struck forward as Drinkwater paused at the top of the companionway.

'I'm goin' below to break my fast, Mr Frey. When the watch changes and you're relieved, give Mr Metcalfe my compliments and tell him we'll exercise the guns during the forenoon.'

'Aye, aye, sir.'

'And keep an eye on our guest,' he added in a low voice.

'Beggin' yer pardon, sir,' the quartermaster asked Frey when the captain had gone, 'but who is 'e?' The man jerked his head at the crumpled figure sitting miserably on the gun-truck.

'Mr Vansittart's a King's Messenger,' Frey explained.

'Bloody 'ell! Can't 'is Majesty find someone more fit to the task, sir?' The old man dropped his voice and muttered, for the benefit of his companions at the wheel, 'Reckon 'e's proof the King's bleedin' barmy.'

Roast Pork and Politics

'Fire!'

Beside him, Drinkwater was aware that Vansittart winced for the eighth time, shocked by the concussion of the starboard battery which was now, after the fourth broadside, almost simultaneous in its discharges.

'Very well, Mr Metcalfe, you may secure the guns and pipe up spirits.' Drinkwater turned to Vansittart who had earlier expressed a wish to 'see the cannon fired'.

'I'm afraid, sir, you'll have little option,' Drinkwater had said at breakfast when he had announced his intention of exercising the gun-crews. 'When we clear for action the bulkheads will be removed and your cabin will cease to exist.'

Vansittart's look of mistrust, of being wary in his nautical inexperience of being mocked, had amused Drinkwater. But so it had proved, and the transformation of the ship had astonished Vansittart. The secluded comfort of his small but neatly appointed cabin was suddenly invaded by a gang of barefoot and grinning seamen even before the bosun's mates had finished their dreadful squealing at the hatchways and while the marine drummer still rattled his snare drum in the ruffle that signalled the ship was beating to quarters.

Volubly protesting, Vansittart's valet Copford had scooped up his master's silver-mounted mirror and brushes, his jade pomade pot and writing-case, together with his books, papers and dispatch box, before the coarse hands of the seamen threw them unceremoniously into a spare chest Mr Gordon, just then officer of the watch, had thoughtfully sent down. The chest of drawers and washstand vanished before Vansittart's eyes and he was left contemplating two huge, 24-pounder cannon of whose existence he had only hitherto been vaguely aware. At that moment, sent from the quarterdeck above, Mr Midshipman Porter had plucked at his sleeve.

'Captain's compliments, sir, and would you care to join him on the quarterdeck.'

It sounded neither complimentary, nor a question; beneath its formal veneer it was a command and it irritated Vansittart. He had only just mastered seasickness; now the wretched comforts of what passed at sea for civilization had been rudely snatched from him and this greasy, red-faced boy was dancing impatiently round like an imp.

'Damn it,' he began, choking the protest off in a masterly effort to retain his *sang froid* before Porter. He had nowhere else to go and he was now being rudely jostled as the powder monkeys ran about the place and the seamen round the guns stretched tackles and hefted rammers and sponges. Mr Gordon appeared, his hanger bouncing belligerently upon his left hip, gesticulating, Vansittart observed, with a hand wanting two fingers. The normally mild officer had a gleam in his eye that lent force to his 'If you please, sir . . .' which dissolved into a shout at his gunners. 'Clear away there, starbowlines, look lively and beat those lubbers to larboard.'

'Careful, damn your eyes,' snarled Porter at a passing landsman who slopped water from his pail over Vansittart's feet. 'This way, sir...'

And Vansittart bowed to the inevitable and allowed himself to be drawn, squelching miserably in sodden shoes, on to the quarterdeck.

For three-quarters of an hour he wondered what all the fuss had been about. On deck, he could no longer see the main batteries properly, though he caught glimpses of activity beneath the boat booms in the waist. The upperdeck gunners manning the quarterdeck 18-pounders seemed to squat idly round their guns for some time while

23

a tirade of shouted orders in which the clipped voices of Frey and Gordon, each in charge of a 24-pounder battery on the gun deck, were interspersed with shouted exhortations from Mr Metcalfe.

The first lieutenant's most offensive weapon was a silver hunter which he consulted with maddening and incomprehensible regularity, dictating numerous time intervals to Porter who ran after him with a slate as he went from waist to quarterdeck and back, pausing now and again to make some remark to Captain Drinkwater.

The captain appeared to take very little interest in the proceedings but stood by what Vansittart was now able to identify with some pride as the mizen weather rigging, addressing the occasional remark to Mr Wyatt, whose face bore a sort of disdain for the present activity. Vansittart knew Wyatt was specifically charged with the frigate's navigation and supposed it was some esoteric point on this to which he and Drinkwater referred.

Periodically there was an awful rumbling from below which Vansittart felt most through the soles of his feet, but it did not appear to affect the men on the upper deck. Quite mystified as to what was happening and ignored by all who might otherwise have enlightened him, Vansittart was compelled to wait foolishly for an explanation.

In the event he was saved the trouble, for after half an hour Metcalfe ran up from the waist, stared at his watch, referred to Porter's slate, muttered something to Drinkwater, and turned his attention to the quarterdeck guns.

Silence was called for and the 18-pounders that had been cleared away earlier were brought to a state of readiness. Metcalfe excitedly called out a stream of orders at which the gunners, with varying degrees of verisimilitude and enthusiasm for so dumb a show, leapt around their pieces. The cause of the rumbling was swiftly revealed as the 18-pounders were run out through their open ports. On the command 'Point!' the gun-captains kneeled beside the breeches of their brute black charges, squinted along the sights and ordered the carriages slewed, adjusting the elevation at the same time. Vansittart looked in vain for a mark, concluded correctly that it was a sham since no boat had put out from the ship, neither had she been manoeuvred, and watched with increasing fascination. Each gun-captain drew away from his gun, raised one hand in signal while the other grasped the lanyard of his fire-lock. When the row of hands had all gone up, Metcalfe yelled 'Fire!' and there was an anti-climactic click as flint sparked ineffectually against steel.

Having repeated this procedure with both quarterdeck batteries and then the half-dozen 42-pounder slide-mounted carronades on the forecastle, Metcalfe trotted back to Drinkwater.

'Very well,' Vansittart overheard the captain say, 'you may load powder.'

For the next few minutes Vansittart's ear-drums were assailed by the battering thunder of the guns. Clouds of acrid grey smoke swept over him and he was dimly aware, through the sudden, bright flashes that pierced the smoke, of dark objects hurled from the guns, first to starboard and then to larboard. At last they fell silent and Drinkwater turned towards him, the infuriatingly amused yet somehow attractive smile playing about his mouth.

'The noise disturbs you, Mr Vansittart?'

'A little, I confess,' Vansittart said, feeling more than a trifle foolish.

'They were only half-charges, don't you know, to con-serve powder. I get no allowance from the Navy Board, damn them.'

'And you fired them at no mark?' Vansittart asked in an attempt to appear knowledgeable. 'I mean you did not intend the shot to hit anything?' He thought of the black dots he had seen in the centre of the discharges.

'No, no, no, we fired at no mark and shot off nothing more offensive then the wads ...'

'But I saw ...'

'Oakum wadding, nothing more. The only ball you see, they say, is the one heading directly towards you, and I hope it won't come to that, eh?'

'Oh.' Vansittart's tone was crestfallen.

Drinkwater felt sorry for the diplomat. ''Tis too lively to try at a target. If the wind falls light I will put out a boat, but the men are untried, a mixture, rough and uncoordin-ated as is usual at the beginning of a commission. At first it is essential, a moment please . . .'

Drinkwater broke off his explanation to attend to Mr Belchambers. Vansittart could not hear what passed between them, but the midshipman's face was dark and Drinkwater's bore a look of disquiet when he turned back to resume.

'At first it is essential to ensure the gun-crews operate in a disciplined manner and serve their guns correctly. One cannot afford mistakes in the heat of battle. You have doubtless seen an excited sportsman loose off a ramrod at game birds, well the same thing may happen here. Perhaps worse. A new charge thrust hastily into an unsponged gun may result in a premature discharge in which the carriage recoils over a gun-captain engaged in clearing a vent.' He paused, then added, 'As it is, one man is suffering from crushed fingers.'

'Mr Belchambers . . . ?'

Drinkwater nodded. 'Yes, he brought me word of it. I ordered the powder largely to gratify the hands. Prolonged dumb show is useful, but nothing makes 'em concentrate like gunpowder. Now I'm doubting the wisdom of my own action.' A rueful expression crossed the captain's face and he smiled. 'A pity,' he concluded.

Drinkwater turned away. Metcalfe was hovering with his insufferable watch, demanding the captain's attention. Vansittart cast about him. Already the guns were resecured and the pipes twittered at the hatchways with their appalling raucous squealing. Suddenly, as the cry 'Up spirits!' went round the ship, Vansittart was aware of a strange buzz, as of a swarm of bees, and realized it was the ship's company, mustering for their daily issue of grog. For the first time since he had stepped on board, Mr Vansittart felt inexplicably easier about his situation.

He went below. Miraculously his cabin had reappeared. Copford was laying his toiletries on the chest of drawers. He looked white and drawn.

'Where the devil were you?' Vansittart asked.

'With the surgeon, sir. In what's called the cockpit. Full o' knives and saws it were, an' they brought some young cully down with his hand all bloody . . .'

26

It was not with the intention of holding a post-mortem that Drinkwater invited his officers to dinner that afternoon. It occurred to him that the time was ripe, both on account of the weather and the fact that the gunnery exercise had been a corporate act different from the heaving and hauling, the pumping and sheer drudgery necessary to clear the chops of the Channel. Whatever its failings, it had been the first step in shaking his crew together as the ship's company of a man-o'-war.

Looking at his officers as they silently sipped their soup, nervously adjusting to the unaccustomed luxury of his cabin, Drinkwater wondered what they feared about him, for their lack of chatter was awesome. Frey might have lightened the mood with his familiarity, but Frey had the deck and Drinkwater had not invited any representatives from the gunroom. He would break his fast with the midshipmen tomorrow morning. For the nonce it was his officers with whom he wished to become better acquainted and their present quiescence was vaguely worrying. Did he intimidate them?

It had come upon him, on recent mornings as he shaved, that he was ageing. He had no idea why this sudden realization of the obvious had struck him so forcibly. Perhaps it was the return to the cares and concerns of command after months of indolence, perhaps no more than the half-light that threw his face into stark relief as he peered at his image in the mirror. Whatever the cause, he had had a glimpse of himself as others saw him. Did that grim visage with its scarred cheek and the powder burns tattooed into one eyelid intimidate?

In repose he wondered what expression he habitually wore. Elizabeth had told him that his face brightened when he smiled. Did he not smile enough? Did he wear a perpetual scowl upon the quarterdeck?

He looked down the twin lines of officers, bending over their soup, concentrating on their manners lest it slop into their white-breeched laps. At the far end of the table Metcalfe laid his soup-spoon in his plate and Mullender loomed up at his shoulder. Others followed suit, the chink of silver upon china the only sound in the cabin, if one set aside the wracking groans of the frigate's fabric, the low grind of the rudder and the surge and hiss of the sea beneath the windows.

The handsome Gordon and the thin-faced chaplain, Simpson, the ruddy Wyatt, the elegant Moncrieff, the purser and the surgeon remained disappointingly unanimated.

'Well, gentlemen,' Drinkwater said, laying down his own soup-spoon, 'what is your judgement of the temper of the men following our exercise at the guns this morning?'

If he had hoped to bring them from their tongue-tied awkwardness by the question, he was sadly disappointed. He sensed an invisible restraint upon them, a disquieting influence, and looked from one to another for some evidence of its source.

'Come, surely someone has an opinion? I never knew a wardroom where criticism of one sort or another was not lavished upon someone.' His false attempt at levity provoked no wry grins. He tried again. 'Mr Gordon, how did the men at your battery respond?'

'Well, sir,' Gordon faltered, shot a glance at the other end of the table and coloured, coughing. The blond lick of his hair fell forward and he threw it back. 'Well, sir, they were well enough, I believe.' He was oddly nervous. 'Their timing improved. According to the first lieutenant . . .'

'They did well enough, sir, for our first exercise,' broke in Metcalfe stridently. 'The starbowlines were faster than those on the port side and loosed both their broadsides in seventy-nine seconds . . .'

Drinkwater was fascinated. The riddle, if he judged aright, was solved by the presence of Metcalfe. Yet these younger men were not intimidated by the first luff, merely silent in his company, as if to speak invited some response. Belittlement perhaps? A mild but persistent humiliation? Did they simply choose not to speak in Metcalfe's presence? Was the man a tyrant in the wardroom? He was clearly a fussy and fossicking individual. It was interesting, too, to hear Metcalfe trot out the word 'port' instead of larboard. True, its usage was gaining ground in the Service, but something in Metcalfe's tone endowed the word with fashionable *éclat*, and more than a little bombast.

'But did you mark any change in their mood, Mr Gordon?'

'You mean after the exercise as compared with before, sir?'

'Yes, exactly.' Drinkwater was aware of a faint air of frustration in his tone.

'They were ...'

'A damned sight smarter at the conclusion.' Metcalfe finished the sentence and Drinkwater detected the corporate affront passing through the officers like a gust of wind through dry grass. Moncrieff, resplendent in the scarlet of the marines, threw himself back in his chair. It might have been for the benefit of Mullender, just then serving them all with thick slices of roast pork, but conveyed a different significance to the vigilant Drinkwater.

'I thought them to be much more cheerful, don't you know. As though they enjoyed loosin' off the cannon.'

Drinkwater turned to the speaker, Henry Vansittart, sitting on his right-hand side and whose presence Drinkwater had ignored in his preoccupation. He might, he thought with sudden guilt, have prompted a conversation with poor Vansittart whom, he knew, felt gauche among these tarpaulin jacks. Vansittart's assessment was exactly what he had hoped Gordon would say, and judging from the mute nods of concurrence, was at least sensed by most of them.

'Oh, they like their bangs, all right, sir.' Wyatt's contribution fell like a brick into a still pool and Drinkwater was glad of it, inapproriate though it was. 'They'll give the Yankees something to remember, never you fear.'

'I do hope it doesn't come to that, Mr ..., oh dear, forgive me ...' Vansittart floundered and Drinkwater hoped his diplomatic skills were not demonstrated by his inability to remember the master's name.

'Wyatt, Mr Vansittart, Wyatt.'

'Of course, of course, how foolish ...'

Wyatt pronounced the name like 'fancy-tart' and thereby brought a smile to the faces of the diners. Drinkwater was sorry for Vansittart, but glad of the joke.   'I agree with Mr Vansittart,' he said, trying not to make the pronounciation of the name too obviously correct. 'As for their fighting ability, we shall see, depending upon our luck. However, we may try them at a mark if we are becalmed, which reminds me, Mr Moncrieff, your marines must be put to some target practice. Tomorrow do you let 'em loose on the bottles we empty today.'

Moncreiff opened his mouth to reply but was prevented.

'Capital idea, sir.'

'I'm glad you approve, Mr Metcalfe,' Drinkwater replied, and was delighted at catching the exchange of hastily suppressed grins between Gordon and Moncrieff. He had certainly learnt more about them than they about him.

'Perhaps, Mr Vansittart, you could enlighten us all as to the current state of relations between ourselves and the United States of America. Do I take it from your reaction to Mr Wyatt's bellicose assertion that we are anxious to avoid a conflict with our quondam cousins?'

'Damme yes, sir. Most emphatically. Whilst I don't doubt for a moment the temper of your men, it would place an insupportable burden on the Ministry to engage in hostilities with them.'

'I think it might place an insupportable burden on His Majesty's Navy,' Drinkwater added, thinking of the difficulties they had experienced manning *Patrician*.

'Aye,' put in Metcalfe, 'we have squadrons in almost every corner of the world in addition to the Channel Fleet. To raise another, or reinforce the ships at Halifax . . .'

'Plans are afoot to send Rear-Admiral York out with four seventy-fours and a brace of frigates, I believe,' Drinkwater said, 'though I agree that this would be insufficient for a blockade, and if we contemplate war then we must enforce a blockade.'

'What force is the American navy?' Moncrieff derided.

'Small, lad,' said Wyatt, helping himself to more wine, 'but they will issue letters-of-marque and have privateers shoaling like herrings.'

'Oh, come Wyatt, privateers . . .'

'Enough of 'em and they'll pick our bones clean, snap

up our trade. Don't despise the Yankees. Remember the *Little Belt*...'

'That was a damned outrage,' protested Metcalfe vehemently, alluding to the unprovoked attack made by the American frigate *President* upon the smaller British sloop, 'a deliberate provocation...'

'What tommy-rot and nonsense, it was a case of mistaken identity...'

'The principal aim of British policy', Vansittart broke in, aware that his lecture, hitherto the only means of ascendancy he had gained over the frigate's officers, had been seized by his audience, 'is to avoid provocation. That is why the offence committed by the *President* was allowed to pass...'

'To our eternal shame,' interrupted Metcalfe.

'Sometimes it is necessary to swallow a little pride, Mr Metcalfe,' Vansittart said, 'in order to guide the conduct of affairs. Some sea-officers consider themselves so far in the vanguard of matters that they rashly compromise our endeavours. Take Humphries of the *Leopard*, for instance, when he engaged the *Chesapeake*; he scarcely endeared us to the Americans.'

'Oh, damn the Jonathans,' snapped Wyatt, out of patience with the pettifoggings of diplomacy. 'They poach our seamen and must be made to spit 'em out again, given a ... what the deuce d'ye call it, Bones?' Wyatt turned to the surgeon.

'An expectorant, I think you mean,' Pym answered drily, adding, ''tis all very well to take men out of Yankee merchant ships, God knows we do it enough to our own, but to attempt to do so out of a foreign man-o'-war and then fire into her when she won't comply...'

The allusion to Captain Humphries' action provoked Wyatt further: 'That's what the buggers deserved! You call 'em foreign, by God! They were no more than damned rebels!' Wyatt protested, dividing the camp. There was a rising tide of argument into which Vansittart plunged.

'They are most certainly not, Mr Wyatt! You'll please to recall they are a legitimately established sovereign state, what ever memories you older gentlemen have of the American War.'

Drinkwater's grin was still-born; he was one of those 'older men'.

'The whole business was a shameful affair,' Vansittart went on, 'the *Chesapeake* was not in fighting trim, half her guns were not mounted and she had no cause to expect an attack . . .'

'Beyond the fact that she had British deserters on board,' Wyatt persisted sarcastically.

'Her captain surrendered,' added Metcalfe with a characteristic lack of logic lost in the heat of the dispute.

'He struck, Mr Metcalfe,' Vansittart said, and Drinkwater realized he was more than holding his own; he was enjoying himself. 'He struck, merely to avoid the further effusion of blood. It was a pity Humphries insisted on searching the *Chesapeake* . . .'

'He found *four* men,' Wyatt snapped, 'four deserters.'

Vansittart turned a contemptuous expression on Wyatt. 'The facts, Mr Wyatt,' he said with a cool detachment, 'indicate three of those men were Americans pressed into our service. Had Captain Humphries contented himself with accepting the surrender and apologizing for the dishonour he had done the American flag by his unprovoked attack, we might have thus avoided the necessity of eating humble pie in the affair of the *President* and the *Little Belt*.' Vansittart stared round the table, a smile of satisfaction playing round the corners of his mouth which he hid by delicately dabbing at it with his napkin. He had achieved a victory over these rough sea-officers and was justifiably pleased with himself. He caught Drinkwater's eye. 'I know many of you to be vexed by the case of Americans born before Independence and therefore theoretically British subjects ripe for impressment into the British fleet. But I hardly think one of you to be so mean-minded as to admit this a *casus belli*, eh?'

'I do not think the Americans will go to war over the plight of their seamen,' Drinkwater said, breaking the silence of Vansittart's triumph, 'though their politicians may make a deal of noise about it. However, there is always the danger that they may imagine us to be in a position of weakness, as indeed we are, with the army in Spain to supply. Suppose they did let loose say five hundred privateers, as Mr Wyatt suggests, to tie up our cruisers with the burden of convoys, and suppose then they attempted, as they did in the last war, to conquer Canada. I would venture to suggest the most disloyal conjecture that they might succeed.'

'Ah, sir, that', said Vansittart, holding up a wagging finger to add import to his words, 'is what concerns His Majesty's government . . .'

'Or that of the Prince of Wales,' Metcalfe interjected sententiously.

'No, sir, the Ministry remains the King's; the Prince, in his capacity as Regent, is, as it were, *in loco sui parentis.*' Vansittart's little joke was lost. The King's supposed insanity combined with his son's extravagant and profligate frivolity and the Duke of York's corruption and malpractice at the War Office, served to cast a shadow over most political deliberations.

'We should also remember Russia,' Drinkwater went on. 'She has seized Finland from the Swedes and her fleet is not to be despised . . .'

'Canada is the keystone to it all,' Vansittart said, almost waving away Drinkwater's words. 'It all depends upon whether the hawks prevail over the doves in the Yankee administration.'

'Let us hope', said the chaplain, speaking for the first time, 'that good sense and Christian charity prevail . . .'

'We always *hope* for that, Mr Simpson,' said Pym the surgeon ironically, 'and are so consistently disappointed, that did hope not spring eternal into the human breast, there would be an end to all your piety.'

A small tribute of laughter followed this and a silence fell as Mullender cleared the table. The ruined carcass of the pig lay dismembered before them. The dinner had not been entirely unsuccessful.

'It is the Orders-in-Council prohibiting trade with the French Empire which will provoke a war,' Drinkwater said. 'The Americans believe it to be an unwarranted interference with their right to trade. Their grain saved the Revolution once, in '94, and they are great boys for

33

profit ... they might yet prove a force to be reckoned with.'

The cloth was drawn and the decanter set before him. He held the lead-crystal glass against the heel of the ship. It had been a present from Elizabeth and he would be most upset if it were lost. He drew the stopper and sent the port on its slow circulation. An anticipatory silence fell upon the company.

When it had completed its circuit he proposed the loyal toast. 'Gentlemen,' he said, solemnly, 'the King.'

'The King,' they chorused.

He raised his glass a second time. 'His Royal Highness, the Prince Regent.'

They mumbled their responses and waited as Drinkwater again lifted his glass. 'And to peace, gentlemen, at least with the Americans.' He bowed towards Vansittart. 'And success to Mr Vansittart's mission.'

'Amen to that,' said the chaplain.

After the officers had left, Drinkwater motioned Vansittart to remain behind. He refilled their glasses while Mullender clattered the dishes in the adjacent pantry.

'I am glad to see you fully recovered from the sickness, Mr Vansittart, and in such good form. I am afraid they are not sophisticates where political matters are concerned.'

'I thought my presence offended them, they seemed so taciturn.'

Drinkwater laughed. 'You marked their odd behaviour then, but discovered the wrong cause.'

'I think not, Captain, though I own to that apprehension initially. It seemed to me they find Metcalfe overbearing.'

'Yes, you are right,' agreed Drinkwater admiringly. Vansittart was no fool, though there was no point in dwelling upon the subject. 'As to their attitude to our present assignment, they have been too closely bred to war and would delight in licking what they consider to be the upstart Yankees.'

'You have reservations, Captain?'

'I am old enough to have served in the last American

war and, in a lifetime of service, have found it to be a foolish man who underestimates his adversary.'

Vansittart nodded, his face suddenly wise beyond his years, borne down by the responsibility of his task.

'You are more than a mere messenger.'

Vansittart looked up, his eyes shrewd. He could hold his liquor too, Drinkwater acknowledged.

'Yes. It is likely that we will give ground on the matter of impressment. It will be a great *coup* for John Quincy Adams who has been alleging our perfidious actions are on a par with murder. He claims several thousand such cases and it will set a deal of lawyers pettifogging over the rules governing neutrals but . . .' he shrugged.

'Needs must when the devil drives, eh?'

'It defuses any action mediated towards Canada. You see, Captain, there is a rumour, gathered by persons close to French affairs, which suggests the Americans will claim certain oceanic rights over the Gulf Stream, and that they are approaching France for the means to build seventy-five men-o'-war . . .'

'And John Quincy Adams has been hob-nobbing with Count Rumiantsev in Russia . . .'

'How the devil d'you know about that?' Vansittart's eyebrows rose in astonishment. 'Ah, I collect: Lord Dungarth.'

Drinkwater nodded. 'He has from time to time seen fit to enlighten me.'

'He seeks to draw Russia back to the old Coalition and reaffirm an alliance with Great Britain again.'

'Yes.' Drinkwater thought of the dropsically obese, one-legged man whom he had first known as a dashing young first lieutenant in the war with the American rebels a generation earlier. 'He has devoted his life to the defeat of the French.'

'It is not entirely that which prompts this appeasement of the Americans, nor the news of Adams and the Russians combining against us. The truth is that a halting of trade with America is having a bad effect on our industries. The mercantile lobby is active in Parliament and though the Luddites are hanged when caught, their cause cannot be thus easily suppressed. Public disorder',

Vansittart said, leaning forward slightly and lowering his voice confidentially, the exaggeration betraying a degree of insobriety, 'is currently tying down more regiments of light dragoons then the French are in Spain.'

Drinkwater knew of the frame-breaking riots. Skilled unemployed men, deprived of their trades by new-fangled machines, had taken the law into their own hands and the law had fought back with its customary savage reprisals. He thought of the Paineite, Thurston, occupied somewhere about the *Patrician*.

He refilled Vansittart's glass. 'So politics are again guided by expedience, eh, Vansittart?' he said. He raised his own glass and stared at the dark ruby port, then looked directly at his young passenger.

'D'you reckon you can do it?'

'Not a doubt, Captain. They shouted loudest about sailors' rights, whatever their true motives. We'll concede that point and all will be well.'

'But for one thing,' Drinkwater said, squinting at his glass again, 'which I doubt you have taken into account.'

'Oh? And what is that?'

'It will encourage our men to desert.'

CHAPTER 3   August 1811

A Capital Shot

In the hermetic life of a ship the smallest matters assume an unreal importance. This is often the case when a voyage has just begun, as with His Majesty's frigate *Patrician*, during the process of shaking down, when men thrown together under the iron rule of naval discipline jostle each other for the means by which to express themselves, to keep and maintain their own sense of identity.

The obligations of duty combined with those of dutifulness to suppress the natural instincts of the officers in a subtler and more dangerous way than among the ratings. The stuffy formalities and the rigid, pretentious hierarchies mixed uneasily with a cultivated and assumed languor in the wardroom. The officers were fortunate in having their cabins. Convention permitted private retreat, but while this was more civilized, it tended to prolong the incubation of trouble.

Elsewhere, on the berth and gun decks, men frequently abused each other and came quickly to blows. Such explosions were usually regulated by the lower deck's own, inimitable ruling, and while fights were swift and decisive, they were rarely bloody or degenerated into brawls. The bosun's mates and other petty officers charged with the maintenance of order knew how far to let things go before intervening.

The midshipmen's berth, by its very proximity and open location in the orlop, generally knew about these disturbances, but a tacit and unspoken agreement existed between the men and the younkers, for the latter too often had recourse to their own fists.

While the officers festered in their differences and disagreements, the fights held in the semi-secret rendezvous of the cable tiers provided a cause for betting and gaming, as much natural releases for men pent up within the stinking confines of one of His Britannic Majesty's ships of war, as the catharsis felt by the protagonists themselves.

The tiny, insignificant causes of disorder, whether in the wardroom, the gunroom or the berth deck, fuelled the ship's gossip, or scuttlebutt. Their triviality was rarely a measure of their importance. This lay chiefly in their ability to rouse sentiment and cause diversions.

In the case of Mr Frey's dislocation with Mr Metcalfe, it united the wardroom almost unanimously behind the third lieutenant. *Almost* unanimously, because Mr Wyatt refused to take sides, his coarse nature impervious to aesthetic considerations, while Mr Simpson the chaplain pretended a charitable neutrality, though Metcalfe's manner deeply offended him.

It was this strained atmosphere that the officers took with them to dinner with Captain Drinkwater and although they might have left it behind them in their commander's presence, it was Metcalfe's peculiar comments about the captain which prevented this. The cause of the trouble had been nonsensical enough. Mr Frey, during his afternoon watch below, had spread a sheet of paper on the wardroom table upon which he was executing some water-colour sketches. He had brought a large number of pencil drawings back from the *Patrician's* circumnavigation. Some of these had been of hydrographic interest and had been worked up, overlaid with washes, and submitted to the Admiralty. Their lordships had expressed their approbation and Frey, by way of diversion as much as seeking further approval, had decided to embellish all his folio of drawings, many of which were competent and fascinating records of the frigate's sojourn on the coasts of China and Borneo. They ranged from a spirited representation of an attack on the stronghold of piratical Sea-Dyaks and the horrors of a typhoon to dreamy washes showing the Pearl River under calm, grey skies, the background pierced with the exotic spires of pagodas and the foreground filled with the bat-winged sails of junks tacking up under the high poops of anchored Indiamen.

Returning from some roving inspection, Metcalfe had entered the wardroom and sat without comment in his customary chair. Tipping it back on its rear legs against the heel of the ship he nonchalantly threw both feet upon the table. One heel rested upon, and tore, the corner of a sheet of Frey's cartridge paper. Frey looked up from his work with brush and paints. 'If you please, sir . . .' he said, at which Metcalfe adjusted his feet and succeeded in extending the tear. Instead of the margin of the paper being damaged, the washed-over drawing was ripped still further.

In the argument which followed, Frey was constrained by his subordinate rank and his outrage, which made him almost mute with indignation. Metcalfe protested Frey had no business 'covering the whole damned table with rubbish', and compounded his vandalism by picking up the drawing by a corner. Already old and browned at the edges, the paper tore completely in half as he held it for the inspection of the others. Frey went deathly pale.

'Have a care, sir . . .' he breathed almost inaudibly and Moncrieff, suddenly alerted to the seriousness of a situation which warranted a challenge, rallied to Frey's support. He lamented the first lieutenant's carelessness and when Metcalfe rounded on him, damning his insolence, Moncrieff coloured dangerously and put his hand on his empty hip.

'By God, sir, had you done that to me I should have drawn upon you,' he hissed as Simpson came forward to restrain him and Pym emerged from his cabin to stare over his glasses at Metcalfe.

The first lieutenant continued to bluster and Simpson expressed regret that Metcalfe had not the manners to apologize. The consensus of opinion had gathered against Metcalfe. He resorted to a damning of them all for being the captain's lickspittle and reviled Captain Drinkwater for an incompetent tarpaulin officer who, by his very age, was barely fit to command a frigate, had been passed over for a line-of-battle ship and clearly deserved no better than to be commander of the glorified dispatch-boat that the *Patrician* had become. This irrational outburst astounded the officers. They stood silent with disbelief as Metcalfe's bravado ran its erratic course and he finally slammed out of the wardroom.

For a moment nobody moved, then Frey began to put his paints and paper away and, as always, the routine of the ship reasserted itself. The watch was called, and Frey prepared to go on deck.

'Thank you, Moncrieff,' Frey said as the marine officer bent and retrieved half the water-colour sketch, 'I mean for your support.'

'I can't take the measure of the man,' Moncrieff said, puzzled and staring at the closed door of the wardroom, 'what does he hope to gain by such conduct?'

Frey shrugged. 'I don't know.'

'You kept your temper very well, Mr Frey,' put in the Reverend Simpson, 'under somewhat extreme provocation.' The chaplain's thin, soft fingers had reached out for one of the sketches. 'These are really very good . . . but not worth fighting over.'

'I collect Mr Metcalfe's distempered spirit may be something to beware of, gentlemen. Well, we are expected for dinner . . .'

Frey cooled off during his watch, his anger subsiding to mere annoyance. He regretted being unable to dine with Drinkwater but could not have sat at the same table as Metcalfe that afternoon. Nor could he, at the end of his watch, return to the wardroom where Metcalfe, being a creature of predictable habit, would be drinking a glass of wine. At such times, the man was at his most truculent and critical, and habitually found some small matter to complain of, a gun in one's battery untidily lashed, a rusty round-shot in the garlands, or a seaman upon whom some misdemeanour could be pinned but in which his divisional officer was implicated. It was remarkable, Frey reflected, how in so short a time Metcalfe has impressed his generally unpleasant character upon the ship.

Resolved not to return to the wardroom, Frey decided instead to visit Midshipman Belchambers in the gunroom on the pretext of giving him some instruction. Immediately upon descending to the gloom of the orlop he realized his mistake. The surprised and furtive looks of men about him, the quick evasive slinking away and the whispered warning of a commissioned presence seemed to Frey's overwrought nerves to echo into the dark recesses of the ship with a sinister significance. Off-duty marines in their berth just forward of the midshipmen's den stopped polishing boots and bayonets. The midshipmen themselves wore expressions of guilt and Frey was just in time to see a book snapped shut, a pencil hurriedly concealed and a stack of promissory notes swept out of sight. He caught Mr Midshipman Porter's eye.

'What are you running a book on, Mr Porter?'

'Er, a book, sir? Er, nothing, sir . . .'

Frey looked about him. The collusion of the midshipmen argued against anything serious being wrong. He had not disturbed a mutinous assembly and would be best advised to turn a blind eye to the matter.

'Mr Belchambers?' he said, affecting a disinterested tone, 'Is he here?'

'First Lieutenant sent for him, sir.'

'Ah . . .' Frey cast a final look round the dark hole. The stale air was thick with the stink of crowded humanity, stores, bilge-water, rust, rot and rat-droppings. He retreated to the ladder.

'Pass word for Sergeant Hudson, will you,' he called mildly to the marine sentry at the companionway. Frey dawdled in the berth deck, wandering forward. Hudson caught up with him as he stood surveying the surviving pigs in the extempore manger just forward of the breakwater set across the ship to stop sea sloshing aft from the plugged hawse-holes.

'Sir, Mr Frey, sir?' The marine sergeant puffed up, buttoning his tunic and jerking his head. Men in the adjacent messes, alerted to something unusual by Frey's presence so far forward, made themselves scarce.

'Hudson, what the devil's going on below?' Frey pretended interest in the pigs and spoke in a low but insistent voice.

'Below, sir? Nothing, sir . . .'

'Don't take me for a fool, Hudson. Something is, or has been going on. When the officers were dining with the captain, I suspect.'

'Ah, well, er, yes, sir . . .'

'Go on.'

'Well, sir, weren't nothing much, sir, only a bit o' fun, like.'

'Gaming, you mean?'

Hudson shrugged. 'Well, a few side bets, sir, you know how it is.'

'On what? Baiting? A fight, a wrestle?'

'Bit of wrestling, sir. Nothing to worry about, sir. If it were I'd be down on it like a cauldron o' coal.'

Frey looked hard at the man. 'If I get wind of an assembly, Hudson, I'll have your hide. We want no combinations aboard here.'

Hudson shook his head and Frey noticed the man had no neck, for his whole body swung, adding emphasis to his indignant refutation of the suggestion. 'No fear o' that, sir, not while Josiah Hudson is sergeant aboard this here man-o'-war.'

'I hope you're right, Hudson.'

'O' course I'm right, sir. 'Tis against regulations in the strictest sense but, well, why don't you place a bet, sir? Won't do no harm and I'll do it for you. You won't be the only officer . . .' Hudson paused, aware he was being indiscreet.

'Really? Who else?' Frey disguised his curiosity.

'Oh, *I* don't know that, sir, but one or two o' the young gennelmen seems to have enough money to be acting as agents.'

The information robbed Frey of the initiative. He turned aft. At the wardroom door he met Mr Belchambers in search of him.

'I believe you were looking for me, sir.'

'Oh, yes, but it don't matter now. Carry on.'

'Aye, aye, sir.'

Belchambers turned for the companionway when intuition caused Frey to call him back.

'What did the First Lieutenant want you for?'

Belchambers stammered uncertainly, his eyes on the wardroom door and the sentry posted there. 'Oh, er, er, a small . . . er, private matter, sir.'

'A private matter between you and the First Lieutenant, Mr Belchambers?' Frey said archly. 'You should be careful your private affairs are not capable of misconstruction . . .'

Belchambers blushed to the roots of his hair. 'I, er, I . . .'

'Did he win?'

'Sir . . . ?'

'Did the First Lieutenant win? I assume you had been summoned to tell him whether he had won or lost the bet you had placed for him.'

Belchambers swallowed unhappily. 'Sir, I was unwilling . . .'

'Don't worry,' said Frey, his voice suddenly sympathetic, 'be a good fellow and just let Mr Porter know I am aware of the situation and I've promised a thrashing to anyone I find running a book.' Belchambers caught the twinkle in Frey's eye. He knew Mr Frey, he was a certainty in a shifting world. Mr Belchambers was learning that ships changed as their companies changed and though he respected Captain Drinkwater, the captain was too remote to know the miseries and petty tyrannies that midshipmen endured.

Whilst Captain Drinkwater was unaware of Belchambers' misery and knew nothing of the improper conduct of his first lieutenant as discovered by Mr Frey, he was troubled by the evident bad blood prevailing among his officers. There was little he could do about it, and at heart he was disinclined to make too much of it. They were bound on a specific mission, their cruise was circumscribed by the Admiralty's special instructions and with the Royal Navy pre-eminent in the North Atlantic he privately considered it most unlikely they would see action. Not that he was complacent, it was merely that in weighing up their chances of meeting an enemy, he thought the thing unlikely. Anyway, if he was wrong, *Patrician* was a heavy ship with a weight of metal superior to most enemy cruisers. Only a line-of-battle ship would out-gun her and she had the speed to escape should she encounter one.

Nevertheless he knew that grievances, once they had taken root, inevitably blossomed into some unpleasantness or other. He would have to wait and see what the disaffection between Mr Metcalfe and his fellow officers produced. For himself, the company of Vansittart proved a welcome diversion. The younger man was pleasant enough, and well-informed; close to Government circles he gossiped readily, though Drinkwater formed the opinion that his own connections with Lord Dungarth proved something of a passport to his confidences. Vansittart knew when to hold his tongue; his present indiscretions were harmless enough.

Mr Frey found his discovery of the secret wrestling match preoccupied his thoughts during the middle watch the following night. Metcalfe's involvement was foolish, the more so since he had implicated Belchambers, who was otherwise an honest lad. It was clear there was nothing he himself could do, though Metcalfe's unwise behaviour would, he felt sure, some time or another cause the first lieutenant to regret the impropriety of his conduct. Metcalfe was not easy-going enough to embroil himself with the dubious affairs of the lower deck. He had already had two men flogged for minor misdemeanours, and while Captain Drinkwater had been compelled to support his subordinate he had passed minimum sentences upon the men concerned.

It was, Frey consoled himself, none of his business, but with that peculiar importance events assume in the small hours of the night, he felt a strong compulsion to probe further into the matter. In the end he waited for Belchambers to make his report at six bells. As the bells struck and the lookouts and sentries called 'All's well' from forecastle, quarter and gun deck, the midshipman of the watch came aft, found Frey in the darkness and touched the brim of his hat.

'All's well, sir, and six bells struck.'

'Very well. Tell me,' he added quickly before Belchambers turned away, 'this business of gaming in the cable

44

tier. Are all the midshipmen involved?'

'Well, more or less, sir,' Belchambers replied unhappily.

'That ain't exactly your kettle o' fish, is it, Mr Belchambers?'

'Not strictly speaking, sir, no . . .'

Frey waited in vain for any further amplification. 'Is it Porter or the First Lieutenant?'

'First Lieutenant's pretty keen, sir,' Belchambers began, as though glad of the chance to speak of the matter, then halted, trying to study Frey's expression in the gloom, failing and adding hurriedly, 'though Porter's the devil if he's crossed, sir, and . . .' He trailed off miserably.

'Have there been many of these bouts?'

'Three, sir, since we left Plymouth. There were several before we commissioned properly . . . dockyard entertainments they called them. I think one or two of the hands took the idea . . .'

'Are they always the same men who wrestle?'

'No, sir.'

'Who was it yesterday?'

'Newlyn and Thurston, sir.' The names meant nothing to Frey; neither man was in his division.

'And there are no other officers present?'

'Not present, no, sir.'

'Then other officers place bets?'

'Yes, sir.'

'Who are they, Mr Belchambers?' Frey's voice hardened in its expression and he wondered he had heard nothing of it in the wardroom.

'Mr Wyatt, sir.'

'Interesting,' remarked Frey almost casually. 'Now, there's something I want you to do for me, Mr Belchambers . . .'

'Sir?'

'Be a good fellow and let me know when there is next to be a bout, even if I'm on watch, d'you understand?'

'Yes, sir.'

There was a note of relief in Belchambers' voice, as though he felt happier for Frey's discovery and offer of alliance. Mr Belchambers trusted Frey.

'And don't say a word to a soul, d'you hear me?'

45

'No, sir, of course not.'

The morning after he had his officers to dinner, Captain Drinkwater invited the midshipmen to breakfast. They seemed a sound enough group of young men. The two master's mates, Davies and Johnson, were a little older, midshipmen waiting for promotion, and not likely to get it, Drinkwater thought, with *Patrician* bound on her run back and forth across the Atlantic and a spell tendering to the Western Squadron at the end of it.

After breakfast he sobered them just as they had begun to unwind with the news that he would inspect their journals within the week. Belchambers, used to Drinkwater's methods, brightened perceptibly. He was clearly the only member of the gunroom who had been keeping his journal up to date. The boy's expression puzzled Drinkwater, and it was not until after they had all gone with their formal and insincere expressions of gratitude that he realized Belchambers had been subdued throughout the meal. He had always been a quiet, sensitive fellow – Drinkwater recalled him fainting at the awful spectre of a deserter being hanged at *Patrician*'s fore-yardarm – but he was usually of a cheerful disposition. Had some of the wardroom malaise spilled over into the gunroom?

Drinkwater took his cloak and hat from the hook beside the door and went on deck. Moncrieff was ordering his marines up and the men were falling in for inspection. A basket full of empty green bottles clinked and the frigate rolled and pitched, her grey canvas spread to the topgallant yards as, braced hard up against the starboard catharpings, they drove to the westward with clouds of spray sweeping over her bluff bow.

Drinkwater recalled his order to Moncrieff and watched Sergeant Hudson checking his men while Corporal Bailey issued cartridge and ball for the practice shoot. Metcalfe stood by watching, having directed a pair of grinning topmen to run a flag-halliard up to the lee main topsail yardarm where they rove it through the studding sail boom and brought the end back on deck. The boom was run out, a pair of hitches thrown over the neck of an empty bottle from the basket, and a moment later it twinkled green and provocative at the extremity of the thin spar.

'Very well, Sergeant, you may drill your men. One at a time at the target. It's accuracy we want, not speed of fire, so take your time, my lads. Carry on.'

Moncrieff, having inspected his men in the belief that ineffective pipeclay and polish inhibited the true martial qualities, retreated to the mizen mast, where a knot of curious officers had assembled, forming round Vansittart who was professing himself something of a wildfowler. Frey, Gordon, Wyatt and Metcalfe watched as Hudson gave some inaudible instructions to his men, told them off in order and formed them into a rough line.

Then, one by one, they stepped up to the hammock nettings, rested their muskets on hammocks or against the iron cranes that supported the nets, took their aim and fired upwards.

Far above them the bottle danced impudently. A slight slackness in the halliard, the working of the ship and the whipping of the spar made it an extremely lively target. Of the thirty-seven privates in Moncrieff's detachment, not one succeeded in hitting the mark, though several struck the studding sail boom and one severed the down-haul of the halliard.

Each shot was keenly watched. Men on deck ceased their tasks, the midshipmen off duty emerged to stare. Every miss was met with a chorus of moans, punctuated by outraged shouts from Wyatt or Metcalfe when splinters flew from the boom. There were five misfires, which Moncrieff disallowed, nodding permission to Corporal Bailey to issue fresh cartridges. He turned to Metcalfe.

'D'your men have to stand and gawp, Mr Metcalfe? Have they nothing better to do?'

'They've nothing better to *watch*, Mr Moncrieff,' Metcalfe chortled facetiously. The marine officer turned away angrily. The first of the five marines given a second chance squinted along the barrel of his Tower musket and took aim with painstaking slowness. The watchers waited, almost holding their breath in anticipation, their good-natured mockery suspended.

'There's no need to worry about breaking this one,

Moncrieff,' Metcalfe called, spoiling his aim, 'we've a whole basket of 'em!'

The frustrated marine glared insubordinately at the first lieutenant's wisecrack. At the end of the five shots, the bottle still swung unmolested. Constrained by the presence of the captain and first lieutenant, the marines shuffled disconsolately off and fell into rank and file.

'You'd better let 'em try again, Mr Moncrieff,' Drinkwater called.

'Aye, aye, sir.' Moncrieff had coloured at his men's failure and Drinkwater heard Metcalfe make some comment to which Moncrieff returned a furious look.

'If you can do any better...' Drinkwater heard Moncrieff snarl.

As the marines reloaded, Metcalfe went below. Drinkwater had dismissed him from his mind, feeling sorrier for Moncrieff who had detached himself from the officers about Vansittart and occupied a miserable no man's land between his colleagues and his men.

'I might ask you gentlemen to try your hands in a moment,' Drinkwater called in a gesture of support for Moncrieff. The marine officer threw him a grateful glance. 'We could tighten the halliard,' he offered.

Moncrieff shook his head. 'It wouldn't be the same ,sir.'

'Perhaps not, but...'

'Thank you, no, sir. It wouldn't be the same.'

'Very well.'

The first marine stepped forward, raised his musket and fired. The snap of the lock and spurt of powdersmoke at the gun's breech transmitted itself to a short, yellow-tipped cough from the muzzle. They stared upwards at the dangling bottle. It spun from the passing wind of the ball, but it remained infuriatingly intact.

'Next!' commanded Moncrieff, superseding Hudson in his anxiety to obtain a hit.

Drinkwater was looking up at the third or fourth shot when Metcalfe reappeared on deck. It was only when these failed and he said in a loud and truculent voice, 'Haven't you succeeded yet?' that Drinkwater saw he was carrying a musket, presumably from the arms rack outside the wardroom.

'With your permission, sir?' he addressed Drinkwater, his expression arch and vaguely offensive.

'Do you ask Moncrieff, Mr Metcalfe.'

'Well, Moncrieff, will you let a fellow have a pot-shot?'

Moncrieff visibly bit off a retort. He had himself been contemplating a shot, but resisted the impulse, for to have missed would have been more irritating and, in any case, the object of the exercise was to train the men. Their shooting had been damned close for Tower muskets with a three-quarter-inch bore and balls whose casting was often more a matter of luck than precision. Let Metcalfe have a shot and damn him. He would be devilish lucky to hit the damned bottle and if he made a fool of himself, then so much the better! He nodded.

Metcalfe walked confidently to the rail, set the musket against his shoulder and raised the barrel. The bottle swung with the wind of the ball's passage and the officers and marines watching let out a hoot of triumph, for he had missed. They were all still laughing at Metcalfe's pride preceding his humiliation, when a second discharge followed. The bottle shattered, its jagged neck left at the boom-end.

Even as a suspicion crossed Drinkwater's mind, the certainty of it had been realized by Moncrieff who was already striding across the deck.

'Let me see that fire-lock,' he cried.

'It ain't a Brown Bess, for sure,' Vansittart opined stridently, moving forward with the others to discover by what malpractice Metcalfe had cheated them.

The speed and accuracy of the second shot had raised all their suspicions. Metcalfe was surrounded by the officers and Drinkwater heard the accusations rain on the first lieutenant.

'It's a damned *rifle . . .*'

'That's a Chaumette breech, damn it . . .'

'Let me see . . . the devil! 'Tis a Ferguson rifle! Where the deuce d'you get this, Metcalfe?' Metcalfe had surrendered the gleaming weapon to their scrutiny and Moncrieff now held it. The question silenced their mild and curious outrage and they stood in a circle, staring at the first lieutenant. A feeling of premonition crept over

Drinkwater as he watched these antics, marking the distastefully smug expression on the face of his second-in-command.

He heard Metcalfe utter the words 'a gift from Captain Warburton', and the mention of his predecessor confirmed his hunch.

'Sergeant Hudson,' he called, suddenly bestirring himself, and the crack of his voice stilled the curious officers examining the rifle.

'Sah!' Hudson was ramrod stiff, his body an admonition to the levity on the quarterdeck.

'There are a dozen or more bottles yet to be shivered. Another round for each of your men and try again.'

'Yes, sah!'

Recalled to his duty, Moncrieff gave back the rifle and bustled to muster his men again. The officers broke up, some still admiring the Ferguson rifle in Metcalfe's hands, others waiting and watching the marines, others wearied of the sport now the first bottle had been dispatched.

Drinkwater went below. As he reached his cabin door he growled to the marine sentry, 'Pass the word for my servant.' A minute later Mullender appeared.

'Mullender, you recollect when we were in the Pacific I had a gun, a rifle . . .'

Patiently Drinkwater awaited the slow workings of Mullender's memory.

'Aye, sir, I do. You fetched it back one day from the Californio shore,' Mullender said slowly, his brow furrowed with concentration.

'Yes, exactly. What did we do with it?'

'Well, sir,' Mullender began, stepping forward and wiping his hands on his apron, 'we stowed it in the settee locker, but . . .'

Drinkwater had the squabbed cushion beneath the stern windows off in a trice, long before Mullender could complete his explanation.

'But after you left the ship, sir, in a hurry like you did, sir, and we heard you wasn't to be coming back, sir, well, that's what we was told at the time and then Captain Warburton and his own man came and I was sent forward, sir . . .'

50

The stern locker was empty, at least of the oiled cloth package Drinkwater now clearly remembered laying there for safe-keeping. He had forgotten all about the rifle, assuming it was lost along with his journals and the polar bearskin he had left in Mr Quilhampton's safe-keeping. When Quilhampton had lost the gun-brig *Tracker*...

Above their heads the bangs of the marines' discharges were suddenly followed by a cheer: a second bottle had been hit!

'It was in here, wasn't it, Mullender? You don't recall it being removed when Mr Quilhampton took my personal effects ashore?'

'No, sir,' Mullender hung his head miserably. 'I forgot it, sir, when I packed, like, 'twas in such a hurry and Mr Quilhampton was bursting to get ashore...'

'It doesn't matter, Mullender,' Drinkwater said, leaving the puzzled steward staring after him as he took the quarterdeck ladder two at a time. Metcalfe was still on deck, the Ferguson rifle held in the crook of his arm. Drinkwater crossed the deck and confronted Metcalfe.

'That was a capital shot, Mr Metcalfe,' Drinkwater said, 'may I see your gun?'

He knew instantly he had seen the rifle before. It had once belonged to a bearded American mountain-man, a man who spent his life wandering across the vast spaces of North America and who had been shot dead at Drinkwater's feet. 'Captain Mack', he had been called, and the long-barrelled Ferguson rifle had been in his possession since he had captured it from a British officer at the Battle of King's Mountain when the gun's inventor himself suffered defeat at the hands of the American rebels. Odd how things turned out.

'If you turn the trigger guard...'

'Yes, I know.' Drinkwater dropped the guard, exposing the breech opening that facilitated the quick loading which had so impressed them all.

'The rifling makes the shot fly true,' Metcalfe tried again, and again Drinkwater quietly said, 'Yes, I know.' In addition to the rifle, Captain Mack had left half a dozen gold nuggets and with the proceeds of their sale, Captain

51

Drinkwater had purchased Gantley Hall.*

'I did not know you were so good a shot, Mr Metcalfe,' he said, handing back the rifle. 'It's a fine piece.'

Metcalfe grinned complacently. 'That is why Captain Warburton kindly presented me with it,' he explained.

'And where did Captain Warburton obtain it?' Drinkwater asked.

'I believe he inherited it, sir.'

'Did he now?'

Above their heads there was the sound of shattering glass and a thin cheer went up from the marines still at their target practice.

*See *In Distant Waters.*

The Paineite

The last of the daylight faded in the west; ahead the sky seemed pallid with foreboding, Drinkwater thought, drawing his cloak the tighter around him and shifting his attention to the upper yards. There would be a strengthening of the wind before morning.

'Very well, Mr Gordon. You may shorten down. Clew up the main course and let us have the t'garn's off her!'

'Main clew garnets, there! Look lively! Stand by to raise main tacks and sheets!'

A bank of clouds gathered darkly against the vanishing day. The twilight of sunset was always the most poignant hour of the seaman's day and, just as the small hours of the middle watch endowed trivial matters with a terrible gravity, this crepuscular hour invested thoughts with sombre shadows.

What was it, Drinkwater thought, that so troubled him? Did this daily marking of time punctuate the passage of his life? Or was it a gale he feared, rolling towards them from the vicinity of Cape Hatteras, the disaffected mood of his officers, or the poor quality of his crew? Once he would have striven with every fibre of his being to lick them into shape; this evening he felt the task beyond him. He was tired, too old for this young man's game. He should not have come back to sea, but quietly farmed his hundred acres, visited the Woodbridge horse fair and sought a pocket borough.

Damn it, he was not old! He could ascend the rigging

with the agility of the topmen now running up to douse the flogging topgallants as they thundered in their bunt-lines. There were men up there far older than himself!

No, he was disturbed by the vague shadow of a new war, for he sensed it as inevitable as much as it was incomprehensible. No matter the *pros* and *contras* of diplomacy adduced by Vansittart; no matter the crude claims and counter-claims advanced by his fire-brand officers, the fact of a war between the United States and Great Britain being in the interests of neither country was obvious. Only Napoleon Bonaparte could profit. Much might be laid at the door of *his* agents in fomenting the suspicion existing between London and Washington.

Despite these considerations, it piqued him to think he had been placed back in command of *Patrician* precisely because he was ageing. The Ministry wanted no hothead frigate captain with only a score of summers to his credit hanging off the Virginia capes, landing a diplomatic messenger on the one hand and impressing American seamen from American ships on the other. He ought to be flattered, he thought, an ironic and private smile twitching the corners of his mouth. He detested the new breed of sea-officer nurtured on victory and assumptions of invincibility. They had never tasted the bitterness of bloody defeat any more than many of them had participated in a victorious action. This current presumption of superiority was a dangerous delusion, but he had heard it expressed enough while he had been ashore in Plymouth. Thank heaven his own officers seemed relatively free of it.

Shortened down, the frigate rode easier, still standing doggedly to windward. Eight bells struck as the watch changed, and in the gathering darkness Drinkwater saw Gordon hand over to Frey. He caught the simultaneous glance of both their heads and the faint blur of their faces as they looked in his direction. He remembered so well the compound of fear and respect he had felt for most of his own commanders, all of them men with feet of clay; old Hope of the *Cyclops*, Griffiths of the *Kestrel* and the *Hellebore*.

Christ, he was morbid! Was this an onset of the blue devils? It was time to go below. Vansittart had sensibly taken to his cot the moment the weather livened up, now he would do the same. The gale would arrive by dawn, time enough to worry then. For the nonce he could drown his megrims in sleep.

And yet he lingered on, his shoulder braced against the black hemp shrouds that rose to the mizen top, feeling the faint vibration of their tension as *Patrician* harnessed the power of the wind and drove her twelve hundred tons into its teeth.

What an odd thing a ship was, he thought, curious in its component parts: fifteen hundred oaks, several score of pine and spruce trees, tons of iron and copper, miles of hemp and coir, tar, flax and cotton. Full of water and stores to support its living muscles and brains which now in part huddled about the deck and in part slung their hammocks in the corporate misery of the berth deck. Men dreaming of homes, of wives, lovers, children; young men dreaming of prize money, old men dreaming of death. Men troubled by lust or infirmities, men scheming or men hating. Men confined by the power confided by Almighty God in the Sovereign Prince King George III, mad by reputation, puissant by the force of the twin batteries of cannon *Patrician* and a thousand ships like her bore on every ocean of the globe.

And he, Nathaniel Drinkwater, post-captain in His Britannic Majesty's Royal Navy, directed this arm of policy, and took Henry St John Vansittart to *pow-wow* in the lodges of the Yankees in the vain hope of averting a war! Would His Majesty's ministers concede the real point of American objection and lift the ordinances against American trade? Or would the greater preoccupations, the maintaining of a naval blockade of Europe and the supply of a British, a Portuguese *and* a Spanish army in the Iberian peninsula, blind them to the dangers inherent in failing to appease the Americans. And if they did comply with Washington's demands, would the Americans be content to the extent of suppressing their desire for Canada?

Two bells struck; the passing of time surprised him, the watch had been changed an hour earlier. It was quite dark now, the horizon reduced to the white rearing crest of the next wave ahead as it surged out of the gloom. Drinkwater was stiff and cramped, his muscles cracked as he straightened up.

The truth was, he wanted to go home. 'Ah, well,' he muttered, 'I have that in common with most of the fellows aboard.'

His left leg had gone to sleep and he almost fell as he tried to walk. 'Damn,' he swore under his breath, hobbling to peer into the binnacle and check the course. The pain of returning circulation made him wince.

'Course sou'west by west . . .' began the quartermaster.

'Yes, yes, I can see that,' Drinkwater said testily. Frey loomed up alongside. Drinkwater was in no mood for pleasantries. 'Good-night, Mr Frey,' he said, then called dutifully from the head of the companionway, 'don't hesitate to call me if this wind freshens further.'

'Aye, aye, sir,' the young officer responded confidently. All's right with the world, Drinkwater thought, heartened by Frey's cheerful tone. Mentally cursing the megrims, he descended to the gun deck and the stiffening marine outside his cabin door.

He had no idea afterwards why he paused there. He thought it might have been a lurch of the ship which prevented him momentarily from passing into the sanctuary of his cabin; on the other hand, the marine, a punctilious private named Todd, made a smart showing of his salute and Drinkwater threw back his cloak to free his hand to acknowledge this and open the door. Whatever the cause he was certain it was no more than some practical delay, not premonition or extra-sensory perception.

Yet in that moment of hiatus he knew something was wrong. Quite what, it took him a moment to discover, but the watchful, expectant look in Todd's eyes rang an alarm in Captain Drinkwater's consciousness. He passed into his cabin and stood, his back against the door, listening.

The ship was unusually quiet.

One became accustomed to its myriad creakings and groanings. One heard instead the noises of people, from the soft murmurs of men chatting in their messes, sitting and smoking at the tables suspended between the guns, or idling on the berth deck, through the louder shouts of abuse or jocularity to the bawled orders and shrilling of pipes. The denser concentrations of humanity, like the marines' quarters or the midshipmen's so-called gun-room, produced their own noise, and the low hum generated by a watch below during the daytime was quite different from that produced, as now, when the watches below should have been asleep, or at least turned in.

What had troubled him outside his cabin door was not a total silence, but a curious modulation somewhere that was not *right*, existing alongside an equally curious *lack* of noise to which he could not lay a cause.

Irritated and a little alarmed, still cloaked though he had tossed his hat aside, he threw open the door and stalked outside. The gun deck was quiet. The men who slept there appeared to have turned in, for the few lamps showed bulging hammocks above the faintly gleaming gun breeches.

He turned abruptly and descended to the berth deck. Immediately he knew something *was* wrong. He sensed rather than saw a movement, but clearly heard the hissed caveat that greeted his intrusion. He moved quickly forward, ducking under hammocks and brushing them with his head and shoulders. Many of those slung were full and he provoked the occasional grunted protest from them, but more were empty and, with a mounting sense of apprehension, he dodged forward, aware of someone moving parallel to himself, trying to beat him but, having to move in semi-concealment, not making such light work of it.

He could hear the source of that strange modulation as he drew up beside the bitts and suddenly saw below him a press of men crowded into the cable-tier. Their faces were rapt, lit by the grim light of a brace of battle-lanterns as the listened in silence to a voice which, though it spoke in a low tone, carried with it such a weight of conviction it sounded upon the ears like a shout.

So strong was the impact of this oration that it, as much as astonishment, made Drinkwater pause to listen. In the wings of the berth deck, his shadower paused too.

'The rights of kings might be supported as an argument; nay, friends, adopted as a principle for good government were it not for the fact that it in all cases without exception reduces us to the status of subjects and, moreover, many of us to abject and necessary poverty. For to glorify one requires a court whose purpose is adulatory, if not purely idolatrous, and which, to support itself, requires the extraction of taxes from the subjected.

'Furthermore, it promotes excessive pride amongst those close to the throne. This in turn excites envy among the middling sort who, gaining as they are power in the manufactures, seek to adopt the manners and privileges of noblemen. Under the heels of this triple despotism are ground the poor, the weak, the hungry, the dispossessed, the homeless and the helpless: men, women and children – free-born Britons every one, God help them!'

Drinkwater drew back in retreat. He had not seen the speaker but knew the man's identity: Thurston, the Paine-ite, the disaffected seducer of men's minds, a suborner, a canting levelling republican subversive . . .

Drinkwater flew up the ladder and Todd snapped to attention, his face an enigmatic mask. Drinkwater had no idea whether or not the marine knew of the combination gathered in the cable-tier, but he surely must have done. Without pausing, saying nothing, but conveying much to the sentry, he sought the refuge of his cabin, his mind a whirl.

He had suspected something of the sort as he had edged forward under the hammocks. A meeting of Methodists, perhaps, even a mutinous assembly, but this, this was intolerable . . .

Why had he done nothing about it?

The thought brought him up with a round turn. The man keeping *cave* had known of his presence, if not his identity; Todd would soon let them know the captain had been down to the orlop and come up again looking as though he had seen a ghost! Good God, what was the matter with him?

And then the appalling thought struck him that Thurston spoke with an irrefutable logic. What little he knew of the Court of St James and the prancing, perfumed and

58

portentious Regent, struck a note of revulsion in his puritan heart . . .

And yet his duty, his allegiance . . .

'God's bones!' he raged. What was he going to do, flog the lot of them? Suppose the bosun's mates refused? And how could he discover who was in attendance and who had turned in? Could he punish Thurston alone, and for what? Speaking a truth that some called sedition? White had been lenient; had White caught the refreshing breath of truth and let the man escape the horrors of the law's worst excess?

'God damn them!' he snarled, finding himself at the decanter stowed in its fiddle. His hand was already on the stopper when he realized he had no time for such indulgence. He *had* to do something, something which was both everything and nothing, something that would not rouse them to spontaneous and hot-headed mutiny, for what Thurston was undoubtedly ignorant of was the fact that he might ignite something of which he was not master. Yet Drinkwater had to signify his displeasure, his disapproval and his power, in order to dissuade them from ever attempting any mass action. He realized what he faced was not mutiny, not something he could quell by summoning the marines and arming his officers. That would be desperate enough, for God's sake!

What he faced was something infinitely worse: its results would be mass desertion in the United States.

Patrician slammed into a wave and Drinkwater felt her bow thrust into the air as she climbed over it and fell into the trough beyond.

'God damn!' he swore again, with a mindless and futile anger. Then he snatched up his hat. Out on the gun deck he knew his visit had disturbed them. There was a low murmur of voices as men hurriedly turned in; he knew he had rattled them. Even if they did not know yet it was the captain who had discovered their meeting, they would guess it had been an officer.

He emerged on to the quarterdeck. All was still well there, he consoled himself. They would do nothing until they arrived in American waters. Unless, of course, they decided to seize the ship . . .

'Sir . . .' Frey began, seeing the captain unexpectedly on deck.

'Call all hands,' Drinkwater snapped, 'upon the instant, d'you hear?'

'Aye, sir . . .' An astonished Frey relayed the order and the bosun's mate of the watch piped and shouted at the hatchways.

Drinkwater drew his cloak around him, stood at the windward hance and watched them turn up.

'Sir . . .?'

'Double reef the tops'ls, Mr Frey, and look lively, a watch to each mast.' Drinkwater cut poor Frey off short and watched for Thurston. The men emerged, many of them stumbling uncertainly, torn unceremoniously from their hammocks by the shrilling of the pipes. Drinkwater was not an inhumane commander and worked his crew in three watches. To be turned up like this suggested some disaster in the offing, perhaps an enemy, and to the uncertainty of those aware their political meeting had been discovered was now to be added this element of panic.

Frey and his bosun's mate were already translating Drinkwater's order: 'Way aloft, topmen! Double reef the tops'ls! Hands by the lee braces, halliards and bow-lines. . .!'

Drinkwater had no difficulty in singling out Thurston. The man made no effort to merge inconspicuously with the mass of the people, but stood stock still for a moment, at the far end of the starboard gangway. There was no one between them, until a petty officer shoved him roughly into his station with a cut of his starter across Thurston's buttocks.

With a sudden feeling of guilt, Drinkwater turned away. Was he one of Thurston's 'middling sort', apeing the manners and seeking the privileges of a discredited nobility? Was the acquisition of Gantley Hall such an act?

'Is something the matter?'

'Eh, what?'

Vansittart stood beside him, the silk dressing-gown

flamboyant even in the darkness of a rising gale.

'Matter, Mr Vansittart?' said Drinkwater, aware of the irony of his situation, 'Why no, we are shortening sail, there's a blow coming on.'

'Oh dear. Then we are to be further delayed.'

'I'm afraid so, but this is one thing we cannot change – the weather, I mean,' he added. Vansittart shuffled away. 'My dear fellow,' Drinkwater said after him in a low, inaudible voice, 'if only you knew by what a slender silken thread the world holds together.'

Far above him men laid out to secure the reef points. Thus far he had the measure of them, and *Deo gratias*, the wind was freshening rapidly!

'Call all hands!'

Drinkwater clapped a hand to his hat as *Patrician* lurched into another wave and the resulting explosion of spray hissed over the weather bow, a fine grey cloud in the first glimmer of dawn. Jamming himself in his familiar station at the mizen rigging he waited for the men to turn up. The bosun's pipes pierced his tired brain and rang in his ears, for he had not slept a wink.

'Another reef, sir?' Lieutenant Gordon struggled up the deck towards him, his cloak flapping wildly in the down-draught from the double reefed main topsail. In the lee of the mizen rigging what passed for shelter enabled the two sea-officers to speak without actually shouting. Gordon's expectant face was visible now as the light grew.

'No, Mr Gordon. All hands to lay aft. And I want the officers and marines drawn up properly. Please make my wishes known.' Drinkwater saw the look of uncertainty at the unusual nature of the instruction cross Gordon's face. 'Do you pass the word, if you please,' Drinkwater prompted. He rasped a fist across his stubbled chin. His eyes were hot and gritty with sleeplessness and he felt a petulant temper hovering. He had spent the night wondering what best to do to stave off the trouble he knew was brewing, trouble far worse than a little bad blood between his officers. He tried to imagine what the wholesale desertion of a British frigate's crew would mean in terms of repercussions. In the United States it would be hailed as a moral victory, evidence of the rottenness and tyranny of monarchy, a sign of the rightness of the emerging cause, perhaps even fuel for the fire of rebellion certain prominent Americans wished to ignite in Canada.

For the Royal Navy itself it would be a dishonour. Already the trickle of deserters from British men-of-war had prompted the stop-and-search policy of cruiser captains, a prime cause of the deterioration in Anglo-American relations. The Americans were justifiably touchy about interference with their ships. The practice of British officers boarding them on the high seas and taking men out of them on the flimsy pretext that they had been British seamen, was a high-handed action, a deliberate dishonour to their flag and a provocation designed to humiliate them. The extent to which this arrogant practice prevailed was uncertain, as was the counter-rumour that trained British seamen made up the gun-crews aboard Yankee frigates; men who would give good account of themselves if it came to a fight, desperate men who resented having been pressed from their homes but who were, nevertheless, traitors.

In this atmosphere of half-truths and exaggeration the defection of *Patrician*'s people would be a death-blow for British hopes of avoiding war. The Ministry in London might be able to overlook the case of 'mistaken identity' which had allegedly occurred the night the USS *President* fired into the inferior *Little Belt*; it would be quite unable to extend this tolerance to the desertion of an entire ship's company. His Majesty's frigate *Patrician* would become notorious, synonymous with the *Hermione*, whose crew had mutinied and carried their frigate into a Spanish-American port, or the *Danae*'s people who had surrendered to the French. Such considerations made Drinkwater's blood run cold, not merely for himself and the helpless, humiliated and shameful state to which he would be reduced, but also for the awful disruption to the mission which would otherwise avert a stupid rupture with the United States.

He had been tortured for hours by this spectre, his mind unable to find any solution, as though he faced an inevitable situation, not something of which luck, or providence, had given him forewarning. His lurking bad temper was as much directed at himself and his lack of an imaginative response, as against the men now emerging into the dawn. In all conscience he could not *blame* them, and therein lay the roots of his moral paralysis. He devoutly wished he did not see their side of the coin, that he felt able to haul Thurston out of their grumbling ranks and flog the man senseless as an example to them all. It would tone down the upsurge of their rebelliousness.

Christ, that was no answer!

How could he blame them? Some had been at sea continuously for years. There were faces there, he remembered, who had stayed at sea when the Peace of Amiens had been signed, loyal volunteers to the sea-service, men who had made up the crew of the corvette *Melusine* when war had broken out again. They, poor devils, had had their loyalty well and truly acknowledged when turned over without leave of absence into the newly commissioning frigate *Antigone*, from which, following their captain, they had passed into this very ship in the fall of 1807. Ten years would be the minimum they would have served.

And to them must be added the droves of unwilling pressed men, come aboard in dribs and drabs from the guardships and the press tenders, but who now made up the largest proportion of *Patrician's* company. Among these came petty criminals, men on the run from creditors or cuckolds, betrayed husbands, men cut loose from the bonds of family, seeking obscurity in the wooden walls of dear old England, fathers of bastards, poxed and spavined wretches and, worst of all, those men of education and expectations whom fate had found wanting in some way or another.

What had they to expect from the Royal Navy? The volunteers had been denied leave, the pressed ripped from their homes, the fugitives and the intelligent found no refuge but the inevitable end of them all, to be worn down by labour, if death by disease or action did not carry them off first.

Nathaniel Drinkwater had faced mutiny before and beaten it, but none of this gave him much confidence, for he had been aware on each of these occasions that he had obtained but a temporary advantage, a battle or a skirmish in a war in which victory was unobtainable. And now, in addition to the catalogue of mismanagement and oppression, the Paineite Thurston had introduced the explosive constituent of something more potent than gunpowder: political logic. Clear, concise and incontrovertible, it had set France afire twenty-two years earlier; it had turned the world on its ears and unleashed a conflict men were already calling the Great War.

Drinkwater found himself again searching for Thurston; the man whom White had sent down in a rare mood of leniency, to stir up the lower deck of the *Patrician* instead of digging turnips on the shores of Botany Bay; Thurston, the man who had smiled and whom Drinkwater conceived might, in vastly different circumstances, have been a friend . . .

And yet the idea still did not seem absurd. He had known one such man before. Perhaps, he thought wildly, they were growing in number, increasing to torture liberally inclined fools like himself until, inexorably, they achieved their aim: the overthrow of monarchy and aristocracy, the reform of Parliament and the introduction of republicanism. That too had happened in England once before, and in English America within his own lifetime.

He recalled the Quaker Derrick, whose fate had been uncertain, lost when the gun-brig *Tracker* had been overwhelmed by Danish gunboats off Tönning and poor James Quilhampton had been compelled to surrender his first command. Derrick had not succeeded because he did not proselytize. Thurston was dangerously different.

God, what a train of gloomy thoughts chased each other through his weary mind! Would Moncrieff never have his infernal marines fallen in? And where the deuce was Metcalfe? Christ Almighty, what a burden *he* was turning out to be!

Why the hell had their Lordships saddled the ship with such a nonentity? He had asked for Fraser, but Fraser, his old first luff, had been ill, and Metcalfe had survived from the last commission when he had served as second lieute-

64

nant. It was true he was a good shot, but that did not make him a good officer.

'May I ask . . . ?'

'No, you may not!' Drinkwater snapped as the first lieutenant materialized in the disturbingly insinuating way he had. Metcalfe fell back a pace and Drinkwater, meanly gratified at the small humiliation thus inflicted, roused himself and stepped forward. In doing so he appeared to drive the first lieutenant downhill, a sight at once mildly comic, but also threatening. The ship's company, whatever the seductions of Thurston's republican polemic, were more certain of Captain Drinkwater's mettle than he was himself.

'Off hats, Mr Metcalfe,' he said quietly, and Metcalfe's voice cracked with sudden nervous anticipation as he shouted the command.

Drinkwater stared at the ship's company and the ship's company stared back. Some of them were shivering in the cold; some eyed him darkly, well knowing why they had been summoned; others wore the look of blank incomprehension and this was chiefly true of the officers, though one or two made a gallant attempt at pretending they knew why the lower deck had been cleared at so ungodly an hour.

Despite the rising howl of the wind, the hiss of the sea and the creaks and groans of the ship, the waist of the *Patrician* was silent. Drinkwater withdrew the small book from beneath his cloak, cleared his throat and began to read in a loud voice.

'If any person in or belonging to the Fleet shall make or endeavour to make any mutinous assembly upon any pretence whatsoever, every person offending herein, and being convicted thereof, shall suffer death: And if any person shall utter any words of sedition or mutiny he shall suffer death . . .'

The words were familiar to them all, for on the fourth Sunday of every month, in place of the liturgy of the Anglican Church, the Articles of War were read to every ship's company in commission by their commanding officer. But this morning was not the fourth Sunday in the month, not did Drinkwater read them all. He excised some of the legal provisos of Articles Nineteen and

Twenty, and cut them to their essential bone; he laid heavy emphasis on certain words and punctuated his sentences with pauses and glares at his disaffected flock. He read with peculiar and deliberate slowness, eschewing the normal mumbling run-through to which even the most punctilious captain had succumbed by the end of the routinely morbid catechism.

'If any person shall conceal any traitorous or mutinous practice or design, he shall suffer death . . . or shall conceal any traitorous or mutinous words spoken by any to the prejudice of His Majesty or Government, or any words, practice or design, tending to the hindrance of the service, and shall not forthwith reveal the same to the commanding officer, or being present at any mutiny or sedition, shall not use his utmost endeavours to suppress the same, he shall be punished . . .'

Drinkwater closed the book with a snap. 'That is all, Mr Metcalfe. You may carry on and dismiss the hands.' As Drinkwater stepped towards the companionway Moncrieff called his men to attention and, with some difficulty on the plunging deck, had them present arms.

Drinkwater must remember to thank Moncrieff for that salute; it was quick-witted of him to invest the departure of Captain Drinkwater from the quarterdeck with the full panoply of ceremony. Drinkwater devoutly hoped its effect would not be lost on the men, aware of the theatricality of his own performance. All those who had listened to Thurston's able and seductive sermon would, he believed, now be pricked by individual guilt and, as he found himself in the shadows of the gun deck, he wondered how many would report the seditious proceedings.

Not many, he found himself privately hoping. He did not yet wish for the dissolution of his crew. Only an honourable peace could permit that.

'Sir, has something occurred?'

Drinkwater laid down his pen and looked up at Metcalfe. For once the man was flustered, unsure of himself. This was a side of his first lieutenant Drinkwater had not yet observed.

'A very great deal, Mr Metcalfe.'

'But when, sir?'

'When you were asleep, or perhaps taking wine in the wardroom, I imagine.' A slight mockery in the captain's voice alarmed Metcalfe.

'But *what*, sir?' asked Metcalfe desperately and Drinkwater admitted to a certain malicious amusement at his expense.

'Tut-tut, Mr Metcalfe, can you not guess? Surely the Articles I read out were explicit enough. What does the scuttlebutt in the wardroom suggest?'

The question further confused Metcalfe, for the opinion in the wardroom, expressed fully by every officer, was that the captain, perceptive though he was, had got wind of the gaming combination, mistaken it for some sort of mutinous meeting and misconstrued the whole affair. In this conclusion, the debating officers were chiefly concerned to unhorse their overbearing mess-president, and they had succeeded, for a covert conference had been observed between Metcalfe and Midshipman Porter, after which torn pages of a note-book had been seen floating astern. Thoroughly alarmed, Metcalfe had sought this unsuccessful interview with the captain.

'Sir, I must request, as first lieutenant, you take me into your confidence.'

'That I am not prepared to do, Mr Metcalfe,' Drinkwater said carefully, aware that he felt no confidence in the man and could not bare his soul. To admit to his second-in-command that he had discovered a seditious meeting would be an admission to Metcalfe of something he wished to remain between himself and those at whom he had aimed this morning's exercise in intimidation. Besides, strictly speaking, he should report the matter to their Lordships, and to inform Metcalfe of the circumstances and subsequently do nothing would be to lay himself open to charges of dereliction of duty. He would have to tell Metcalfe *something*, of course.

But his refusal to confide in Metcalfe had struck his subordinate's conscience and, unbeknown to Drinkwater, no further explanation was necessary. Metcalfe assumed the worst as far as he, a self-interested man, was concerned. In his guilty retreat he gave up both his chance of a clue that it was not his malpractice of betting on the crew's wrestling which had caused the morning's drama, as well as Captain Drinkwater's rather ingenious explanation of why he had acted so extraordinarily.

It was to Gordon that he spoke about Thurston. The memory of the Quaker Derrick had brought its own solution; what had been done once might be done again. 'The man is in your division and seems a likely character, a man of some education and no seaman.'

'I'm afraid I know little about him, sir,' Gordon admitted.

'You should,' Drinkwater said curtly. 'Anyway, to the point. I have no clerk, and want a writer. You may send him aft at eight bells.'

As for an explanation of the morning's events digestible enough for the officers, it was Frey to whom he revealed his fabricated motive.

'It was necessary,' he afterwards told Frey as they paced the quarterdeck together that afternoon when a watery sunshine marked the passing of the gale, 'because as we approach the American coast, I wish to dissuade the men from any thoughts of desertion.'

'But you spoke only of mutiny or sedition, sir,' commented the shrewd Frey.

'I intend to spring the Articles on desertion upon another occasion. This was but a preamble.'

They exchanged glances. Frey was undeceived, and for reasons of his own he passed on this intelligence only to those whom he knew to dislike the unfortunate Metcalfe.

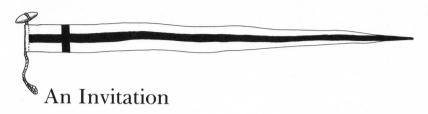

An Invitation

'By the mark thirteen!'

Drinkwater looked at the American chart. 'Very well, Mr Wyatt, you may anchor the ship.'

'Aye, aye, sir.' Wyatt raised his speaking trumpet. 'Main braces there, haul all aback!'

The knot of officers on the quarterdeck stared upwards as the main topsail and main topgallant came aback and flattened against the mast and the maintop.

'By the deep twelve!' the leadsman's chant continued. 'A quarter less twelve!'

Patrician lost what way she had been carrying in the fickle breeze blowing off the green river-banks and bringing with it the nostalgic land scents of grass and trees. The hands hauled the fore and mizen yards aback and the frigate glided to a stop, submitting to the rearward thrust of her backed sails and the current of the river. Wyatt and Drinkwater each selected a transit ashore, Drinkwater a lone tree which drifted into line with the corner of a white Palladian mansion standing majestically amid a broad and luscious swathe of grass. The two objects remained in line for a moment and then began to reverse the direction in which they had closed: their drawing apart signified that the frigate was moving astern over the ground. Wyatt caught his eye and he nodded.

'Let go the cat stopper!' Wyatt called and there was a thrumming as the short rope ran out, followed by a splash and then the vibrating rumble as the cable ran out through the hawse-holes.

The ship would take some time to bring up to her cable and Drinkwater pulled his Dollond glass from his tail pocket, levelling it momentarily at the noble house and its beautiful sweep of parkland. It made a mockery of his scrubby Suffolk acres and the homely architecture of Gantley Hall. He watched as a groom, a tall negro, brought a chestnut horse round the corner of the house from what he assumed was a stable block.

'Castle Point, Captain.'

Drinkwater was not certain whether Vansittart, resplendent in plum-coloured velvet, meant this as a statement of fact, or a query as to whether or not they had reached their destination. He swung his glass to the ship ghosting up two cables' lengths distant from them. She too followed the same procedure, backing her sails and letting go her anchor.

'Aloft and stow!'

'Aloft and stow!'

The orders were piped and called simultaneously from each ship and it was clear a race was to be made of it. The topmen leapt into the rigging, setting the shrouds a-trembling in their haste to be aloft, urged on by Metcalfe's usual loud, unnecessary exhortations and the active chivvying of the bosun's mates.

Drinkwater watched the other vessel. She was no more than a sloop, a twenty-gun ship, but at her peak, lifting languidly in the light breeze, flew the stars and stripes of the United States of America. She had laid-to athwart their hawse off the Virginia capes, her guns run out, and had sent a lieutenant across by boat demanding to know the reason for their presence in American waters. By his bluster the officer had clearly been expecting a show of arrogant truculence on the part of the British commander. It transpired that within the previous two months a pair of British frigates had been cruising off the capes, stopping and searching American merchantmen for both contraband cargoes bound for Napoleonic Europe and British deserters. Hard-pressed for men, they had inevitably poached a handful of seamen which had infuriated

Yankee opinion, disturbed the peaceful prosecution of trade and insulted the sovereignty of the United States. The *Patrician*, it seemed, appeared as another such unwelcome visitor, and this time Mr Madison's administration had seen fit to have a guardship off the capes to ward off such an impertinence, if not to challenge openly any such mooted interference with American affairs upon her own doorstep.

Much of the American officer's bluster was understandable. After the unfortunate incident between the *Chesapeake* and the *Leopard*, the British government had not reacted when the USS *President* fired into the much smaller British sloop, the *Little Belt*. The British press, however, had made much of the incident, screeching for revenge, and the Ministry's restraint must have seemed to the Americans uncharacteristic, wanting only an opportunity to reverse the odds and hammer the upstart navy of the young republic. The materialization of the *Patrician*, clearly a frigate of the heaviest class possessed by the British navy, could therefore have but one interpretation to the commander of the patrolling sloop. He had sent his first lieutenant to find out.

Drinkwater received the young man with considerable courtesy, invited him below and introduced him to Mr Vansittart, whom he had ensconced in his own cabin. There was, Drinkwater observed, a regrettable air of condescension about Mr Vansittart, trifling enough in itself, but obvious enough to provoke a reaction from the American lieutenant, whose corn-pone homeliness was laid on a little for Vansittart's benefit.

Nevertheless, Lieutenant Jonas Tucker went back to his ship with a request for Vansittart's passport to be honoured. The two ships lay-to together for half an hour within sight of Cape Charles and Cape Henry awaiting the American commander's sanction before Lieutenant Tucker returned with his senior officer's compliments. Drinkwater refused his offer of pilotage as being not consonant with the dignity of the British flag, but diplomatically accepted an escort into Chesapeake Bay.

'If you will follow our motions, sir,' Tucker had drawled, addressing Drinkwater and ignoring Vansittart, who had accompanied him on to the quarterdeck, 'and bring to your anchor here.' He unrolled a chart and Drinkwater bent to study it.

'Off Castle Point?' Drinkwater had asked.

'Just so, sir.'

Drinkwater had looked up, 'Mr Wyatt, do we have Castle Point on our chart?'

'You may have the loan of this one, sir,' said Tucker.

'Thank you.' Drinkwater had accepted the American's offer. 'We will salute the American flag, Lieutenant, immediately upon anchoring, if you will reciprocate.'

'I guess that will be an honour, sir,' Tucker had replied with insincere formality, and had taken his departure.

They had doubled Cape Charles, standing south towards Cape Henry to avoid the Middle Ground before hauling the yards and swinging north-west into the bay. Ahead the American sloop led them in. They cleared the Horse Shoe shoal and The Spit, between which the York river debouched into the bay and where thirty years earlier Cornwallis had surrendered to Washington and Rochambeau, effectively ending the American War and ensuring independence from Great Britain. They steadied on a northward course, forming in line ahead, finally entering the mouth of the Potomac and anchoring two miles below Falmouth township, off Castle Point.

The rumble of the veering cable ceased with the application of the compressor bars. *Patrician* brought up to her anchor and immediately from her forecastle the first boom of the salute reverberated around the anchorage. Clouds of pigeons rose in a clattering of wings from the adjacent woods and a flock of quacking duck and wildfowl flew up from the reedbeds fringing the river. The concussion of the gunfire echoed back and forth, returned by the classical façade of the mansion. The exact, five-second intervals between each explosion were timed by Mr Gordon, so that the twenty-one discharges sounded like a cannonade, only to be repeated and amplified by the gunners of the Yankee sloop they now knew to be the USS *Stingray*.

As the last echoes faded away, Drinkwater turned to Vansittart.

'Well, Vansittart, it's up to you now.' He paused to stare through his glass again at the American ship, continuing to speak. 'I imagine our friend will provide a boat escort, but you can take my barge up to Washington. 'Tis a goodish pull, but unless we can obtain some horses...' A solitary figure was staring back at them. Drinkwater lowered his glass and raised his hat by the fore-cock. The American commander ignored the courtesy, but continued to stare through his own telescope.

'Perhaps he didn't see you,' Vansittart consoled.

'Oh, he saw me all right,' Drinkwater replied. The thought of horses made him swivel round and refocus his glass. The Negro was walking away from the mounting block and Drinkwater was just in time to see the big chestnut break into a canter and disappear into the trees to the right of the house. He caught a fleeting glimpse of a woman in grey with a feathered bonnet riding side-saddle. 'I wonder', he remarked, 'why we have been brought to an anchor here...?'

'Even I, in my ignorance, know "goodish pull" to be something of a euphemism, Captain,' said Vansittart, grinning. 'It must be forty miles to Washington.'

'I'm glad to see our somewhat land-locked surroundings have persuaded you to recover your good humour,' Drinkwater riposted, but both men were interrupted by Midshipman Belchambers reporting the approach of a boat. Ten minutes later Lieutenant Tucker once again stood on the quarterdeck.

'Captain Stewart presents his compliments, gentlemen. He intends to let the Administration know of the arrival of Mr Vansittart himself without delay. He hopes to return shortly with the Administration's response.'

'Would he be kind enough, Lieutenant Tucker, to convey a letter from myself to Mr Foster?'

'Mr Foster, sir?'

'His Britannic Majesty's ambassador to your government,' Vansittart explained.

Tucker shrugged. 'I guess so, sir.'

'If you would give me five minutes.' Vansittart withdrew below.

'Well, sir,' Drinkwater said, attempting to fill the five

minutes with polite if meaningless small-talk, 'it is beautiful country hereabouts.'

'It sure is,' said Tucker bluntly, awkwardly adding, lest
he seem too abrupt, 'real beautiful . . .'

'Plenty of wildfowl,' said Metcalfe, coming up and
joining in with the cool effrontery he often displayed.
Drinkwater, irritated at the intrusion but equally relieved
to have his burden halved, recalled Metcalfe's expertise
with the Ferguson rifle. They were standing staring
ashore at the parkland surrounding the Palladian mansion when from the trees whence she had disappeared
earlier, Drinkwater saw the lone horsewoman reappear.
Her horse was stretched at a gallop and the plumed hat,
which he had noticed earlier, was missing. She brought
the horse to a rearing halt a pistol-shot short of the
river-bank and Drinkwater thought she was waving at
them. Beside him Lieutenant Tucker chuckled.

'Reckon Belle Stewart's just had a scare,' he remarked.
'That goddam gelding of hers must've had a rare fright
from the salutin' cannon.'

'She's shaking her fist and not waving, then,' Drinkwater said.

'She could be doin' either, Cap'n, she could be doin'
either. She might be shakin' her fist, 'n' she might not. She
might be wavin' at her brother, Cap'n Stewart, Master
Commandant of the United States Sloop o' War *Stingray*,
but then again, she might be a-shakin' it at you for a-firing
all those guns.'

'I'd say we were both equally guilty,' Metcalfe said,
matching Tucker's condescending drawl.

Drinkwater ignored the implied slight. 'Ah, I see.
Captain Stewart resides hereabouts, then,' he said, indicating the house.

'Well, not exactly resides . . . his sister does the residin',
but I guess it was in his mind to get a horse here.'

'I understand. And will that facility be extended to Mr
Vansittart, d'you think?'

'I don't know, Cap'n. Matter of fact, I don't know
exactly what's in Cap'n Stewart's mind, sir.'

Vansittart reappeared with his letter and Lieutenant
Tucker took his departure. Drinkwater, Metcalfe and

Vansittart lingered, watching the return of the American boat and then, sweeping round the sloop's stern, the departure of a second boat from the *Stingray*. She was a smart gig with white stars picked out along her blue sheerstrake. Red oars with white blades swung and dipped in the dark waters of the Potomac river. Upright in her stern stood a midshipman, hand on tiller, beside whom sat a sea-officer. He was, Drinkwater guessed, the same man who had scrutinized them from the quarterdeck of the *Stingray*. Drinkwater walked aft to the taffrail and stared down as the gig pulled close under *Patrician*'s stern. Vansittart and Metcalfe joined him. Again he lifted his hat.

The midshipman, curious about the heavy British frigate, was looking up at the three men and could not have missed the private salutation. They saw him turn and address a remark to the officer sitting next to him. No flicker of movement came from the immobile figure; he continued to stare straight ahead, just as his oarsmen, bending to their task, stared astern, over the shoulders of their officers, as if the British ship did not exist. The officer must have made some remark to the midshipman, for the boy solemnly raised his own hat.

'That's a gesture of the most sterile courtesy,' Vansittart objected.

'That, I fear, is Master Commandant Stewart,' Drinkwater concluded, 'and I hope he don't exemplify the kind of response you're going to get in Washington, Vansittart.'

Vansittart grunted.

'I collect that we should blow the insolent ass's piddling sloop out of the water while it lies so conveniently under our guns,' Metcalfe interjected, with such pomposity that Drinkwater understood the motive for his earlier intrusion. Metcalfe was eager to ingratiate himself with Vansittart. Drinkwater wondered how much of this insinuating process had already been accomplished during their crossing of the Atlantic. The idiocy of the remark was so at variance with the first lieutenant's earlier caution that Drinkwater was compelled to remark upon it. 'I thought, Mr Metcalfe, you were opposed to provokin' hostilities with the United States.'

'Well, I consider . . .' Metcalfe blustered uncomfortably, clearly having abandoned reason in favour of making an impression, but could find nothing further to say.

'I think we may forgive a little rudeness from so young a Service, mayn't we, Mr Vansittart?' Drinkwater said archly, catching the diplomat's eye.

'I think so, Captain Drinkwater. Particularly from the commander of a ship whose company had their sails furled half a minute before our own.'

Metcalfe opened his mouth, thought better of saying anything further and stumped away with a mumbled, 'By y're leave, gentlemen . . .'

'*Touché* Vansittart,' Drinkwater murmured.

Vansittart and Drinkwater idly watched the *Stingray*'s gig ground on a bright patch of sand lying in a shallow bay. The horsewoman in grey walked her now quietened mount towards the boat and they watched the mysterious Captain Stewart address her, saw her turn her horse and, with Stewart walking beside her, return to the house. She looked back once at the two anchored ships, then both disappeared inside. Shortly afterwards a man rode off on horseback.

'So there goes Captain Stewart, bound for Washington.'

'Is it unusual for a, what d'you call him . . . ?'

'Master Commandant,' Drinkwater explained, 'their equivalent of Master and Commander; a sloop-captain, in fact.'

'I see; is it usual then for such a curious beast to be absent from his ship under the circumstances?'

'The circumstances being your arrival, I should say it was essential,' Drinkwater said.

'Might he not be suspicious of your taking men out of his ship?'

'To be truthful, Vansittart, I am more concerned to stop my men deserting to his.'

'D'you think it likely?' asked Vansittart, displaying a mild surprise.

'Certainly 'tis a possibility. Did you not mark the furling of the sails? You noticed we were slower.'

'I, er, assumed it not to be significant . . .'

'The last tucks in the fore t'gallant were deliberately

delayed. I conceive that to have been a mark of sympathy with the Yankees.'

'A form of insolence, d'you mean?'

'Something of the kind.' Drinkwater raised his voice, 'Mr Metcalfe! Mr Moncrieff!'

When the two officers had approached he said, 'Gentlemen, I wish you to consider the possibility of desertion to the American ship or', he looked towards the longer distance separating the frigate from the lush greensward sweeping down to the Potomac, 'directly ashore. Mr Moncrieff, your sentries are to be especially alert. They must first challenge but thereafter they may fire. They are to bear loaded weapons.' He turned to the first lieutenant. 'Mr Metcalfe, we will row a guard-boat day and night. The midshipmen to be in command. There will be no communication whatsoever with either the shore or the American ship.' He paused. 'I am sorry for the Draconian measures, gentlemen, but I'm sure you'll understand.'

'Of course, sir,' Moncrieff nodded.

'Yes, sir,' Metcalfe acknowledged.

'You will be pleased to pass on to all the officers that the desertion of a single man in such circumstances', he gestured at their idyllic, land-locked situation, 'may not be a disaster in practical terms for the ship, but it will be a considerable embarrassment to the Service. I therefore require the lieutenants and the master to maintain their watches even though we are anchored. Is that understood?'

'Aye, aye, sir,' Metcalfe said woodenly.

'You *are* taking this seriously,' Vansittart said, after the two officers had been dismissed.

Vansittart's apparent flippancy revealed the maritime naïvety of the man. Vansittart had not been witness to Thurston's oratory; nor would he have been so susceptible, Drinkwater thought, coming as he did from a family long in the public service. Mr Vansittart would have scoffed at Captain Drinkwater's misgivings. Such guilty considerations had kept Drinkwater from revealing anything of his private thoughts. Besides, he did not need to be told his duty and he had at least the satisfaction of knowing that Thurston was kept obedient and under his immediate eye. 'Oh yes, indeed I am,' he said, 'I cannot tolerate a single desertion. The consequences acting upon the remainder of the people would be most unfortunate.'

They passed an uneasy night. The knocking of the guard-boat's oar looms against the thole pins, the routine calls of the sentinels that all was well, and the airless, unaccustomed stillness of the ship after her ocean passage, combined with Drinkwater's anxiety to keep him awake, or half-dozing, until dawn, when sheer exhaustion carried him off.

They estimated that Captain Stewart, at best, would not return until the following evening. The parallel existences of the two ships passed the hours: the trilling of the pipes, the shouting of orders and the regularity of the bells, each chiming just sufficiently asynchronously to remind their companies they each belonged to different navies, lent a suspense to the day. Occasionally a boat put off from the American ship and her midshipmen doffed their hats to those rowing their tedious duty round *Patrician*. The absence of so crude and despotic a routine about the *Stingray* was a permanent reproach to the British and a source of delight to the Americans.

Towards late afternoon, however, the returning American cutter, instead of taking a sweep round the circuit of the guard-boat, cut inside, making for *Patrician*'s side. A midshipman, smart in blue, white and gold, a black cockade in his stovepipe hat, came smartly up the side and, saluting in due form, handed a note to the officer of the watch, Lieutenant Frey. Frey took the missive below to Captain Drinkwater.

'Enter.' The September sunshine slanted into the great cabin, picking up motes of dust in the heavy air. Drinkwater, his shoes kicked off and in his shirt sleeves, was slumped in a chair dozing before the stern windows.

'What is it?' he murmured drowsily, his eyes closed.

'Message from the shore, sir.'

'Read it, then.'

Frey slit the wafer. 'It's an invitation, sir ... er, Mr Zebulon and Mistress Arabella Shaw of Castle Point request the pleasure of the company of the Captain of the

English frigate and his officers, at six of the clock . . .' Frey broke off, a note of excitement testimony to the boredom of his young life. 'There'll be food, sir, and music, and', he added wistfully, 'company.'

'I suppose you'd like me to accept on your behalf, Mr Frey.'

'Well, yes please, sir.' The merest suggestion that Drinkwater might refuse clearly alarmed Frey.

'Zebulon who?' Drinkwater queried in a disinterested voice.

'Er,' Frey studied the invitation again. 'Shaw, sir.'

Drinkwater was silent for a while. 'You were with me on the *Melusine*, weren't you?'

'Yes, sir,' replied Frey, impatiently wondering where this line of questioning was leading them and rather hurt that it was necessary.

'We didn't have much opportunity for social life in the Greenland Sea, did we?'

'Not a great deal, sir.'

'And the natives were not particularly attractive, were they?'

'No, sir, their huts weren't quite like the wigwam ashore there, sir.' Ducking his head Frey could see a white corner of the stables adjoining the classical frontage of Castle Point.

'I wonder why they call it Castle Point . . .?'

'There are some battlements, sir.'

'Are there? Well, well.' Gantley Hall had no battlements. 'You'd better call Thurston . . .'

'I'll write the reply myself, sir, if you like,' Frey said, then thinking he was being too forward he added, 'there's a midshipman from the Yankee sloop waiting on deck . . .'

'Is there, by God?' Drinkwater said, sitting up, rubbing his eyes and feeling for his shoes. 'Then we'd better jump to it and not keep young Master Jonathan waiting . . .'

'I beg your pardon . . .'

'Don't be a fool, Frey. I know full well you want to stretch your legs, and preferably alongside a rich Virginian belle in the figures of a waltz. It's a damned sight better than takin' the air on the quarterdeck, ain't it?'

Drinkwater gestured for the note; Frey gave it to him.

79

The paper gave off a faint fragrance and was covered in an elegant, feminine script. Presumably the patrician hand of Mistress Shaw. Going to his desk he drew a sheet of paper towards him, lifted the lid of his ink-well and picked up the Mitchell's pen Elizabeth had given him.

'To Mister and Mistress Zebulon Shaw...' he murmured as he wrote, wondering what manner of man and wife owned so luxurious a property. The bare untitled names reminded him of the virtues of republicanism. Perhaps it was as well he had not summoned Thurston to pen this acceptance. When he had sanded it dry he gave it to Frey.

'There, Mr Frey, and remember we are ourselves ambassadors in our small way.'

'Aye, aye, sir,' replied Frey, grinning happily and retreating as hurriedly as decency permitted.

The Widow Shaw

'Lord, Lootenant, you *are* hot!'

Arabella Shaw looked up at the handsome face of the English officer.

'And you, ma'am,' Lieutenant Gordon replied with equal candour, 'are beautiful.'

He smiled down at her, blaming his own goatishness on her soft body and its capacity to arouse. He clasped her waist tighter as they whirled together in the waltz. She judged him to be a year or so short of thirty, at least ten years her junior, but with a chilling absence of two fingers on his left hand. She could feel the lust in him, pliantly urgent. He might have excused his obtrusiveness by claiming an overlong period at sea, but he pretended it did not exist and she acknowledged this intimate flattery by lowering her eyes.

Mr Gordon took this for surrender; not, he realized, of the citadel, but of an outwork, a ravelin. He gathered her closer still, enchanted by the scent of her hair in his nostrils, her exotic perfume and the swell of her breasts against his chest.

Mistress Shaw endured his rough attentions and curt-seyed formally as the music stopped. As he returned her to her seat, she quietly cursed her own weakness for suggesting this evening. Her widowhood had begun to irk her and she had felt the impromtu ball an occasion enabling her to cast aside more than a year of mourning, besides helping her father-in-law do what he could to stop the imminent rupture between the United States and Great Britain. He had enthusiastically adopted her suggestion of inviting the officers of both naval ships to a rout.

She had to admit her own motives were far less philanthropic. It had been curiosity which tipped her judgement in favour of making the suggestion; curiosity to see the English officers. She had been a girl at the time of Yorktown when the hated redcoats had surrendered sullenly against overwhelming odds. Defeat had not robbed them of their potent terror to a young mind and the childish impression had remained. She still thought of them as bogey-men inhabiting the dark, threatening spectres to be conjured up when children were disobedient. And once again they were at large, plundering American ships off their own coastline and carrying off innocent sailors like the Barbary pirates with whom her country had already been at war. Tonight she had thought, with a *frisson* of fearful delight, she would see these mythological beings for herself and she was half-disappointed, half-relieved that they were not the pop-eyed, dissolute, viciously indolent exquisites she had expected.

There had been, too, the added inducement to exhibit a new gown, a gay, uninhibited contrast with the black bombazine which for so long had hidden her figure. To this was added a patriotic justification, for the gown had been smuggled from Paris to replace her widow's weeds and she wore it in defiance of the British blockade. The wicked desire to try its effects on English sophisticates (as she imagined them to be) had honed her anticipation. She had had enough of the male society of Virginia. The rich, elderly and often dissolute men who had shown an interest in her had seemed either opportunist or calculating. Their expressions of regard had been too contrived for sincerity, or their desires too obvious for a permanent attachment. None had struck an answering longing in her own heart. For her all men had died with her husband, whose mutilated body they had found already putrefying beside his exhausted horse. They said the stump of an Indian arrow in his back had killed him when mounting, and not the dreadful, nightmare gallop of a terrified mount whose rider had fallen backwards with one foot caught in a stirrup.

They reached the table and Gordon's mangled hand gave her a sharp reminder of the mortality of men. She was suddenly sorry for him and ashamed of her soft breasts that jutted, *à la Marie-Louise*, to tantalize him. She sat and sipped from her glass while Gordon, handsome and eager, hovered uncertainly. She was about to ask him to sit too, since his awkwardness was unsettling her, when he was superseded. A tall, gaunt young Scot in the scarlet and blue facings of her childhood fancy, a glittering gorget and white cravat reflecting on a pugnacious chin, elbowed Gordon aside. She sensed some tacit agreement, for Gordon withdrew unprotesting and bowing. She felt cheap, not wicked, as if the subtleties of wearing the gown were lost on these boors and had merely made of her a whore. The lobsterback officer was bending over her hand.

'Quentin Moncrieff, ma'am, Royal Marines, at your service. The band is about to strike up, I believe, and I would be obliged if you would do me the honour . . .'

The leg he put forward was well muscled, the bow elegant enough, and, as if to emphasize his authority, the music began again, silencing the buzz of chatter. She submitted, Moncrieff led her out and almost at once she regretted Gordon's honest lust as Moncrieff's flattery assaulted her.

Both had the same end in view; she had clearly been pointed out as a widow, perhaps in a moment of weakness by the rather gauche-looking American officers grouped around one table muttering amongst themselves and regarding their visitors with suspicion. She supposed she had upset them by dancing exclusively with the British; it was a good thing her brother was not here, though Lieutenant Tucker would doubtless keep him informed.

Moncrieff's remarks blew into her ear. Oh yes, they knew her for a widow all right, a woman who in their opinion must, by definition, need a man and who, moreover, would be discreet in having one. She did not know a sizeable wager rested upon her virtue.

She was tiring of the evening as a self-satisfied Moncrieff led her back to her table. She tried to recall what she had said to him, but found the intimidating glares of Lieutenant Tucker and his cronies only made her reflect what a pity it was that events always had the contrary result to what had been intended. She was beginning to wish she had not suggested the evening in the first place as much as regretting the *décolletage* of the French gown. Inspiration saved her from surrender to yet another eager young officer who appeared to head a queue of blushing midshipmen.

'Mr Moncrieff,' she asked in her low drawl, 'would you be kind enough to introduce me to your captain?'

She had missed the arrival of the British officers. They had been prompt – some talk of a race between the boats of the two ships, she believed, though where she had learned the fact, unless it was from Moncrieff's panting eagerness to pour his heart's desire into her ear, she could not be sure – and her maid had not done her hair properly so *she* had been late. Her father-in-law had greeted them all and the ballroom was already filled with chatter and the glitter of uniforms by the time she had joined them.

'The Captain, ma'am? Why ... er, of course.'

She sensed the response to discipline, felt the effect of iron rule even here, in the privacy of Castle Point. Moncrieff ceased to be himself and became merely an officer, correct, precise and formal. She felt a momentary pity for him and his colleagues, a wildly promiscuous desire to touch them all with herself and release them from the thraldom of lust and duty.

Moncrieff surveyed the company as the music began again and Lieutenant Tucker, his arm about the waist of Kate Denbigh of Falmouth township, prepared to out-do the British and show them how a Yankee officer danced the polka.

'This way, ma'am.'

Moncrieff was eager to be rid of her now, eager to slide his own arm round the slender waist of a younger, less worldly woman than the Widow Shaw. He led her to an open French window where a solitary figure stood, half merging with the heavy folds of a long blue velvet curtain.

Moncrieff coughed formally. 'Sir? May I present Mistress Shaw . . .'

The captain did not turn, indeed he did not appear to have heard and she thought the authority of a British captain too elevated to acknowledge an American widow hell-bent on escape from his officers. His indifference riled her far more than their concupiscence and she felt humiliated in front of Moncrieff. She played a final desperate card and dismissed the marine officer.

'Thank you, Mr Moncrieff.'

Lamely Moncrieff carried out the final ritual of his duty: 'Captain Drinkwater . . . Mrs Shaw . . .' He bowed, disappointed, and withdrew.

She hung there, flushing, resenting this necessity of suspension between the two men – two Englishmen!

'I was admiring the view, ma'am,' the captain said, almost abstractedly and without turning his head. 'The moonrise on the Potomac . . . yours is a very beautiful country.'

He turned then, catching her wide-mouthed, angry and flushed. She was, he saw, voluptuously handsome, her black hair a legacy of Spanish or Indian blood, her skin creamy from some Irish settler. Too lovely to contemplate, he thought with a pang, and swung abruptly away, disturbed despite his fifty years.

She saw a stoop-shouldered man, whose epaulettes failed entirely to conceal something odd about his shoulders. He was of middle height with still-profuse and unpomaded hair. The iron-grey mane was drawn back and caught behind his head in an old-fashioned, black-ribboned queue which she longed to tug, to chastise him for his rudeness.

'You are not dancing, Captain?' she said desperately at this infuriating indifference.

He was aware of his ill-manners and turned to face her properly. 'Forgive me, ma'am. No, I am not dancing. Truth to tell, I dare not . . .'

His forehead was high, his nose straight and his face at first seemed to be a boy's grown old, an impression solely due to the twinkle in his grey eyes. But his skin was weathered and lined, and the thin scar of an ancient wound puckered down his left cheek.

She responded to the dry twist of his mouth, her anger melting now she had his attention. '*Dare* not, sir? Do I understand a British captain is afraid?'

He grinned, and again there was the suggestion of boyishness, disarming the mild jibe. Drinkwater himself warmed to the gentle mockery which reminded him of his wife, Elizabeth.

'Terrified, ma'am . . .'

'Of what, pray?'

'Of betraying my incompetence before my officers.' They laughed together.

'They sure are a scarifying lot,' she said. 'I have just escaped their clutches.'

'Ah,' said Captain Drinkwater, looking her full in the face and seeing for the first time she was no longer a girl. 'And am I to understand you feel safer here, eh?' He did not wait for a reply, but went on. 'If I attended to my duty I should remonstrate that your gown has an obvious origin, which I disapprove of, but I am not yet too dried up to be so ungallant.'

'I am glad of that,' she said, now strangely irritated by the success of her ploy in wearing it, 'but we conceive it to be no right of yours to blockade our coast.'

'Ma'am, in all seriousness, we have not yet *begun* to blockade your coast.'

His eyes wandered past her bare shoulder as he tried to mask the gall her remark provoked and to forget the terrible cost in British lives that the blockade of Europe was costing. What its extension to the seaboard of the United States would mean could only be guessed at. It was not the roaring glory of death in battle that was corroding the Royal Navy, but the ceaseless wear-and-tear on ships and men condemned, officers and ratings alike, to a life deprived of every prospect of comfort or privacy. It was over a twelvemonth since Collingwood had died at his desk aboard the *Ocean*. Five years after Trafalgar and without leave during the whole of the period, Nelson's heir had followed his own brother, whom Drinkwater had once met, to an early grave. It was a bitter pill to swallow, to be deprived of Elizabeth and yet to see this woman done up in the height of Parisian fashion. He sighed, aware she was no more mistress of her own destiny than he was of his. Providence ruled them all and it was no excuse for discourtesy. There were parsons and squires aplenty in Kent and Sussex who roistered to bed full to their gunwhales with cognac. Had he not seen himself, on the island of Helgoland, the lengths to which men would go to trade in proscribed goods? There were too many transgressors to offend this woman on the far side of the Atlantic. He made amends as best he could.

'I regret I did not catch your name, ma'am.' He made a small bow. 'Nathaniel Drinkwater, Captain in His Britannic Majesty's Navy, at your service.' He recited the formula with a tired ruefulness he hoped would pass in part for apology, in part for explanation.

'Arabella Shaw,' she replied, 'widow . . .' She did not know why she had revealed her status, except perhaps to prick his stiff British pride and ape his own portentousness.

'I'm sorry, ma'am, I had no idea.' He looked gratifyingly confused.

'It seemed common knowledge among your officers.'

'Hence your escape?' he asked and she inclined her head. 'Then I apologize for their conduct and my own failure to render sympathetic assistance.'

'Lord, Captain, you make me feel like a derelict hulk!' She was smiling again and he was feeling an unaccountable relief.

'You are familiar with a nautical metaphor?'

'I am no stranger to boats, Captain, while my brother is a Master Commandant in our *un*-Britannic navy.'

Comprehension dawned upon him and it was Drinkwater's turn to flush. 'Forgive me . . . Mrs Shaw, of course, I am sorry, I had not realized, you are the daughter of the house . . .'

'Daughter-in-law, Captain. Unfortunately I was not here to receive you . . .'

'We were inconsiderately early,' he said quickly and then turned to look round the dancers. His eye fell upon the bald head of their host. 'I thought the tall lady in brown silk with Mr Shaw . . .'

'Oh, she'd like to become Mrs Shaw, but she is actually still Mrs Denbigh, from Falmouth, a widow and a somewhat designing woman with two pretty daughters . . .'

'Ah, and you are the young lady whose horse we startled this morning . . .'

'With your preposterous cannon, yes, I spoke to my brother Charles about that. Why on earth you should have wished to disturb the peace and tranquillity of half Virginia with such nonsense passes my comprehension!'

He remembered Captain Stewart walking at the head of the chestnut and talking to its rider. Righteous indignation lent colour to her cheeks.

'I think a flag of truce is in order, Mistress Shaw, do you not?'

'Is that what you have come here for? A flag of truce, or something more durable? My father-in-law sees no advantage in a war.'

'What about your brother?'

She shrugged. 'He seems to be like most men – eager to fight.'

'He would not be so eager had he spent his lifetime thus.'

The conviction in Drinkwater's tone made her look at him with renewed interest. 'I know you to have brought a diplomatic mission . . .' She looked round the ballroom.

'No, he is not here. He has some notion of propriety that it would not be politic for him to step ashore until he has official approval . . .'

'So you too are against an open breach between our countries?'

'Certainly. And so, I think it is not indiscreet of me to say, is he.'

'I am glad of that. You must meet my father-in-law later. Come, show me the moonlight on the Potomac, Captain Drinkwater.'

She slipped her arm in his with sudden, easy familiarity, and they stepped through the French windows on to a battlemented terrace which crowned the rising ground upon which the house was built.

'My late husband's grandfather intended to build a castle on the hill here, hence its name. It was barely started when he was killed at the Battle of the Brandywine. This terrace is called "The Battery", though it mounts nothing more offensive than a flower urn or two.'

'Your husband's grandfather had a fine eye for landscape, ma'am; it reminds me of an English deer-park.'

'*Your* English deer-park, perhaps?' she asked shrewdly.

He laughed, thinking of Gantley Hall and its two modest farms. 'Lord no, Mrs Shaw, my own house boasts nothing more impressive than a walled garden, a kitchen garden and an orchard which would fit upon the terrace here.'

Mrs Shaw nodded to another couple taking the air. 'And is there a wife, Captain Drinkwater, to go with all this domesticity?'

He looked at her, about to ask if it mattered either way, while she waited, herself annoyed that it did. He nodded, turning the knife in the unguessed at and, for her, unexpected wound. 'And a son and daughter. Do you have children, Mrs Shaw?'

She shook her head and digested the fact in silence, comparing it with her own bereavement and catching the wistful note in his voice.

'If you miss them, Captain,' she asked softly, 'why do you come here?' There was a hint of Yankee hostility in the question.

'That is a question I frequently ask myself, Mrs Shaw.'

She sensed his retreat and found it surprisingly hurtful. Silence settled on them again and after a while she shivered.

'Shall we go in?' he asked.

They turned back to the brilliantly lit ballroom. He was already remote again, ready to detach her as they approached the French windows. She stopped short of the light spilling on to the *pavé*.

'Do you ride, Captain?'

He halted, surprised. 'Ride? After a fashion, an indifferent bad fashion, I'm afraid.'

'Would you care to see some more of my beautiful country tomorrow?'

He thought of the enchantment inherent in such an invitation, the release from the isolated and tedious splendour of his command, the surrender to landscape, to fecund greenery after the harsh tones of sea and sky. Then he thought of the ship and the discontent seething between her decks, of men mewed up by force, of the guard-boat and the sentries with their orders, *his* orders to shoot . . .

He had left a disgruntled Metcalfe aboard this evening; how could he leave them again and go gallivanting about on horseback in full view of the ship's company?

She took his hesitation for imminent refusal. She knew her brother's return from Washington was as likely to bring rebuttal to the English peace overtures as acceptance, that the English frigate might overnight become an enemy and be compelled to put to sea. A sense of panic welled up within her, a sudden, overwhelming urge to see this man again; she tried to find something wittily memorable to say to him and compel him to change his mind.

'I promise my habit will be less contentious, Captain,' she said, furious that her voice trembled.

He could not ignore her, or cast her aside. He told himself he had been more than off-hand with her earlier, that her father-in-law wanted peace and was clearly a man of substance and influence, a man to be encouraged; he told himself that such a meeting might aid the peace process just as he told himself a dinner party at Castle Point might include Captain Stewart and therefore open a discussion of potential interest to a British naval officer.

'Have you a mount docile enough for a sailor?'

'Certainly,' she laughed, 'provided you will lead me in to dinner.'

He inclined his head and bowed, grinning widely. 'I'm honoured, ma'am.'

She smiled and dropped him a curtsey, and they re-entered the ballroom to be engulfed in the gaiety of the scene.

The moon was almost at its culmination when they left Castle Point. The early hostility between the officers of the British and American ships had been skilfully averted by Mr Zebulon Shaw. The protestations of peace and amity, the toasts proposed, seconded and swallowed in assurance of the fact, and the fulsome, wine-warmed expressions of mutual goodwill had healed the incipient rift between the two rival factions. A breach of manners towards their host had thus been avoided. Furthermore, Drinkwater's presence had curbed the taunts of the Americans and intimidated his own people. As far as Drinkwater knew, none of his officers had disgraced themselves, the virtue of the local maids remained intact, if intact it was at their landing, and with the exception of Mr Frey whose farewell had been overlong, all had come away merry, but light-hearted.

It would doubtless have warmed Mr Shaw's heart, Drinkwater thought as he waited to board the gig, if he could have seen Frey finally rejoin his companions, for he strode down the path to the water in company with Lieutenant Tucker, apparently the best of friends. It was only later that Drinkwater learned the cause of this unlikely alliance. While Tucker courted Miss Catherine Denbigh, Mr Frey had been smitten with her sister Pauline.

As for his own farewell, it had consisted of the promise of a meeting on the morrow.

And too long a glance between Mrs Shaw and himself.

CHAPTER 7   September 1811

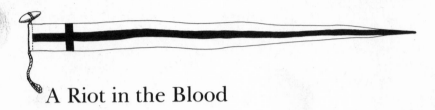

A Riot in the Blood

His acceptance of Mistress Shaw's invitation troubled
Drinkwater the following forenoon. He did not advertise
his forthcoming absence from the ship, indeed he busied
himself with the routine of paperwork to such an extent as
almost to convince himself he had no appointment to
keep. Mullender guessed something unusual was afoot,
since the captain called for his boots to be blacked, but
Mullender, being incurious, gave the matter little thought,
and although Drinkwater had a coxswain, the man had
never replaced Tregembo as a servant and confidant.

Oddly it was Thurston who almost by default came
closest to the captain's soul that morning. Called in to
make up the ship's books and to assist in the standing
routine inspections of the purser's and surgeon's ledgers,
Thurston fell into conversation with the captain.

Until then he had kept a respectful silence and attended
to his duties, aware of the awful punishment Drinkwater
had it in his power to dole out. He was conscious that the
captain was neither inhumane nor illiberal, in so far as a
post-captain in the Royal Navy could be expected to be
either, having been guided in this matter by older heads
who were less willing to heed the trumpets of revolution
and had pointed out the virtues of service to the common
weal. Thurston was intelligent enough and by then experienced enough to know the sea-service was different
from life ashore and that, for cogent reasons, libertarian
concepts were inimical to survival at sea. He had therefore

learned to tread warily where Captain Drinkwater was concerned.

Drinkwater, on the other hand, now regarded Thurston with more interest than suspicion. By keeping the man to hand and working him hard, by altering his status from pressed man to captain's clerk and by making him a party to a measure of the frigate's more open secrets, Drinkwater had sought to seduce the revolutionary by responsibility.

Prompted by his guilty conscience, he addressed Thurston while the clerk cleared away pen, ink and sand.

'Well, Thurston,' he began, 'are you settled in your new employment?'

'Well enough, thank you, sir, under the circumstances.'

'What circumstances?' asked Drinkwater, puzzled.

'Of being held against my will, sir.'

Drinkwater gave a short cough to mask his surprise at the man's candour. 'I believe you to be luckier than you deserve, Thurston. You could have been transported.'

'That is true, sir, but that would have been a greater injustice. It in no way mollifies my outrage at being carried to sea. Both punishments, if punishments they be, are unjust.'

'Sedition is a serious matter,' said Drinkwater, regretting starting this conversation yet feeling he could not dismiss its subject lightly, despite the increasingly pressing nature of his engagement. 'You do not truly advocate rule by the mob?'

'Of course not, sir, but the mob is a consequence of the ill construction of government. By exalting some men, others are debased, until this distortion is inconsistent with natural order. The vast mass of mankind is consigned to the background of the human picture, to bring forward, with greater glare, the puppet-show of state and aristocracy.'

'A puppet-show, you say,' Drinkwater said, somewhat nonplussed.

'Indeed, sir, there is no class of men who despise monarchy more than courtiers.'

'You have had much experience of courtiers, have you, Thurston?' Drinkwater asked drily.

'My father was in the service of a duke, sir. It amounts to the same thing,' Thurston answered coolly.

'Ah, I see, so you do not want mobocracy?' Drinkwater said, returning to the safer ground of his earlier remark.

'No. Governments arise out of a man's individual weakness. He places himself and his own in the common stock of society. Locke says for the preservation of his property, but also for the security of his family. He becomes a proprietor in society and draws upon its common capital as a right, thus it follows that a civil right flows from a natural right. If all men behaved with equal respect the one to another, then an equilibrium would exist within society. Each man would give and take according to his means and abilities, thus the differences whose abolition is so much feared by those who misunderstand, would themselves be a natural, earned and unenvied consequence of civil rights, a right in themselves; but no man would want, be beggared or dispossessed, for he would by right hold that of the common stock to which he was entitled.'

'And if he failed to gain that stock, or to hold it . . . ?'

'He *could* not fail to gain it, it would be his by natural right. You only raise the matter of loss because you have lived under English law and know it to be possible even when a man does not actively break the law. Dispossession by enclosure, by loom and seed-drill and steam-engine, have severally destroyed the hopes of many, because artful men have seized upon this common stock and called it their own; they have then held it by the immoderate use of superstition and power, created a monarchy under which their privileges stand and are upheld by the law.' Thurston paused.

'That is all very well . . .'

'You know the doggerel, sir, I'm sure,' Thurston went on relentlessly:

'The law doth punish man or woman
That steals the goose from off the common,
But lets the greater felon loose,
That steals the common off the goose.'

'That is clever, Thurston . . .'

'As it is true, sir. I do not seek to justify the excesses of a mob, even when it is made up of men without hope. But I do not condone the maintenance, at the expense of the unfortunate, of a parasitic court, of a self-perpetuating legislature, an unjust judiciary, the practitioners of sycophancy, nor all the recipients of privilege, those jacks-in-office who extract the last penny from a man in order that he may prove himself a free-born Englishman!'

Drinkwater wondered if, as a post-captain, he was himself included in that awful list as a recipient of privilege? Did Gantley Hall exist in even its moderate freehold at the expense of a dispossessed yeomanry? Yet he knew to what inequities Thurston referred. From the prevarications and vastly tedious pettifoggings of the High Court of Chancery, to the perquisites and bribes recognized as being necessary to further the public service, no area of life seemed exempt. He looked at his desk. If he and Thurston did not attend to their business properly, if these very books were not properly kept, then a mean-minded Admiralty clerk might postpone their clearance at the end of a commission. Such a delay meant his ship's company would not be paid, further exacerbating an already unjust system which failed to pay men for their labour until a commission ended, forcing them to resort to usurers who bought up their 'tickets' at discount rates, advancing the poor devils cash at far less than face value. It was customary for captains to pass a little money over with their books, to expedite the matter.

'How many widows' men have we entered for this morning, Thurston?' Drinkwater referred to the allowed practice of bearing upon a man-o'-war's books a number of non-existent men to provide a sum for relieving the hardships of the dependants of those lost or killed at sea by disease or action.

'The regulation six, sir.'

'I could make it twelve ... and either pocket the difference myself, or distribute it among the needy.'

'Sir, I had not meant anything personal . . .'

'I had not thought so, but either act would be illegal, within the strict letter of the regulations.'

'You suggest that I should wait for a better life in

95

heaven then, sir?' Thurston asked, with a curious bitter hardening of his face.

'Do you truly think this world is capable of improvement?'

'Most assuredly so, sir.'

'They thought so in France, yet they have ended up with an Emperor Napoleon and have trampled on half the nations of Europe . . .'

Thurston shrugged, apparently undisconcerted by this irrefutable logic. 'They are the French, sir, and have merely trampled upon *courts*,' he said. Drinkwater suppressed a laugh with difficulty. Time was drawing on and he was more anxious than ever to escape the oppressive confines of the ship. 'They order things very differently hereabouts . . .' Thurston's eyes wandered wistfully through the stern windows to the sweep of green grass and deciduous woodland bordering the river. 'Very differently.'

'Thurston, you know very well why I had you made into my clerk, don't you?'

'I think so, sir.'

'You know so, sir . . . and you know why I cannot tolerate your spreading your creed aboard this ship.'

'I know that, sir, and I pity you.'

'Have a care, Thurston, have a care, you may not find things would fall out quite as you wish even in Utopia. I am aware some men think you dangerous, while others think you mad. I am aware too that cranks are small things which make revolutions . . .' The pun brought a smile back to Thurston's face, 'but the word on ship-board also signifies unstable and top-heavy, so have a care. Do you understand?'

'Oh, I understand, sir.'

They faced each other for a moment, the one, unresponsible and armed with the truth; the other worn down by obligations and compromised by the nature of the world.

'Pass word to call away my barge, if you please.'

On Drinkwater's insistence they rode away from the house directly inland. He had first enquired if there was news of

Stewart's return with Vansittart's passport and having thus acquitted himself of the last demands of duty he gave himself up to pleasure with a rare and uncharacteristic enthusiasm.

Vansittart reading his novel and patiently awaiting the acceptance of his credentials; Metcalfe, irritated by his non-participation in the previous evening's rout and further annoyed by Drinkwater's departure this morning; Frey, moonstruck and vacant; even Thurston righting all the world's ills with his honest and impossible creed – all could go hang for an hour or two. He had given them enough to keep them busy. A wood and watering party sent off under adequate guard, a restowing of the hold and a rattling down of the rigging should guard against the devil finding work for idle hands . . .

It did not occur to him as he kicked the roan mare after the spirited chestnut gelding that he was the only one whose hands were, at least metaphorically, empty.

'Do we go alone?' he had asked as she walked the leading horse round the rearward corner of the house and so cut off the view of the river.

She had turned and patted a bulging saddle-bag. 'I have a luncheon here,' she called gaily, 'or do you think me in need of a chaperon?' The notion caused her to burst out into a peal of laughter and spur her horse.

For a moment or two Drinkwater was too preoccupied by the need to stay in the saddle to think of anything else. He was aware his dignity was non-existent as he struggled to get the rhythm of the trotting horse, urging the beast to canter as much to stay in the saddle as to keep up with his hostess. It was only when the mare obliged and Drinkwater recalled the tricks he had learned on a similar horse of Sir Richard White's, that it occurred to him Mistress Shaw was wearing breeches.

The day was fine and sunny, with small puffballs of cumulus clouds trailing downwind under the influence of a fresh breeze which made the leaves of the trees rustle delightfully. He had never fully mastered the skills of horsemanship, unlike his father and his younger brother. The former was long dead but Ned, he supposed, was still at large, somewhere in Russia, an adopted Cossack.

97

And here *he* was, in Virginia, behaving like a fool in hot pursuit of a delightful rump as it bounced ahead of him and, dear Christ, went over a hedge!

'God's bones,' he swore, recalling his mother's adage that pride invariably preceded a fall. There was no need for fate to be so literal, he thought desperately as the hedge drew rapidly closer. And then with a sense of mounting panic he realized it was not a hedge. This was not enclosed England, but wide and wonderful Virginia. He was confronted by a row of bushes which, he realized with sudden certainly, ran alongside a little brook. He was too late to rein in; he felt the mare gather herself and, at the last moment, remembered to lean forward. The mare crashed through the brushwood and stretched herself for the brook beyond. He saw the bright flash of water and then his whole frame shook as the mare landed and the bony structure of her shoulders steadied and received his weight. The horse stumbled, recovered, and began to pant as it breasted the rising ground beyond the brook. Relieved, Drinkwater took stock of his surroundings. Mistress Shaw had halted her horse on the summit of the hill. He pulled up alongside her.

'You promised me . . .' he panted.

'A docile mount, not an easy ride,' she laughed, cutting him short.

'Thank God your horse knows the lie of the land.'

'Betsy would die rather than throw you,' she said, leaning forward and affectionately patting his mount on her neck. The mare whinnied softly and the chestnut threw up his own head and jingled a protest at this favouritism.

For a moment they sat on their horses and regarded the view in silence. Drinkwater was surprised how far and how high they had come. He could see the roof of Castle Point, and beyond, on the silver-grey waters of the Potomac, the two ships with the bright spots of their rival ensigns at their sterns.

'They look so insignificant from here, don't they,' she said. It was not a question, nor could he argue with the fact.

'They are,' he said suddenly, and the sense of liberation

the words gave amazed him. In a sudden impulsive movement he had jerked Betsy's head round to the west and kicked his unspurred heels into her flanks. Without looking back he worked the mare up to a gallop, dropping down towards more trees on the far side of the hill.

She watched him for a moment, holding her own restively eager horse in check until the foam flew from its mouth. Her heart was hammering inexplicably and she knew her hesitation was useless; yet she felt compelled to wait, not knowing the reason for this foolishness. When she could stand it no longer, she gave a yelp, flicked the reins and let the chestnut have its head.

The two ships were instantly hidden behind the summit.

'You remind me of a magnolia we have at home,' he said. 'It grows against a south-facing wall and produces flowers of a singular loveliness.'

'We have them here in Virginia,' she said, blushing and busying herself with the game pie. 'Do you open this.'

He sat up and took the bottle and corkscrew while she knelt and laid two plates upon the spread cloth.

'You have more than a magnolia at home, Captain,' she said pointedly, after a long pause, her voice strained.

'And still you remind me of it,' he said, placing the uncorked bottle on a level corner of the cloth, 'magnolia, home and beauty.'

'Have you killed, Captain?' she asked suddenly, looking at him squarely, her expression intent.

'In cold blood, or action?' he prevaricated, wondering why she had so cruelly turned his love-making aside.

'Does it matter?'

He shrugged. 'Perhaps not to you . . .'

'You men think by setting such moral questions in grades of dreadfulness to make them acceptable.'

'I am somewhat wearied of moral judgements being made against me today. You are not the first woman to ask that question of me. I am a sea-officer, for better or worse. I have my duty.'

'Does it not bother your conscience that you murder with some proficiency?'

'Of course; but adultery is a sin as proscribed as murder, madam, yet is indulged in with little thought by people who do not conceive themselves as wicked. It has been a matter of amazement to me that one who moralizes about the evils of the latter can so easily practise the former. I am a sinner, but hesitate to throw stones.'

She had coloured and bit her lip, then said, 'I had not expected such flippancy.'

'Would you have me bare my soul to a stranger?'

'Perhaps,' she said, looking at him again, 'the stranger would wish to be otherwise.' She poured the wine into two glasses and handed him one.

'And what would the stranger be? An adulterer, or merely a magnolia?'

'Perhaps both.'

Later she propped herself on an elbow and looked down at him as he stared impassively at the clouds moving slowly above the trees.

'You regret what has happened, don't you, Nathaniel?' He remained silent, staring upwards. 'Do not, I beg you, if only for my sake. For you 'twas but a riot in the blood.'

He turned and looked at her, and saw her eyes were brim full of tears.

'I think we are both too old for such . . . such rioting to be passed over thus easily.'

'It doesn't signify . . .'

'On the contrary,' he said gently, 'even madness has its own place under heaven.'

'Do you feel any different now?'

He smiled sadly. 'Not all men spend in the same manner as they piss, Arabella. Perhaps I wish I did, it would make my infidelity the easier to bear.'

'I do not think', she said, her voice trembling, 'you should reproach yourself. I am not . . .'

He took her hand and smiled at her. The boyish attractiveness had gone, replaced by something she could not describe, but which would, she knew with the certainty of true foreboding, haunt her future loneliness. 'My darling . . .' she breathed.

They arrived back at Castle Point at sunset. As they approached, walking their horses for fear they might arrive too soon, yet both aware their arrival was inevitable, the sound of shots rang out. Seized by a sudden awful thought that his absence had precipitated wholesale desertion, he pushed the mare forward until he saw Moncrieff's scarlet coat floundering through a reedbed waving a duck above his head. Relieved, he watched the wildfowling party which appeared to consist of Moncrieff, Metcalfe and Davies, one of the master's mates, until Arabella drew level with him.

'They are fowling,' he said, 'I hope with your father-in-law's permission.'

'You are forgetting me already,' she reproached him.

'When I heard those shots I feared for my life,' he remarked grimly, then turned towards her. Her hair was dishevelled and her cheeks were wet with tears. 'My dear,' he said, his voice thick with emotion, 'you make me reproach myself . . . please, do not cry, I am not worth it.'

She sniffed noisily. 'We must ride back to the house. Let us at least look as if the day was enjoyable.' And she drove her spurs into the chestnut's flanks so that the galled horse reared up and then leapt forward into a gallop.

Drinkwater followed as best he could, but she was already dismounting as he drew rein in the gravelled courtyard before the stables. The negro groom was rubbing down a large black stallion and, as the horses whinnied at each other and the stallion stamped, Zebulon Shaw came towards them.

'Bella . . . Captain Drinkwater, I trust you enjoyed your excursion.' He clapped his hands and a little negro stable-boy ran out and took the two bridles. Shaw spoke to his daughter-in-law and she turned to her guest.

'My brother is back and wishes that you and Mr Vansittart join us for dinner. He has brought the answer we wish for.' Her triumph was tempered by the formality about to overlay the day's intimacy.

'It is surely good news, Captain Drinkwater,' Shaw said.

'Surely, sir,' Drinkwater replied, easing himself out of the saddle. He looked at Arabella. 'It is for the best, I think,' he added in a low voice.

101

She caught his eye and then bit her lip, just as Elizabeth was wont to do, turned away and went into the house.

'Shall we say in two hours, Captain?' asked Shaw, looking from the retreating back of his daughter-in-law to the large turnip-watch in his red fist. 'Charles has retreated to his ship refusing the ministrations of our servants to wash the dust off him, but I reckon he'll be ashore again by then.'

'I'll fetch Vansittart, Mr Shaw, and perhaps we can make some travelling arrangements for him . . .'

'Of course, of course,' Shaw waved aside any trifling difficulties of that nature. ''Tis in a good cause, Captain, the noble cause of peace.'

'Indeed, sir, it is.'

It was almost dark when he reached the water's edge at the same time as the returning shooting-party.

'Have you had a good bag?' he asked and was caught up in the jocular repartee of their high spirits. Metcalfe seemed to have forgiven Drinkwater his absence and had gathered an impressive bag. Already the events of the afternoon were become a memory.

He paused on the quarterdeck and looked back at the shore. The white façade of Castle Point was grey in the gathering dusk. A few lit windows blazed out, some hid behind curtains. Was Arabella concealed behind one, washing him from her voluptuous body and dressing for the evening?

'*Post coitus omnes triste est,*' murmured Drinkwater to himself, and went unhappily below.

CHAPTER 8   September 1811

The Master Commandant

The sudden transition from the company of Arabella
Shaw to that of his high-spirited officers with their bag of
duck and snipe gave Drinkwater little time to reflect upon
the events of the day. Even in the odd moments that
followed his return to *Patrician* in which his mind had the
opportunity to wander, other, more pressing matters
supervened. In any case, the day was not yet over and his
subconscious subdued his conscience with the certainty of
being in Arabella's company again that evening.

   The shots of the wildfowlers which had so alarmed him
reawakened his fear of mutiny, tapping the greater guilt
of absence from the ship which, in its turn, combined with
the knowledge that Captain Stewart had returned to his
own ship prior to their meeting over dinner, and made
Drinkwater consider his coming encounter with the Yankee. From what he had gleaned of Stewart's character so
far, and in particular the American's hostile taciturnity,
the evening promised more of confrontation than con-
viviality. The fact that Drinkwater had already established
an intimacy at Castle Point gave him a *frisson* of expectation. Such was his state of mind that he was both ashamed
and, less creditably, gratified by this, a feeling of elated
excitement further enhanced every time he caught sight
of the American sloop through the stern windows of his
cabin. It was fading in the twilight, merging with the
opposite river-bank, but he remained acutely aware of its
presence. Not since he had joined *Patrician* in Cawsand

Bay had he felt so full of vigour.

There was a knock at the cabin door. 'Come!'

'Is there anything . . .' Thurston began, but Drinkwater cut him short.

'No, thank you, Thurston. I am dining ashore tonight.' He unrolled his housewife, drew out his razor and began stropping it. 'There is one thing,' he said as Thurston was about to withdraw, 'be so kind as to ask Mr Vansittart to join me for a moment, would you?'

He began to shave. Vansittart entered while he waited for Mullender to prepare his bath. He passed on Zebulon Shaw's invitation, adding, 'We can make all arrangements for your travelling through Shaw; he's a most obligin' fellow.'

The diplomat's self-imposed quarantine, though doubt-less proper, seemed a little foolish under the circumst-ances. Shaw was quite clearly opposed to war and if not an Anglophile, he was worldly enough to regard open hostili-ties between two countries as in nobody's interests. Vansit-tart might, Drinkwater reflected, profit much from his conversation by way of a briefing before leaving for Washington and he expressed this opinion while he shaved. Vansittart, his elegant legs crossed and a glass of the captain's Madeira in his hand, lounged on a chair and contemplated the dishevelled Drinkwater.

'But supposing, my dear fellow,' Vansittart said in a superior tone suggesting he was already conducting nego-tiations on the part of His Majesty's government, 'suppos-ing this fellow Shaw has his own axes to grind.'

'I don't follow . . .' Drinkwater stretched his cheek and drew the razor carefully over the thin scar left by a sword cut.

'Well, let us hypothesize that his pacific intentions are governed by his desire not to have some aspect of his personal economy interrupted by war; or perhaps he has some disagreement with a congressman from New Eng-land who is of a contrary opinion . . .'

'Suppose he has?' broke in Drinkwater, sensing the looming prevarications and evasions, the tortuous and meaningless sophistry of political blustering. 'What the devil does it signify? If he serves our purpose in bringin'

104

the weight of his opinion in favour of headin' off a rupture, he serves our cause...'

'Ah, but nothing,' Vansittart said smoothly and with a hint of patronizing, 'is quite as simple as that.'

Drinkwater looked at the urbane young man. He had been right about the proximity of the land. It had had its effect upon Vansittart, even though he had yet to step ashore. He was no longer a bewildered ignoramus, lost among the technical mysteries of a man-of-war, but a member of an élite upon whose deliberations the fates of more ordinary mortals depended. Already Vansittart's imagination inhabited the drawing-rooms of the American capital and the success his intervention would achieve.

'We are none of us exempt from our personal entanglements,' said Drinkwater pointedly, a small worm of uneasiness uncoiling itself in his belly, 'and now if you'll excuse me...' He wiped his razor clean.

Mullender was pouring the last of the hot water from the galley range into the tin bath and the cabin was filling with steam. Drinkwater began pulling his shirt over his head. Mixed with the smell of his own sweat a sweet fragrance lingered.

Vansittart watched for a moment, saw the scarred lacerations and mutilation of Drinkwater's right shoulder and hurriedly rose, tossing off his glass. 'Well, I shall have the opportunity of judging this Shaw for myself,' he said. 'In any event my bags are packed, so I will leave you to your ablutions.'

'I shall be half an hour at the most.'

Drinkwater sank back into the delicious warmth of the bath. 'Well, Mullender,' he said, 'what news have you?'

'Mr Moncrieff has presented you with a brace of ducks, sir.'

'That's very kind of Mr Moncrieff.' He entertained a brief image of Arabella sitting down to a dinner of roast duck with him in the intimacy of the cabin, then dismissed the notion as dangerously foolish.

'Do you want the boots again today, sir? As they're muddy I'll have to clean them.'

'No, no, full dress...'

105

''Tis already laid out, sir, and I've the sponging of your old coat in hand, sir.'

They had lain upon the old, shabby undress coat he had worn for the expedition. The reminder made him move restlessly, slopping water in his sudden search for the soap.

He stood before the mirror with comb and brush, an uncharacteristic defensive vanity possessing him. He suppressed his conscience by convincing himself it was to make an impression on Stewart that he dressed with such care. Mullender moved one of the lanterns and the silk stockings and silver buckled shoes, the white breeches, waistcoat and stock seemed to glow in the reflected lamp-light. He handed the comb and brush to Mullender who, with a few deft and practised strokes, quickly finished the captain's hair off in a queue.

'I suppose I should have it cut,' Drinkwater said.

'Wouldn't be you, sir,' Mullender said with finality, drawing the black ribbon tight and levelling its twin tails. Drinkwater held his arms out and Mullender helped him on with the coat. He felt the weight of the heavy bullion epaulettes, one on each shoulder as befitted a senior post-captain, and his gold cuff lace rasped that on his lapels as he adjusted the set of the garment. Mullender pulled the long queue clear of the collar and flicked at Drinkwater's shoulders before stepping back and picking up sword and belt.

'No sword tonight, Mullender, thank you.'

'Aye, sir,' grunted Mullender, clearly disapproving of Drinkwater's tact.

'Call away my barge, if you please.'

Mullender opened the cabin door and spoke to the marine sentry. Drinkwater took one final look at himself in the mirror and picked up his hat.

'Barge crew called, sir,' Mullender reported, 'and Mr Metcalfe said to tell you what looks like a Yankee schooner has just anchored on the far side o' that Yankee sloop.'

'Very well,' Drinkwater said absently and swung round.

'We must get that bulkhead painted,' he remarked suddenly. Mullender looked up.

'Sir?'

106

'That bulkhead, get it painted!' snapped Drinkwater, abruptly leaving the cabin.

'What now?' Mullender muttered, and sighed, scratching his head uncomprehendingly. He did not see, as Drinkwater saw, the faint discolourations where once the twin portraits of Elizabeth and his children had hung.

'Sir, the Yankee has just gone over the side, if you hurry...'

They could hear the squealing of the pipes floating over the still water from the dark shape of the *Stingray*, her tall masts and yards black against the dark velvet of the night sky with its myriad stars. He could see nothing of the schooner beyond her. Metcalfe's almost childish urgency irritated Drinkwater.

'I don't want to make a damned undignified race of it,' he said curtly. 'Let the bugger go ahead...' Metcalfe opened his mouth to say something, but Drinkwater was in no mood now to bandy words with his first lieutenant. 'Do you make sure the sentries present arms as he goes past. We are not at war with the United States, Mr Metcalfe, and I'll see the courtesies extended while we are within American waters.'

Metcalfe's mouth shut like a trap and he spun on his heel, but Moncrieff had already dealt with the matter. The American gig, a chuckle of phosphorescence at her cutwater, the faint flash of her oar blades rising and dipping, approached them in a curve to pass under the *Patrician*'s stern. The dim light of a lantern in her stern-sheets reflected upon the face of Captain Stewart and his attendant midshipman.

Moncrieff called the deck sentinels to attention. 'Present arms!' The American boat swept past, Stewart and the midshipman unmoving.

'Insolent devil,' said Moncrieff in a voice that must have been heard in the still darkness. 'Shoulder arms!'

'Are you ready, Vansittart?' Drinkwater enquired as a grey shape joined them.

'I am indeed, Captain Drinkwater.'

'After you, then.' Drinkwater gestured and Vansittart

peered uncertainly over the side. Midshipman Belchambers looked up from the barge.

'Just hold on to the man-ropes, sir, and lean back . . .'

He saw her first, in a full-skirted dress of watered green silk the origin of which was not Parisian. Her raven hair was up and a rope of Bahamian pearls wound round her slender neck. She looked remote, proper, Shaw's daughter-in-law-cum-hostess and not the creature who . . .

'Captain Drinkwater, good of you to come.'

'Your servant, sir. May I present Mr Henry Vansittart . . . Mr Shaw.'

'Mr Vansittart, you are very welcome. Captain Drinkwater, you have met my daughter-in-law. Mr Vansittart, may I present Mrs Arabella Shaw . . .'

Bows and curtsies were exchanged, Vansittart bent solicitously over Arabella's hand and Drinkwater turned away. He found himself face to face with Master Commandant Stewart.

He had his sister's features and the likeness shocked him. Yet there was nothing effeminate in the American officer's handsome face, on the contrary, his dark features conveyed the immediate impression of a boldness and resolution which, as he confronted the Englishman, were unequivocally hostile. Drinkwater had the unnerving sensation that, despite his own superiority in years and rank, the American held himself in all respects the better man. A cooler head than Drinkwater possessed at that instant might have considered this impression as a consequence of underlying guilt on his own part and an overweening pride and youthful contempt on the American's. At that moment, however, the impact was uncanny and overwhelming, and Drinkwater endeavoured to conceal his inner confusion with an over-elaborate greeting that the American attributed to condescension.

'Captain Stewart, I presume. I am your servant, sir, and delighted to make your acquaintance.'

The younger man's face split in a lupine grin. From the moment his topman reported the approach of the British frigate, Stewart had been both affronted by the British man-o'-war's presence in American waters, and hoping for some means by which he, the most junior commander on the American Navy List, might personally tweak the tail of the arrogant British lion. Captain Drinkwater, a greying tarpaulin officer of no particular pretension, offered him a perfect target. Stewart would not have admitted fear of any British naval officer, but he nursed an awkwardness in the presence of those urbane and languid sprigs of good families he had once met in New York. Vansittart was so clearly an example of the class, if not the type. In needling Drinkwater he felt he opened a mine under British conceit, laid under so easy and foolish a target as Captain Drinkwater, the more readily to wound Vansittart. The prospect of this revenge for past humilia-' tions, real or imagined, amused and stimulated him.

'You presume a great deal, Captain. As for being my servant that's fair enough, but your delight concerns me not at all . . .' It was a gauche, clumsy and foolish speech, but made to Drinkwater in his present mood and made loud enough for all the company to hear, it had its desired effect, bolstering Stewart's pride and leaving the witnesses nonplussed as they, in full expectation of a sharp-tongued response, left Captain Drinkwater to defend himself.

But Drinkwater blushed to his hair-roots, dropping his foolishly extended hand. Vansittart's inward hiss of breath, of apprehension rather than outrage, broke the silence.

'Gennelmen, a glass,' Shaw drawled, motioning to a negro servant in a powdered wig and a ludicrous canary-yellow livery. He bore a salver upon which the touching rims of the glasses tinkled delicately.

'I thought rum appropriate to the occasion,' said Shaw, clearly practising a joke he had rehearsed earlier and which was now quite inappropriate to the occasion.

'Indeed, ' Vansittart waded in, 'almost the *vin du pays*, what? Your health, ma'am, and yours, sir, and yours, Captain Stewart. That's a fine ship you command, by the by.'

'Indeed it is,' replied Stewart, clearly enjoying himself and never taking his eyes off Drinkwater, 'the match of any ship, even one of reputedly superior force.'

The sarcasm brought Drinkwater to himself. He mastered his discomfiture and met the younger man's eyes. 'Let us hope, Captain Stewart, the matter is not put to the test.'

'It wouldn't concern me one damn jot, Captain, were it to be put to the test tomorrow morning.'

'Come, come, gennelmen,' said Shaw, stepping between the two sea-officers and smiling nervously at Vansittart, 'damn me, Vansittart, we will have our work cut out to keep such hotheads from tearing each other to pieces. 'Tis as well they put these fellows under orders, or what would become of the peace of the world?'

Drinkwater caught Arabella's eye. Was it pity he saw there, or some understanding of his humiliation?

'I think it you, Charles, who is the greater hothead,' she scolded, half in jest. 'I don't believe Captain Drinkwater to be a man to underestimate his enemy.'

Was the remark taken as one of mere politeness, or an indiscretion of the most lamentably revealing nature? Drinkwater could not be sure how each of them perceived it, for his prime concern was to seize the lifeline she had flung him, to put the company at their ease, to detach himself from Stewart's sarcastic goading.

'I have held that as a guiding principle throughout my career, ma'am.'

'You have seen a good deal of action, have you not, Captain?' Vansittart rallied to him, equally eager to defuse the atmosphere, but painfully aware of Drinkwater's lack of finesse in such circumstances.

'I believe so,' Drinkwater answered.

'What – Frenchmen?' put in Stewart, unwisely.

'Some Frenchmen, yes, but Dutchmen, Russians – and Americans.' He paused, feeling he had regained some credibility. 'War is not a matter to be entered into lightly, no matter how excellent one's ship, nor the fighting temper of one's people.'

Stewart had swallowed his rum at a gulp and it emboldened him. 'Oh, ship for ship, we'd lick you, Cap'n . . .'

Drinkwater experienced that sudden cool detachment he usually associated with the heat of action, after the period of fear before engagement and the manic rage with which a man worked up his courage and in which most men conquered or perished in hand-to-hand slaughter. For him this remote and singular feeling lent him strength and an acuity of eye and nervous response which had carried him through a dozen fierce actions. He suddenly saw this boorish boy as being unworthy of his temper, and smiled.

'Perhaps, ship for ship, you are quite right, Mr Master Commandant, but I beg you to consider how few ships you have and the inevitable outcome of a concentration of force upon this coast. A blockade, for instance; do you comprehend a blockade, Mister Stewart? No, I think not. Say twelve of the line cruising constantly off Sandy Hook, another dozen off the Delaware, another off the Virginia capes, with frigates patrolling in between, cutters and schooners maintaining communications between the squadrons, ships being relieved regularly, and water and wood being obtained with impunity from your empty and unguarded coastline ... come, sir, that is not a happy prospect, you'll allow?'

Drinkwater observed with a degree of pleasure how Stewart resented the use of his proper rank and Drinkwater's pointed abandonment of his courtesy title. The added irony of begging his listener's consideration was lost on Stewart in his inflamed state, for while Drinkwater spoke, he snapped his fingers and took another glass of rum.

'You couldn't do it,' he said thickly when Drinkwater finished speaking, 'your men wouldn't stand for it ...'

'We'd still be damned foolish to put it to the test, Charles,' temporized Shaw, 'hell's bells, you professional gennelmen are a pair of gamecocks to be sure. Arabella, my dear, we'd better fill their bellies with something less inflammatory than firewater ...'

Vansittart laughed loudly and Mistress Shaw caught the manservant's eye and addressed a few words to him.

'Whether or not you gennelmen trade shot for shot rather depends upon the efforts of Mr Vansittart here,' Shaw said, taking the diplomat's elbow familiarly, 'and we have concluded all the necessary arrangements for you to proceed to Washington, Mr Vansittart. A schooner has just arrived this evening to convey you up to Baltimore and I understand a chaise is at your disposal thereafter. I, for one, hope the news you bring for Mr Foster enables us to conclude a peaceful settlement of our dispute. Foster's a better man than either Jackson or Erskine were in the subtleties of representing the British government over here, so there's some hope!' Shaw raised his glass and was about to propose a toast to peace when Stewart snorted his objection. Shaw put out a placating hand as Stewart made to protest. 'Oh sure, Charles,' he went on, 'I understand your anger, Great Britain *has* undoubtedly acted the part of the bully and I'm sure Captain Drinkwater, being a fair-minded man, will acknowledge that his country's foreign policies have not always been honourable, whatever justification – mainly expedience, I guess – is advanced, but it don't mean we *have* to fight.'

'Men were taken out of my own ship,' Stewart protested.

'The *Stingray?*' queried Vansittart quickly.

'No,' said Shaw, 'Charles was master of a Baltimore schooner between naval appointments,' he explained. 'We have more officers than ships . . .'

'*Naval* ships,' Stewart said with a heavy emphasis.

'How many guns do your merchant ships mount?' Vansittart asked, anticipating the question forming at the same instant in Drinkwater's mind. Not for the first time, Drinkwater acknowledged the sharpness of Vansittart's intelligence. Yet he did not want Vansittart to overplay his hand. Such a rapid tattoo of queries might make Stewart clam up and, in his perceptive state, Drinkwater wanted the already mildly intoxicated young man to talk a great deal more. Perhaps he might, with advantage, stir this pot a little.

'They make excellent privateers, Vansittart,' he said, 'I recall during the last American war . . .'

Stewart, who had long since swallowed his third glass of rum, grinned. This British captain was not merely ancient, he was also cautious! 'Cap'n Drinkwater is right,' he said with a hint of mimicry, 'they make *excellent* privateers, and we could have 'em swarming like locusts over the ocean.' Stewart held up his free hand and snapped his fingers. 'And a fig for your blockade! You'd have to convoy *everything*!'

'Well, sir . . .' Vansittart began but was interrupted.

'Gentlemen,' Arabella broke in, the yellow-coated servant at her shoulder, 'dinner is served.'

They sat down to dine in the same room as they had used the previous evening, but now gravity not gaiety was the prevailing mood. Zebulon Shaw remained a gracious host and Vansittart a sociable guest but Stewart sank into a moody contemplation of the man who epitomized his conception of the enemy. As for Drinkwater, he did his best to contribute to the conversation and to maintain a somewhat pathetic contact with Arabella. He was largely unsuccessful, for Vansittart divided his easy attention between Shaw and his daughter-in-law.

Drinkwater could not afterwards recall what they had eaten. A spiced capon, he thought, though his abiding memory was a complex feeling of self-loathing, of irritation that Stewart's slowly increasing drunkenness was accompanied by the man's unceasing scrutiny, and of jealousy that Arabella should flirt so with Vansittart, a boy young enough to be her son.

He was in a foul mood when she rose and declared she would withdraw and leave them to their spirits and cigars. As she swept out with a smiling admonition to her father-in-law not to deprive her for too long of the society of so many gentlemen, Drinkwater felt bereft, unaware of a tender and pointed irony in her words.

'This is a superb house,' Vansittart remarked as he drew on his cigar.

'It was my father's conceit to build a castle, such as an English peer might have. He began in '76, three weeks after the declaration of independence, but', Shaw blew a fragrant cloud of tobacco smoke at the ceiling, 'man proposes and God disposes.'

'I don't follow . . .'

'He was killed at the Battle of the Brandywine a year later,' Shaw explained. 'Although a lieutenant in Wagonner's Virginia regiment in Scotch Willie Maxwell's brigade, he had been sent with a message to Wayne at Chadd's Ford where he stopped a Hessian ball. He died instantly . . .'

113

'I am sorry to hear it, sir,' Vansittart replied.

Shaw shrugged. 'Oh, I bear no ill-will, time heals all things and he died in good company.'

'He died fighting the English,' slurred Stewart.

Shaw seemed embarrassed at the interruption and addressed Drinkwater. 'You served at the time, Captain, did you not?'

'Aye, sir. I served in Carolina – and lost friends there. It had become a filthy business by then. The circumstances of death were less glorious. There was a midshipman whose end was foul.'

'How so?' Stewart put the decanter down and looked up. His intake of wine had been steady throughout the meal and beads of sweat stood out on his forehead. A prurient curiosity blinked through his blurring eyes and Drinkwater wanted to wound the cocksure fool, to disabuse him of his misconceptions of war.

'He was captured and mutilated, Captain Stewart,' Drinkwater said quietly.

'I think we should join . . .' Shaw began, but Stewart ignored his host.

'Whadya mean – mutilated?'

Vansittart half-rose, but his face was turned expectantly towards Drinkwater. The curiosity of the two younger men sent a sudden shudder of revulsion through Drinkwater. The one sought glory in war, the other thought of the business as a gigantic game in which whole divisions of men might be moved across continents as a matter of birth-right.

'We found him with his own bollocks in his mouth, Captain Stewart.'

'I am sorry about Charles,' Arabella said as they stood once more on the terrace.

'It was nothing.'

'For a moment I thought . . .'

'That I would call him out?' Drinkwater chuckled, 'God's bones, no . . . I am too old for that tomfoolery.'

'I am glad to hear it.' She pressed his arm and they stood in silence. The moon was riding clear of a low bank of cloud and the stridulation of cicadas filled the air. In

114

the room behind them Stewart had fallen asleep; Vansittart and Shaw were deep in discussion.

'I am sorry,' she said suddenly.

'For what?'

'I feel now that I should not have asked you to come this morning.'

'My dear, what has passed between us has passed. We may or may not be judged, I don't know . . .'

'Remorse will turn you against me.'

'I can never be anything more to you than I was today, you know that. But I shall never be anything less.'

'I marked you as a man of constancy.'

'You must have faith in your intuition . . .'

'Nathaniel, suppose there are consequences?'

A cold sensation wrapped itself about his heart. 'Is it likely?'

'It is not impossible,' she whispered fearfully.

'I will give you an address in London. I will not abandon a child.' He paused. Pride cometh before a fall, he recalled. The modest competence, the acquisition of Gantley Hall, his wife and family – how he had jeopardized them by his casual dalliance with this woman. A riot in the blood, she had called it . . .

But looking at her he yearned to kiss her again.

'Arabella . . .' She turned her face towards him when a movement at the end of the terrace caught his eye.

'Who the devil . . . ?'

'It's me, sir, Frey.'

Gently he detached himself from her, aware, even in that prescient moment when he knew something was wrong, how reluctant she was to let him go. 'Mr Frey? What the devil do you here?'

'Eight men have run, sir. Made off in the blue cutter left alongside from the watering party.'

'God damn and blast it!'

CHAPTER 9 September 1811

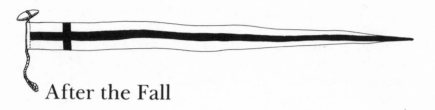

After the Fall

'What's to be done, sir?'

'Quiet, boy!'

Midshipman Belchambers' whispered query was hissed into silence by the first lieutenant. Metcalfe fidgeted, clasping and unclasping his hands, then ran a crooked finger round the inside of his stock. He felt Frey's eyes upon him in the preternatural chiaroscuro of the moonlit quarterdeck and concluded that he did not like Frey: he and Captain Drinkwater were, what was it? Too close, yes, that was it, too close; the bonding of long service affronted Metcalfe's hierarchical sensibilities, disturbed him where it had no right to. He felt the silent reproach in Vansittart's presence among them, conceiving the young diplomat one of Drinkwater's party when, by all the social conventions and familial traditions, Metcalfe knew he should not be so constantly at Drinkwater's side. Belchambers was another, a lesser example of the first. He snapped the eager boy to cringing silence and faced aft, unaware of the irrationality of his train of thought, as apparently expectant as all the other officers ranged on deck, awaiting the reaction from the shadowy figure standing right aft at the taffrail.

Captain Drinkwater stared astern, towards the confluence of the Potomac with Chesapeake Bay wherein drained the waters of a dozen rivers. The moon rode high, clear of the clouds, apparently diminished in diameter due to its altitude, yet lending a weird clarity to the dismal scene. Captain Drinkwater had been lost in this

116

contemplation for almost ten minutes, while his officers waited on the quarterdeck and below them the ship seethed. Barely a man slept after the hue and cry had been raised and Metcalfe, Gordon, Frey, Moncrieff and his marines, with drawn swords and hand-held bayonets, had called the roll and scoured the ship.

'For God's sake...' Metcalfe muttered, much louder than he intended. He met Vansittart's eyes and shrugged. 'The buggers could be anywhere,' he said, as if Vansittart had asked him a question, 'anywhere, damn them.'

'Do you search for them tonight?'

Metcalfe jerked his head aft, but still Drinkwater remained motionless, his hands clasped behind his back, his head facing away from them. All decisions waited upon the captain's pleasure now he was back on board.

It had been in Drinkwater's mind to vent his temper upon those responsible for the desertions: Metcalfe as his own deputy, the officer of the watch and his subordinates, down to the marine sentries and the men in the guard-boat.

But he knew he would be guilty of a grave injustice if he did, and he was already guilty of so much that day that the prospect of adding to the woeful catalogue of folly appalled him.

Standing beneath the pale splendour of the moon he felt himself a victim of all the paradoxes visited upon mankind. And yet his sense of responsibility was too keen to submit to so cosy a justification; the harsh self-condemnation of his puritan soul rejected the libertine's absolution.

In the cool of the night his old wounds ached intrusively, the body sharing the hurt of the mind. Mentally and physically he gave himself no chance of surrender to passion, refused to acknowledge the mutual hunger in, and irresistible attraction between himself and Arabella. Perhaps, had he remained in Arabella's presence, he would not have judged himself so harshly, would have placed events in their perspective. But Frey had been the agent of fate and brought the news of providence's swift retribution.

'Pride', he again and again recalled his mother saying,

'always comes before a fall,' and now he remembered another saw she was fond of, a social pretension in its way, almost an aspiration: 'Remember, you are not born to pleasure, Nathaniel, it is not for us. We are of the middling sort . . .'

He had heard the phrase recently and, in remembering, he confronted his own ineluctable culpability. Thurston had used it only that morning. A sudden anger burst in upon his brain. He should never have let Thurston have his head and spew his republican cant so readily! God, what a damned fool he had been to listen; to listen and to be half-convinced the fellow spoke something akin to the truth!

Well, he had his bellyful of the truth now, to be sure, he thought bitterly, victim of his own stupid, expansive weakness, a weakness doubtless induced by the bewitching prospect of a day in Mistress Shaw's company. God Almighty, he had been gulled by a damned whore!

And supposing he had left her pregnant, or worse, she had left *him* poxed . . . ?

He broke out in a cold sweat at the thought. Fate had an uncanny way of striking a man when his guard was down and it had certainly conspired to strike him today.

Forward the ship's bell tolled two. It was already tomorrow, one o'clock in the morning, two bells into the middle watch, almost the lowest, most debilitating hour of the night.

He looked at the moon. It would be setting over Gantley Hall, already the first pale flush of the morning would be turning the grey North Sea the colour of wet lead, glossing the ploughed furrows of his oh-so-proudly acquired acres.

With an effort he mastered his temper, his dark fears and forebodings. 'I am grown selfish, morbid and gloomy,' he muttered to himself, 'and there is work to do.' There was always work, always duty, always the submission of the self to the common weal. It was the great consolation. The thought steadied him, drove back the gathering megrims and the whimpering self-pity that threatened, for one desperate, lonely moment, to overwhelm him.

No, he could not visit his anger upon men who had

been merely neglectful of their duty. Doubtless the deserters had employed a degree of guile, slipping into the moored boat and shoving off as the guard-boat vanished round the far side of the frigate. Davies, the master's mate in charge, had heard nothing, nor seen anything. Yes, he had agreed, his men had been pulling somewhat lethargically and the current had, he admitted, swept them down a little too far from the ship than he would have wished, but he had forgotten how many circuits they had made during his watch . . .

Drinkwater could guess the rest. A distracted or dozing sentry, maybe even a colluding one, and who could blame the poor devils when some men had long been away from the kind of comforts he had so liberally indulged in the preceding day?

But eight men had run . . . He began to think logically again, thrusting aside the earlier train of thought. The ache in his old wounds throbbed into the background of his consciousness.

There must be those among them who remembered hanging a man for desertion before *Patrician* left for the Pacific. There was even less cause for mercy upon the present occasion. At least then the victim had the not unreasonable excuse of running to find out whether the tales of his wife's infidelity were true.

The thought of marital infidelity made Drinkwater sweat again. He had betrayed his wife and been unjust to Arabella; she was no wanton and, he reflected, he was no libertine. He took heart from the thought.

Eight men had run and it was time to tackle the problem, but in such a way as allowed him to control events. Yesterday, for that is how it was now, part of the unalterable past, yesterday had been a day during which he had lost control, been swept up by events, relaxed and forsaken his duty; perhaps for a few hours he had been merely himself, in all the lonely isolation of an individual human soul, but now, today, and from this very minute, he must be what he was: a sea-officer. He squared his shoulders, swung on his heel and strode forward.

'Gentlemen,' he said coolly, 'we are here to see Mr Vansittart lands safely and with every prospect of success

in his task. He is to board the schooner which arrived here
at sunset and will do so at six bells in the morning watch.
That is seven o'clock by your hunter, Vansittart, if you
made the last correction for longitude. My barge is to be
used for the transfer, Mr Belchambers in command. Do
you understand?'

There was a mumbled chorus of comprehension.

'Very well, then I suggest those of us not on duty should
get some sleep.' He stepped forward and they drew apart.

'Sir, what about . . .' Metcalfe began.

'Let's deal with that in the morning, shall we? Good-
night, gentlemen, I trust you will sleep well.'

'They will be laughing at us over there this morning,'
Drinkwater said and Moncrieff, Gordon, Metcalfe and
Frey all looked at the *Stingray*, visible in part through the
stern windows. 'More coffee . . . ?'

If the officers assumed their invitation to breakfast was
an invitation to a council of war, they were disappointed.
Their commander's detached and almost negligent
approach was reminiscent of the night before.

Indeed, Metcalfe, going below to turn in, had expressed
the opinion that Drinkwater seemed about to let the
matter slide and to bid good riddance to the eight who
had run. Such pusillanimity was, he concluded, quite
within the captain's erratic character and would have a
bad effect on the men. They could, he asserted with an
almost cheerful conviction, look forward to more desertions if he proved correct in his assumption. In the
prevailing gloom no one had seen fit to contradict him. He
was, in any case, given to extreme expressions of opinion
and no one took much notice of him. It was only over the
coffee and burgoo that they recalled the matter and
thought Metcalfe might, after all, have a point. Close to
the land as she was, the ship might well become ungovern-
able and the thought made them all uneasy.

There was no doubt the Yankees would find the event
most amusing.

'What *are* your intentions, sir,' Moncrieff ventured
boldly, anxiety plain on his open face, 'now Mr Vansittart
has gone?'

Drinkwater sat back and regarded the company. Metcalfe looked his usual indecisive, critical self, an air of mock gravity wrapping his moon face in a cocoon of self-importance. Gordon and Frey looked concerned, ready to act upon orders but too junior to have any influence upon events. Only Moncrieff, the ever-resourceful marine lieutenant, had physical difficulty in holding his eager initiative in check.

Drinkwater smiled. 'What do you suggest, Mr Frey?'

Frey's Adam's apple bobbed. 'Well, sir, I should, er, send out a search party . . .'

'Mr Gordon?'

'I agree, sir, perhaps to scour the countryside, check the buildings on the estate here . . .'

'Run downstream, they'd have used the current to put as great a distance between us and them and they know there are towns and villages for miles along the banks of the bay . . .'

'Very good, Mr Moncrieff. Mr Metcalfe?'

'I agree with Moncrieff, sir, and they already have a head start of', he pulled out his watch, 'almost ten and a half hours.'

'Do we know exactly what time they got away?'

'Well no, not exactly, sir, but . . .'

'Very well. The launch, with a corporal's guard and provisions for three days, is to leave for a search along the shore. Mr Frey, you are to command. Mr Gordon, you may run along the Potomac shore in the remaining cutter. Take a file of marines, but contrive to look like a watering party, not a war party. I don't want trouble with the local population. Be certain of that. Under the circumstances I would rather lose the men than have a hornets' nest stirred up to undermine Vansittart's mission. That is an imperative, do you understand?'

'Aye, sir.'

'Aye, sir.'

'Very well, you may carry on.'

Frey and Gordon scraped back their chairs. Metcalfe and Moncrieff made to rise too, but Drinkwater motioned them to remain seated. After the junior lieutenants had gone Drinkwater rose, lifted the decanter of Madeira from its fiddle and, with three glasses, returned to the table.

'I was surprised no one mentioned the *Stingray*,' he said as the rich, dark wine gurgled into the crystal glasses.

'The *Stingray*, sir?' Moncrieff said with quickening interest, 'They wouldn't dare . . . I mean how the deuce . . .?'

'When I went ashore, the blue cutter was alongside the starboard main-chains. Davies, the master's mate rowing guard, said they dropped too far downstream before they rounded the stern, but even then I suspect they were too stupefied by the monotony of their duty to notice immediately the cutter was missing in the darkness. They probably fell downstream *every* circuit they made. But being downstream they commanded a fair view of the larboard side of the ship and, with the light southerly breeze then blowing, the ship was canted across the current sufficient to render the starboard, not the larboard side the more obscured . . .'

'And the *Stingray* was in, as it were, the shadow of the ship, lying to starboard of us, begging your pardon, sir,' Moncrieff added hurriedly. 'God damn it, of course! They pulled directly for the *Stingray*!'

'What makes you so sure, sir?' asked the unconvinced Metcalfe. Drinkwater's clever assessment undermined his own carefully argued case for the captain's general incompetence.

'I've a notion, shall we say, Mr Metcalfe? Nothing more.' But it was more, much more. He did not explain that something in Captain Stewart's over-confident demeanour had laid a suspicion in his mind. He had only just realized that himself, but now it gripped his imagination with the power of conviction.

'What about the boat, though?' persisted Metcalfe, unwilling to give up his theory.

'Oh, I expect Frey will find it downstream somewhere. The current and the wind will probably have grounded it on the Maryland shore.'

'Damn it, I think you're right, sir.' Moncrieff's eyes were glowing with certainty.

'Thank you, Moncrieff,' Drinkwater said drily. 'And now I think I'd better write to Mr Shaw and explain why marines and jacks are likely to be seen trampling over his land this morning. Perhaps you'd pass word for Thurston...'

'He was among the eight, sir,' said Metcalfe, his theory bolstered by Drinkwater's forgetfulness. 'I told you last night.'

'Oh yes, I had forgot.' Drinkwater felt a sensation of shock. He had been too self-obsessed last night to assimilate that detail. If Metcalfe's nervously delivered report had contained the information, it had simply not sunk in. It was not Arabella who had gulled him, he thought now, kinder to himself and therefore to her, she had merely let passion run away with her, as he had done himself; but Thurston had most assuredly duped him, lectured him and then pulled wool over his preoccupied eyes!

'But if you are right, sir, what do you intend to do about the Americans?' Metcalfe asked, prompting, aware that if Captain Drinkwater did not do something then he would most assuredly dishonour the flag.

'I am going to dissemble a little, Mr Metcalfe.'

'Dissemble, sir?' It was a policy Metcalfe had neither considered himself, nor thought his superior capable of.

'Yes. They are not going to sail until we do; they will sit as post-guard upon us until we depart. Let us bluster about our searches and, while we can, keep a watch upon her deck. You have a good glass, Mr Metcalfe?'

'Aye, sir, a Dollond, like yours.'

'Very well, busy yourself about the quarterdeck without making your spying too conspicuous. How many of these eight men would you recognize?'

'Well, Thurston, sir, and a man called King, foretopman, one of our best...'

'I know Carter, sir,' put in Moncrieff, 'and the Dane Feldbek...'

'And there were the two Russians, the fellows from the *Suvorov*, Korolenko and Gerasimov,' Drinkwater added, remembering now how Metcalfe had stumbled over the pronunciation of their names, 'you'd recognize them, surely?'

'Yes, of course, sir,' Metcalfe hurriedly agreed, surprised at Drinkwater's access of memory.

'Well, that is six of them,' Drinkwater said, finishing his wine and rising from the table. 'They cannot keep 'em below indefinitely.'

Moncrieff and Metcalfe rose at this signal of dismissal. Drinkwater turned to stare out through the stern windows at the American ship. Sunlight picked out her masts and yards and the thin, pale lines of her immaculately stowed sails. Her ports were open and her guns run out. There were signs of men at exercise about her decks, the glint of cutlasses and boarding pikes.

'What will you do if and when we spot them, sir?' asked Metcalfe from the doorway.

'Mmmm?' Drinkwater grunted abstractedly, still gazing at the Yankee sloop.

'What will you do, sir, *vis-à-vis* the Yankee?'

'Ain't it a first lieutenant's privilege to lead cutting-out parties, Mr Metcalfe?' Drinkwater replied absently, turning back into the cabin.

Metcalfe had difficulty seeing the captain's expression, silhouetted as he was against the sun-dappled water in the background, but Drinkwater stepped forward and Metcalfe was shocked to see a look of implacable resolve fixed upon Drinkwater's face. 'Almost', he said to himself, 'as if he had been staring at an enemy.'

Frey's party found the missing cutter. It had grounded on a spit fifty yards from the Maryland shore.

'I don't know where they landed, sir,' he reported later that day, 'but that boat had been drifting.'

'We know where they landed, Mr Frey,' Drinkwater said, nodding at the sloop they could see through the stern windows.

'The *Stingray*, sir?' queried Frey in astonishment.

Drinkwater nodded. 'We've seen both the Russians using the head,' he said drily. 'I daresay if we wait long enough we'll see all eight of them bare their arses in due course.'

'So, er, what do you intend doing, sir?'

Drinkwater drew in his breath and let it out again. 'Well, I believe the Americans call it playing possum, but you've a little time before dark. I want you to go and beat up a bit

124

of shore-line. Pull round a little, let our friends over there think we're hoodwinked.' Drinkwater rose and leaned forward, both hands spread on the table. 'I don't want to do *anything* to jeopardize Vansittart's mission. On the other hand, the ship's company must not be allowed to think we are taking no action, so make no mention of the fact that we know about the presence of the deserters aboard the *Stingray*, do you understand?'

'Perfectly, sir. In fact the men may already know.'

'Good, now be off with you and conduct yourself like a man who's just had a flea in his ear and been told not to come back empty-handed.'

'Aye, aye, sir.'

Frey turned and was about to open the cabin door when Drinkwater added: 'You *can* come back though, Mr Frey, and with all your boat's crew, if you please.'

'Aye, aye, sir,' Frey replied with a grin.

Half an hour before sunset Drinkwater called away his barge. The knowledge that the deserters were aboard the *Stingray* gave him some comfort, for Stewart would keep them closer watched than Metcalfe. Whether or not Stewart would keep his secret until after *Patrician's* departure or make some demonstration embarrassing to Drinkwater remained to be seen. The man harboured a deep resentment against the British and, it was obvious, saw the *Patrician's* commander as the embodiment of all he disliked. But there was also an ungovernably passionate streak, a rash impetuosity to offset a deep intelligence; that much Drinkwater had deduced from the man's indiscreet drunkenness. Much might also be read from his sister . . .

However, he must dissemble, to gull as he had been gulled, to convince his people that he would not tolerate desertion.

Shaw received him in his dressing-room.

'I had your note, Captain Drinkwater.'

'I apologize for troubling you and hope that my men have not been over-intrusive upon your land, Mr Shaw.'

'Not *over*-intrusive, no,' Shaw replied, his resentment clearly aroused by the minor invasion of the day.

125

'I apologise unreservedly, sir, if any damage has been caused . . .'

'No, no,' Shaw waved aside the suggestion that anything more than his sense of propriety had sustained injury.

'And I apologize at the inconvenience of the hour, it is intolerable of me . . .'

'Please sit down, Captain. Will you join us for dinner? Arabella will be delighted to see you; she sure enjoyed your company yesterday.'

'Thank you, no, sir,' Drinkwater said, remaining standing. He longed to see Arabella again, for all the pain and remorse it would cause him. 'My official affairs are, alas, more pressing. Perhaps I may wait upon Mistress Shaw at a later date, but for the nonce I must perforce ask you to convey my felicitations to her. My presence is, er, a matter of some delicacy . . .' Drinkwater shot a glance at Shaw's negro valet.

Shaw dismissed the man. 'Come, sir, you have time to sit and take a glass.'

'Obliged, sir.' Drinkwater was not loathe to comply. Shaw poured from a handy bottle on a side-table. They mutually toasted each other's health. 'The point is', Drinkwater went on, leaning forward in his chair to give his words both urgency and confidentiality, 'this affair of deserters is a damnable nuisance. I *must* make every effort to regain 'em, for my Service, my reputation and general appearances, not to mention *pour discourager les autres*,' he said in his poor French, 'but I wish to do nothin' which might provoke a suspension of negotiations, Vansittart was most tellin' upon this point. It seems, from your discussions with him last night, there are men in Washington seekin' some new impropriety on our part, like Humphries' cavalier behaviour towards the *Chesapeake*, to make a *casus bellum* . . .'

'That is surely true, Captain. They are mostly from New England, hawks we have styled them, perhaps foolishly, for a hawk has a greater appeal than a dove, I allow. But I don't follow why . . .'

'I know where the men are, Mr Shaw . . .'

'You do?' Shaw's eyebrows rose with astonishment. 'Where?'

'Aboard the United States sloop-of-war *Stingray*.'

'The hell they are!'

'I feel sure thay have been given asylum by Captain Stewart . . .'

'Have you sent word to Charles? Asked for them back?'

'Mr Shaw, you saw Captain Stewart's attitude to British interests last night. I am not insensible to the fact that he may be personally justified in all his resentments, but I am convinced he would refuse *me* the return of my men as a matter of principle. Why, I think he would delight in it.'

'He certainly has a thirst for glory.'

'And took against me personally, I believe.'

Shaw nodded. 'I fear so, Captain. Then you want me to approach him, to persuade him to relinquish your deserters?'

'Yes, if you would. It would be the simplest answer.'

Shaw sighed and rubbed his chin. 'What would you do with them? You would have to punish them, would you not?'

'Aye, sir, but I am not an inhumane man. Whatever I decided I would not carry out in American waters and properly I can do nothing until they have been court-martialed.'

'I don't follow . . . would you act improperly?'

'I could deem them guilty of a lesser crime and hence a lesser punishment . . .'

'And simply flog 'em? Pardon me, but the forces of Great Britain have a certain reputation for brutality. I too lived before the Revolution, Captain.'

'I believe General Washington ordered corporal punishment for breaking ranks and deserting, Mr Shaw. It is a not uncommon, if regrettable thing in war.'

'But my country is not at war and I want no part in precipitating any such misery on another . . .'

'I admire your sensibilities, Mr Shaw, but my country *is* at war.' Drinkwater mastered his exasperation. Shaw, it seemed, wanted to be all things to all men. He thought of Thurston, the idealist without responsibility. Now this wealthy man could keep his conscience clean by stepping round the problem. I am of the middling sort, he thought ironically, the sort that thrust the affairs of the world

127

along day by day. 'I can only give you my word of honour that I will be lenient . . .'

'Be more specific, sir. To what extent will your leniency diminish your sentence of retribution?'

'I will order them no more than a dozen lashes.'

'Good God, sir, a *dozen*?'

'How many do you give your slaves, Mr Shaw?' Drinkwater was stung to riposte, regretting the turn the conversation had taken.

'That is an entirely different matter,' Shaw snapped. Then, struck by a thought and measuring the English officer, he added, 'Hell! Don't get any ideas about making up your crew from my plantation.'

Drinkwater attempted to defuse the atmosphere with a grin. 'I could promise them a nominal freedom aboard a man-o'-war,' he remarked drily, 'but I would not, you have my word,' he added hurriedly, seeing the colour rising in Shaw's face.

Shaw blew out his cheeks. 'Damn me, sir, this is a pretty kettle o' fish.'

Drinkwater seized this moment of weakness. 'I want only to avoid a collision, Mr Shaw. If you cannot be advocate perhaps you could merely ask; let Stewart know I am aware he is harbouring my men. The burden of conscience will then be upon him, will it not?'

'That is true . . .'

Drinkwater rose, 'I have kept you from your table, sir, and I am sorry for it. Perhaps you might consider consulting Mistress Shaw, in any event please present my compliments; she struck me as a woman of good sense. It is my experience that most women know their own minds, and what is best for their menfolk too.'

Shaw rose and held out his hand. Both men smiled the complicit understanding of male confraternity.

'Perhaps I will, Captain, perhaps I will,' Shaw said smiling.

And partially satisfied, Drinkwater walked down towards the boat upon the lush, shadowed and terraced lawn. There existed stronger and more instantaneous bonds than those of chauvinism, bonds whose strength and extent were mysteries but whose existence was undeniable.

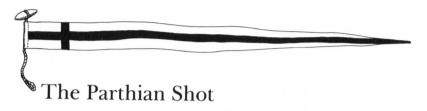

The Parthian Shot

They lay in this limbo of uncertainty for eight days, one, it seemed to those disposed to seek signs amid the random circumstances of life, for every deserter. The fall of the year came slowly, barely yet touching these low latitudes, so the very air enervated them and the pastoral beauty of the scene was slowly soured by idleness and a lack of communication with the shore.

The Patricians, unpatrician-like, still pulled their miserable guard round themselves, while the Stingrays regularly ferried their commander ashore. It was clear to Drinkwater that although Shaw might have spoken to Stewart about the advantages accruing to an honest, open, applepie handover of the British deserters, the appeal had fallen on deaf ears. Since they now caught no more than an occasional glimpse of their men, Drinkwater knew that Stewart was guarding his prizes closer still.

To keep the pot boiling Drinkwater dispatched Frey in the launch for a three-day expedition along the Virginia and Maryland shores and Stewart had, perforce, to send a shadowing boat. As for Arabella, Drinkwater saw her three or four times as she rode out. Once they exchanged greetings, she with a wave, he with a doffing of his hat, but on the other occasions, distance prevented these formalities.

The lack of hospitality on Shaw's part discouraged Drinkwater and, when he sent an invitation to Shaw and his daughter-in-law to dine as his guests aboard *Patrician*

(Lieutenant Gordon's questing boat-party having disturbed a covey of game birds), it was declined on the grounds of Mr Shaw's absence.

Drinkwater tried to convince himself all parties awaited the outcome of negotiations before re-establishing amicable relations, but he knew the matter of the deserters had come between them all. As for Arabella herself, he thought she wished to distance herself from him and respected her wishes. Besides, he had no desire to make a fool of himself.

'Why did Vansittart have to go via Baltimore, sir?' Frey asked on his return. He had made his report and he and Drinkwater had been consulting a chart, Frey tracing his aimless track along the shores of Chesapeake Bay. 'The Potomac leads directly up to Washington.'

'A matter of formalities, I suppose,' replied Drinkwater absently, filling two glasses. 'Perhaps they did not wish him to see the defences of Washington, or reconnoitre so obvious an approach.'

'He'll come back the same way, then?'

'I imagine so. I've really no idea.'

'I wish *we* were back, sir,' Frey said suddenly.

'Back? Where?'

'In home waters, off Ushant, in the Mediterranean, the Baltic, anywhere but here. God, we're not liked hereabouts.'

'We're an old enemy, Mr Frey ... Tell me have you executed any watercolours lately? I believe you were working on a folio ...'

'Oh, those, no, I have abandoned the project.' Something wistfully regretful in Frey's tone prompted Drinkwater to probe.

'Not like you to abandon anything.'

'No, maybe not, sir, but this occasion proved the rule.'

'The wardroom's not the most conducive place, eh? Do 'em in here, I could do with a little society.'

'Begging your pardon, sir, but I don't think that a good idea ...'

'Oh, why not ...? Ah, I see, presuming on our previous acquaintance, eh?'

'Something of the sort, sir.'

'Who? Not Moncrieff . . .' He knew already, but wanted to see if Frey's admission would back his hunch.

'No, no, not Moncrieff, sir, he's a good fellow . . .'

'Well, Wyatt then, he's no aesthete, though I'd have baulked at calling him a Philistine.'

'No, old Wyatt's a marline-spike officer, not well-versed, but experienced. I find the first lieutenant . . .'

'A difficult man, eh?'

'An inconsistent man, sir,' Frey admitted tactfully, the wine having its effect.

'Ah, diplomatic, Mr Frey, I must remember your talents in that direction. Perhaps you should have gone to Washington in place of Vansittart. He is certainly a curious fellow.'

'Vansittart, sir?' Frey frowned.

'No,' Drinkwater grinned, 'Metcalfe . . .'

It was good to see Captain Drinkwater smiling, Frey thought as he finished his glass, it reminded him of happier times. There was something sinister about this interminable wait, knowing the deserters were within easy reach of them and that they possessed superior force and could scarcely be condemned for insisting their own be returned to them. Frey had, moreover, heard it expressed in a deliberate lower deck stage whisper meant for his ears, that was it not for Captain Drinkwater himself being in command, there would have been more than a handful of deserters.

Drinkwater, regarding his young protégé, wondered what sort of impositions Frey suffered in the wardroom. He had written Metcalfe off as an adequate but fossicking officer whose chief vice was irritation. It had not occurred to him that he was a contrary influence.

'Well, well, I had no idea.'

'There is something else, sir, something you should know about.'

'What is it?'

'The men are *very* restless, sir. I am concerned about it if we are forced to wait much longer.'

'Be patient, Mr Frey. I like this state of affairs no better than you or the hands, but we are tied to Vansittart's apron strings.'

131

And with that Frey took his dismissal. So downcast was his mood, he thought Drinkwater merely temporizing and failed to catch the faint intimation of a purpose in the captain's words.

Mr Pym was as new to *Patrician* and her commander as most of the other officers. However, he was not new to the Royal Navy, having been an assistant surgeon at Haslar Naval Hospital when Mr Lallo, the ship's former surgeon, was found dead in his cot. Pym had accepted the vacancy in a frigate ordered on special service with alacrity. He was an indolent, easy-going man who found his wife and seven children as heavy a burden upon his tolerance as his purse. He had subdued his wife's protests with the consolation that he could at last drop the 'assistant' from his title and would receive a small increase in his emolument. Having thus satisfied her social pretensions, he had packed his instruments with his beloved books and contentedly joined *Patrician*.

Mr Pym was a quiet, private man. He possessed a kind heart, though he saw this as a vice since it had trapped him into a late marriage and ensured his broody and doting wife fell pregnant with dismal regularity, a circumstance which surprised and flattered his ageing self. He guarded this soft-heartedness, having learned early in his career not to display it aboard ship. Furthermore, like most easy-going and indolent men he was basically of a selfish disposition. The charm he possessed was used to ward off invasion of his privacy, and this latter he employed chiefly in reading. Books were Pym's secret delight.

He played cards with Wyatt, partly because they were of an age, but also by way of a break, a form, he told himself, of exercise between his voracious bouts of reading. As for his duties, he attended to these easily, holding a morning surgery, after which he spent the day as he pleased. Once a week, for the purpose of presenting the sick-book and discussing the state of the ship's company's health, he waited upon the captain.

Professionally he was not over-taxed. There were the usual crop of diseases: mostly skin complaints and an asthmatic or two, a few rheumatic cases, men with the

132

usual minor venereal infections, coupled with a baker's dozen of the inevitable hernias found aboard any man-of-war. There was nothing, it seemed, of a surgical, nor indeed of a general medical nature to interest Pym, and this rather disappointed him.

He had, as a young man, studied at St Bartholomew's under the lame, scrofulous, supercilious and misanthropic physician Mark Akenside. Under Akenside's influence, he had aspired to greatness at an age when all things seem possible to the young and they have yet to discover the limitations of their energies, gifts and circumstances.

Early in life he had fallen into bad company, a mildly dissolute life and debt. The Royal Navy put distance between himself and his creditors, gave him back his character and kept him out of harm's way; but ambition continued to nag, and believing success came from change rather than effort, he accepted a post at Haslar. Here he found himself relegated to the second class and sought consolation in marriage with its consequent burdensome family. The appointment to *Patrician* presented him, therefore, with a new opportunity.

As with many unimaginative and idly ambitious men, Pym failed to see any opportunity fate cast in his way. Obsessed with the end itself, he missed anything which might, with a little application, have provided him with the means. His books were too good a diversion, too absorbing a hobby. They tied up his mind, leaving it only room to brood upon his failure.

Until, in the hiatus of lying at anchor in the Potomac, he finished them.

To this disaster was now added a trail of men with imagined complaints. The artificial nature of exercises designed to keep them busy fostered a resentment only fuelled by the desertions. It was common knowledge on the lower deck that Thurston and his companions were aboard the *Stingray*. This, and the continuing useless search parties when each man was tempted from his duty by both the abuse offered when they came into contact with Americans and the healthy prosperity of the local population, combined to keep the pot of discontent simmering. Nor did the weather help. Warm and largely windless, the poorly ventilated berth deck became stifling, despite the burning of gunpowder and sloppings of vinegar solution.

'They are', Pym announced to the dining officers, 'rotten with the corrupting disease of valetudinarianism.'

'What's that?' asked Wyatt, his mouth full.

'Malingering,' Metcalfe explained.

Pym made a mock bow to the first lieutenant for stealing his own thunder which Metcalfe, helping himself to another slice of roast snipe, did not see but which tickled Frey's sense of humour so that he first laughed and then choked.

Metcalfe looked up. 'What's so damned funny?'

Frey spluttered and went purple. 'God, he's not laughing!' Moncrieff rose and slammed a hearty palm between Frey's shoulder blades. The piece of wing dislodged itself and flew across the table on to Metcalfe's plate.

'God damn you for an insolent puppy,' Metcalfe exploded, and in the same instant Pym received inspiration and enlightenment. He knew Metcalfe had not seen his own rudeness for he had been looking at the first lieutenant when he produced his little sarcasm. He knew his own mood was due to his having run out of books. A vague idea was stirring that a sure cure to his problem was to write one of his own, though the thought of the necessary effort bothered him. Parallel with these undercurrents of thought had been a detached observation of the first lieutenant's conduct. In this as in much else, Pym was lazy, blind to the clinical opportunity the concupiscence of a frigate's wardroom gave him. He merely concluded Metcalfe would, like so many other naval officers of his era, end up raving in Haslar.

'Though he don't drink much,' he had observed to Wyatt when they had been gossiping.

'Perhaps he's poxed,' Wyatt had suggested in his own down-to-earth manner.

'Or has incipient mercurial nephritis,' Pym had humbugged elevatingly.

But now, watching Metcalfe while the others stared at Frey recovering his breath and his composure, Pym thought him mad from another source and the seed of an idea finally germinated in his mind.

'I say, Metcalfe,' Moncrieff growled as Frey exchanged near-asphixiation for indignation.

'I . . . ain't . . . a . . . damned . . . puppy!' Frey gasped.

'You even talk like the man,' Metcalfe went on, and Pym realized Metcalfe's train of thought was somehow not normal. Here again was the recurrence of this obsessive disparagement of Captain Drinkwater, and Pym wondered at its root. Metcalfe's condemnation of the captain had become almost a ritual of his wardroom conversation, ignored by the others, tolerated only because he was the first lieutenant. Captains had a right to be eccentric, disobliging even, and first lieutenants an obligation to be unswervingly, silently loyal. That was how the writ ran in Pym's understanding.

Poor Frey, unaware of any irregularity in Metcalfe's personality beyond the generally unpleasant, thought the first lieutenant must have heard something about the confidences he and Drinkwater had exchanged earlier. He resolved to have words with Mullender, forgetting in his anger that Mullender had not been in the pantry, and disgusted that Metcalfe had such spies about the ship.

'Take that back, sir . . .'

'Steady, Frey . . .' Moncrieff advised.

'Stap me, you're all in this.' There was a bewildered wildness in Metcalfe's eyes. 'Why are you looking at me, Pym? Don't *you* think such insolence is intolerable?'

And so the patient delivered himself to the quack and Pym received the means by which he was to achieve fame. 'To a degree, yes, Mr Metcalfe. I concur you've been badly treated,' Pym went on, mentally rubbing his hands with glee and ignoring the astonishment of his messmates' faces. 'Come, sir, don't let your meat spoil. Afterwards you and I shall take a turn on deck.'

For a moment Metcalfe stared at the surgeon, something akin to disbelief upon his face. Pym, in a rare and perceptive moment, interpreted it as relief. Metcalfe bent to his dinner and over his head Pym winked at the others.

Pym was not objective enough to recognize the crisis

Metcalfe had reached. He preened his self-esteem even while planning his therapy and probing his patient's mind. Overall lay a vague image of his discovery in print, a seminal work dislodging Brown's *Elements of Medicine*. He would complement Keil's *Anatomy*, Shaw's *Practice of Physic*; alongside Munro on the bones and Douglas on the muscles, they would set Pym's *On the Mind*. Yet amid this self-conceit and at the moment imperfectly glimpsed, Pym had caught sight of a great paradox. Within Metcalfe he sensed a twin existence . . .

And already the opening words of his treatise came to him: *Just as, in utero, a foetus may divide and produce two unique human beings, so in the skull, twin brains may develop, to dominate the conduct and produce responsive contrariness and a lack of logical direction . . .*

Pleased with the portentious ring of the phrases he abandoned them, setting the composition aside as Metcalfe, unsuspicious, soothed by Pym's solicitude, confirmed the growing certainty in Pym's ecstatic imagination.

'Damn the man, Mr Pym,' Metcalfe was saying, 'what is he about? The men have run and we know where they are.'

'Quite, quite, Mr Metcalfe, what do you propose, that we should take them by force and precipitate a crisis at this delicate juncture?' Their situation had been much rehearsed in the wardroom during the week and Pym laid out the logic to see where Metcalfe diverged from its uncompromising path, for he was familiar with a method used to cure the megrims by first rooting out their source.

'We should beat 'em, Pym', Metcalfe said fervently, 'blow 'em from the water, pound 'em to pieces . . .' The wildness was back in Metcalfe's eyes now and Pym felt disappointment. This was a normal, naval, fire-eating madness after all.

'Perhaps,' he said disconsolately, 'we are to take our leave without raising the matter.' He paused, seeking to lead Metcalfe's thoughts along a different path. 'It is clear to me and all the others you dislike Captain Drinkwater, though he seems reasonable enough to me . . .'

Metcalfe grunted but offered no more.

'Well, I suppose you require his good opinion for advancement...' the surgeon suggested slyly.

'Me, Pym? What the devil for? I may make my own opportunities, damn it.'

'Well,' said Pym shrugging, a sense of failure, of approaching boredom, of finding the task he had set himself too difficult making him lose interest. It had seemed a good idea earlier, but perhaps that was the wine. He failed to recognize Metcalfe's massive self-delusion and reverted to a clinical examination. Stopping his pacing, he compelled Metcalfe to do the same. The two turned inwards and Pym looked deliberately into Metcalfe's eyes, while saying with exaggerated and insincere concern, 'How can you be sure of that, Mr Metcalfe? It seems to me the war is a stalemate. All the opportunities seem to have evaporated.'

'If we were to fight *them*,' Metcalfe replied, jerking his head in the direction of the *Stingray*, 'then things would soon be different.'

'But,' said Pym frowning, suspending his clandestine examination of Metcalfe's pupils and rekindling his theory, 'I thought you once expressed a contrary opinion, or was that', he affected a conspiratorial expression, 'merely a matter of dissembling; of, shall we say, seeking the captain's good opinion?'

Metcalfe stared back at the surgeon. 'Good opinion?' he murmured, almost abstractedly, and Pym's heart leapt with enthusiasm again. 'Oh, yes, perhaps ... yes, perhaps it was.'

And Metcalfe, like a man who had suddenly remembered a forgotten appointment, abruptly walked away. Pym watched him go. 'It's not going to be easy,' he muttered to himself, but later that afternoon he fashioned a new quill-nib and began to write: *I conducted my first series of clinical observations, engaging my patient in conversation designed to draw out certain convictions, simultaneously examining his eyes for luetic symptoms. He displayed a vehement conviction at first, which yielded to a meeker and contrary opinion when this was suggested, thus exhibiting a predisposition towards influence ...*

Pym sat back very pleased with himself and at that

moment the quarter sentry called out that the schooner aboard which Vansittart had left for Baltimore was in sight.

'It is good news,' Vansittart said, sitting back in the offered chair and taking the glass Drinkwater held out. 'I think we shall simply rescind the Orders-in-Council where the United States are concerned, provided they do not press the matter of sailors' rights. There seems little pressure to do so in Washington, whatever may be said elsewhere.'

'I daresay seamen are as cheaply had here as elsewhere,' Drinkwater observed, marvelling at this change of diplomatic tack. 'Did you meet Mr Madison?'

'Alas, no, Augustus Foster handled all formal negotiations, but I learned something of interest to you.'

'To me? What the devil was that?'

'Captain Stewart is shortly to be relieved of his command.'

'Why? Surely not because of his indiscreet . . . ?'

'No, no, nothing to do with that,' Vansittart affirmed, swallowing a draught of Madeira. 'It seems to be Navy Department policy to rotate the commanders of their, how d'you say, ships and vessels? Is that it? Anyway, he won't be allowed the opportunity of quenching his fire-eating ardour one way or another now.'

'Well, there is my consolation for eating humble pie and holdin' my hand.' Drinkwater explained about the location of his deserters. 'And it don't taste so bad either. So we may weigh at first light?'

'No. Stewart left word that we should drop downstream at, how d'you say? Four bells?'

Drinkwater grunted non-committally. It would be unwise to seek a meeting with Arabella. He had existed for eight days without her and he had no right to any expectations there. They both had their bitter-sweet memories. It was enough.

Besides, he was meditating something which would hardly endear him to any American.

An hour before dawn Drinkwater turned all hands from their cots and hammocks. The bosun's mates moved with

138

silent purpose through the berth deck, their pipes quiescent, their starters flicking at the bulging canvas forms, stifling the abusive protests.

'Turn out, show a leg, you buggers, no noise, Cap'n's orders. Turn out, show a leg, no noise . . .'

'What's happening?'

'Man the capstan, afterguard aft to rouse out a spring, gun crews stand to.' Mr Comley, the boatswain, passed the word among the men tumbling out of their hammocks.

'Come on, my bullies, lash up and stow. Look lively.'

'We're gonna fuck the Yankees,' someone said and the echo of the statement ran about the berth deck as the men rolled their hammocks. Whatever their individual resentments, the abrupt and rude awakening shattered the boredom of the routine of a ship at anchor. An expectant excitement infected officers and men alike as they poured up through the hatchways, their bare feet slap-slapping on the decks as they ran to their stations like ghosts.

Wrapped in his cloak against the dawn chill Captain Drinkwater stood by the starboard hance and watched them emerge. Any evolution after a period of comparative idleness was a testing time. Men quickly became slack, lacked that crispness of reaction every commander relied upon. Eight days of riding to an anchor could, Drinkwater knew, have a bad effect.

In the waist Metcalfe leaned over the side as a spring was carried up the larboard side. Drinkwater waited patiently, trying to ignore the hissed instructions and advice offered to the toiling party dragging the heavy hemp over and round the multiplicity of obstructions along the *Patrician*'s side. Finally they worked it forward and dangled it down until it was fished from the hawse-hole and dragged inboard to be wracked to the cable. He knew, from the sudden relaxation of the men involved, when they had finished, even before Midshipman Belchambers ran aft with the news.

'Mr Wyatt requests permission to commence veering cable, sir.'

'Very well.'

Aft on the gun deck the spring would have been hove

taught and belayed; now the slacking of the anchor cable would cause the ship's head to fall off, some of the weight being taken by the spring.

Drinkwater turned and spoke to the nearest gun-captain. 'Campbell, watch your gun, now, tell me when she bears.'

'Aye, sir,' the man growled, bending his head in concentration.

'Mr Metcalfe, be ready to hold the cable.'

Metcalfe waited to pass the word down the forward companionway.

'Gun's bearing, sir.'

'Hold on,' Drinkwater called in a low voice and bent beside Campbell's 18-pounder. He could see the grey shape of the USS *Stingray* against the darker shore, her tracery of masts, yards and the geometric perfection of her rigging etched against the grey dawn. *Patrician* adjusted her own alignment and settled to her cable.

'She's a mite off now she's brung up, sir,' Campbell said and Drinkwater could smell the sweat on the man.

'Veer two fathoms,' Drinkwater called, straightening up. It would be enough. He turned to Frey. 'Your boat ready, Mr Frey?'

'Aye, sir.'

Drinkwater looked at the growing glow in the east, an ochreous backlighting of the overcast which seeped through it to suffuse the sky with a pale, bilious light.

'We'll give it a minute longer,' Drinkwater said, raising his glass and staring at the American ship upon which details were emerging from the obscurity of the night.

'We'll not want a wind outside,' someone muttered.

'What's happening?' a voice said and a score of shadowy figures shushed the coatless Vansittart to silence. 'For God's sake . . .'

'Quiet, sir!' Metcalfe snapped, fidgeting as usual.

'I forbid . . .' Vansittart began, but Frey took his elbow.

'It's a piece of bluff, sir. The Captain wants his men back before he goes.'

'But . . .'

'Shhhh . . .' Drinkwater's figure loomed alongside him and Vansittart subsided into silence.

'Very well.' Drinkwater shut his telescope with an audible snap. 'Off you go, Frey.'

With a flash of white stockings, a whirl of coat-tails and a dull gleam of gilt scabbard mountings, Frey went over the rail into the waiting boat.

Drinkwater returned to the hance and again levelled his Dollond glass. He could see a figure on the *Stingray*'s quarterdeck stretch lazily. 'Any moment now,' he said, for the benefit of the others. The cutter cleared the *Patrician*'s stern and rapidly closed the gap between the two ships.

In the stillness the plash of her oars sounded unnaturally loud to the watching and waiting British. Then the challenge sounded in the strengthening daylight.

'Boat, ahoy!'

'Hey, what the hell . . . ?'

'They've noticed our changed aspect,' Drinkwater observed, again peering through his glass. An officer was leaning over the side of the American sloop as the cutter swung to come alongside. Frey was standing up in her stern and they could hear an indistinct exchange. The cutter's oars were tossed, her bow nudged the *Stingray*'s tumblehome and Frey nimbly ran along the thwarts between the oarsmen. A second later he was leaping up the sloop's side.

'It's a master's mate . . . no, there's a lieutenant on deck without his coat . . . looks like Tucker, aye, 'tis, and there are men turning up.' The squeal of pipes came to them, floating across the smooth water.

'What's Frey saying, sir?' Metcalfe asked in an agony of suspense, frustration and resentment, because Drinkwater had briefed the third lieutenant without mentioning anything to his second-in-command, though everyone grasped the gist of Frey's purpose. For Metcalfe it was one more incident in a long series of similar slights.

'Why, to request an escort downstream, Mr Metcalfe,' jested the preoccupied Drinkwater, glass still clapped to his eye.

'Not to demand the return of our men?' Metcalfe's dithering lack of comprehension, or dullness of wit, irritated Drinkwater. 'That as well, Mr Metcalfe,' he added sarcastically.

Metcalfe turned on his heel wounded, his hands out-spread, inviting his colleagues to share in his mystification. Drinkwater had ordered him from his bed an hour earlier, told him he wanted the ship's company turned-to at their stations, a spring roused out, run forward and hitched to the cable and thought that sufficient for him to be getting on with. Frey's briefing was a different matter. It had to be precise, exact, not subject to committee approval; besides, there had been no time for such niceties, however desirable. As Metcalfe turned he caught Gordon nudging Moncrieff at the first lieutenant's dis-comfiture. The ridicule struck Metcalfe like a blow.

'Ah, here's Captain Stewart...'

Drinkwater's commentary had them craning over the hammock nettings. A group of pale figures in their shirt-sleeves were grouped round the darker figure of Lieutenant Frey in his full-dress. And as their attention was diverted to the *Stingray*, Metcalfe slipped below.

'Good mornin', sir.'

Lieutenant Frey, unconsciously aping his commander's pronunciation, gave the emerging American commander a half-bow.

'Captain Drinkwater's compliments, sir, and his apolo-gies for disturbing you at this hour. He is aware you had arranged with Mr Vansittart via the master of the schoon-er that we should weigh and proceed in company at four bells, but he insists upon the immediate return of the British deserters you have been harbouring. Truth is, sir, we have known about their presence aboard your ship for several days; saw 'em, do you see, through our glasses. Captain Drinkwater was particularly desirous of not com-promising Mr Vansittart's mission and hoped you'd re-turn 'em yourself, but his patience is now run out to the bitter end and, well, you *will* oblige, sir, won't you? Otherwise...'

'Otherwise what?'

Frey had enjoyed himself. He was not sure if he had the message word-perfect, but the gist of it, delivered at the run, as Drinkwater had ordered, had been surprisingly easy. Stewart, clogged with sleep, had twice or thrice tried to interrupt him, but Frey had had the advantage and each successive statement had demanded Stewart's sleep-dulled concentration. In the end, despite himself, he had succumbed to the coercion.

'Otherwise what?' he repeated angrily.

Frey heard Tucker mumble something about a spring and a cable.

'Otherwise, sir, the most unpleasant consequences will arise. You lie under our guns.' Frey, his hat in his hand, stepped aside and, with a theatrical flourish about which he was afterwards overweeningly boastful, he indicated the unnatural angle of the *Patrician* and the ugly, black foreshortening of her gun muzzles.

'Why you goddammed . . .' Stewart's face was flushed and his eyes staring as he transferred them from Frey to the *Patrician*, then back to Frey.

'I believe, sir,' Frey continued, overriding Stewart's erupting anger, 'your removal from your command might be a consequence of interfering with the speedy return of a British emissary after such a happy accommodation has been reached by our two governments.'

Whether or not Stewart knew he was due to be re-placed, or that the matter was a mere possibility, Frey had no idea. It was to be his last card and it appeared to work. The American captain clamped his mouth in a grimace and let his breath hiss out between his teeth. The muscles of his jaw worked furiously and when he spoke his voice cracked with the strain of self-control.

'Turn 'em over, Jonas.' Stewart turned on his heel and made for the companionway. Lieutenant Tucker hesi-tated, stared after his commander, then shrugged and repeated Stewart's order to the officers and men gather-ing about them.

'Bring up the King's men,' he sneered and sparked off a chorus of muttered curses and imprecations. Frey's cool affront began to quail before this unrestrained hostility.

'Fuck King George,' someone called out, an Irishman, Frey thought afterwards. As if stiffened by that rebel obscenity, Stewart paused, 'like Achilles at the entrance to his tent', Frey later reported, and addressed the British officer.

'Tell your Captain Drinkwater, Lieutenant,' Stewart said venomously, 'that if ever our two countries *do* find themselves at war, this ship, or another ship, *any* other ship commanded by Charles Stewart will prove itself more than a match for one of His Britannic Majesty's apple-bowed frigates!'

'His gauntlet thrown down, he disappeared like Punch, sir,' Frey reported later, 'though his people thought this a great joke, and then I was involved in receiving the deserters . . .'

The reluctant downcast shambling of the half-comprehending Russians, the fury and abuse and scuffling necessary to get the others down into the boat and the obvious distress of the American seamen in having to carry out so nauseating a duty upset Frey. He was a young man of sensitivity and not yet entirely brutalized by his Service.

'Obliged, sir,' he said at last to Tucker, aware that the moral ascendancy he had so conspicuously flaunted a few moments earlier had now passed to the American officer and the cross-armed men ranked behind him. It was a moment or two before he realized he had only received seven men. He stared down into the boat where recaptured and captors were confronting each other none too happily.

He turned to Tucker. 'Where's Thurston?'

Tucker shrugged and grinned. 'I dunno. Maybe he weren't cut out for the sea-life, mister. Maybe he ran away from us too. Anyway he ain't to be found.'

The men ranged behind Tucker seemed to surge forward. Honour could be satisfied with seven out of eight. Frey knew when he was well-off and clamped his hat on his head.

'I'm obliged, Mr Tucker. Good-day.' And stepping backwards, his hands on the man-ropes, he slid dextrously down to the boat. 'Shove off!' he ordered curtly. 'Down oars! Give way together!'

An hour and a half later His Britannic Majesty's frigate *Patrician* broke her anchor out of the mud of the Potomac river, let fall her topsails, hoisted her jib and fore-topmast

144

staysail and unbrailed her spanker. With her foreyards
hauled aback and her main and mizen braced up sharp,
her bow fell off and she turned slowly downstream,
squaring her foreyards as she steadied on course and
gathered way to pass the United States sloop-of-war
Stingray.

'Good riddance,' Frey breathed with boyish elation after
his virtuoso performance of the morning.

Captain Drinkwater crossed the deck and levelled his
glass at the sloop. Her crew were spontaneously lining the
rail, climbing into the lower rigging.

'Frey,' he suddenly called sharply.

'Sir?' Frey ran up alongside the captain.

'Who's that fellow just abaft the chess-tree?' Drinkwater
asked, holding out his glass. Frey peered through the
telescope.

'It's Thurston, sir!'

'Yes it is, ain't it . . .' Drinkwater took back the glass and
levelled it again. They were almost alongside the American ship; in a moment they would have swept past.

Frey hovered, half-expecting an order. Behind him
Moncrieff hissed *'There's Thurston!'* and the man's name
passed like wildfire along the deck.

On the *Stingray's* quarterdeck Lieutenant Tucker, now
in his own full-dress uniform, raised a speaking trumpet.

'Captain Stewart desires that you anchor until the
appointed time of departure, sir.'

As the two ships drew closer a rising crescendo of abuse
rose from the *Stingray's* people. It seemed to the watching
Frey that they pushed Thurston forward, goading the
British with his presence and their taunts. For his own
part Thurston stood stock-still, aloof, as though wishing to
be independent of the demonstration, yet the central
figure in it.

'Damned insolent bastard!' Frey heard Wyatt say.

'Cool as a god-damned cucumber, by God,' agreed
Moncrieff.

'Silence there!' Drinkwater snapped as a ripple of
reaction spread along *Patrician's* gangway and down into
the ship. 'Eyes in the ship!' Men were coming up from
below, men who had no business on the upper deck. 'Send

145

those men below, Mr Comley, upon the instant, sir!'

The noise, like a ground-swell gathering before it breaks, echoed back and forth between the two hulls as they drew level.

'Silence there!' he called again and a jeering bellow of mimicry bounced back from the Americans.

Suddenly Thurston fell backwards with a piercing cry. The Americans surrounding him gasped, then their jeering changed to outraged cries as the *Patrician* drew away.

'What the devil . . .?' Drinkwater cried in the silence that fell instantly upon the *Patrician*'s people. He was aware that amid the shouting there had been another noise, heard a split-second before Thurston fell with a scream.

'There! Does that please you, Captain Drinkwater?' a voice cut the air.

Lieutenant Metcalfe straightened up beside the transom of the launch on the boat booms. A wisp of smoke curled up from the muzzle of the Ferguson rifle.

PART TWO

The Commodore

'America certainly cannot pretend to wage war
against us; she has no navy to do it with!'
The Statesman,
London,
10 June 1812

'What became of him?'

Drinkwater stirred from his reverie and looked at his wife working at her tapestry frame. Between them the fire leapt and crackled, flaring at the updraft in the chimney. Its warmth combined with the rum toddy, a good dinner and the gale raging unregarded outside to induce a detached stupor in Captain Drinkwater. To his wife he seemed to be dozing peacefully; in reality he was on the rack of conscience.

'I'm sorry, my dear, what did you say?'

'What became of him?'

'Who?'

'Mr Metcalfe. You were telling me about him.'

'Of course, how stupid. Forgive me . . .'

'There is nothing to forgive, you dozed off.'

'Yes,' Drinkwater lied, 'I must have . . .'

A gust of wind slammed against the side of the house and the shutters and sashes of the withdrawing room rattled violently. Between them the fire flared into even greater activity, roaring and subsiding as it consumed the logs before their eyes, a remorseless foretaste of Hell, Drinkwater thought uncomfortably.

'God help sailors on a night like this,' he remarked tritely, taking refuge in the cliché as he stirred himself, bent forward and threw another brace of logs into the fire-basket. 'Metcalfe is in Haslar, the naval hospital at Gosport.'

'I know, Nathaniel,' Elizabeth chid him gently. 'Is he mad?'

Drinkwater pulled himself together and determined to make small talk with his wife. Her brown eyes regarded him over her poised needle and he felt uncomfortable under their scrutiny. Had she guessed anything? He had asked himself the same question in the weeks he had been home, examined every facet of his behaviour and concluded she could only have been suspicious because of his solicitude. He cursed himself for his stupidity; he was no dissembler.

'The doctors at Haslar were content to conclude it, yes, but our surgeon, Mr Pym, thought otherwise.'

'And yet the poor man was delivered up . . .'

'We had no alternative and, to be candid, Bess, I fear I agreed with the bulk of medical opinion. The man was quite incapable of any rationality after the incident, his whole posture was preposterous . . .'

Drinkwater recalled the way Metcalfe had stood back, the Ferguson rifle crooked in his left elbow, his right hand extended as though for applause, a curious, expectant look upon his face, an actor upon a stage of his own imagining. His whole attitude had been that of a man who had just achieved a wonder; only his eyes, eyes that stared directly at Drinkwater himself, seemed detached from the awful reality of the act he had just perpetrated.

Like everyone on *Patrician*'s upper deck, Drinkwater was stunned; then a noise of indignation reached them, rolling across the water from the *Stingray*. A moment later it was taken up aboard *Patrician*. Thurston had been popular, his desertion connived at: his murder was resented. The undertones of combination and mutiny implicit in the events of the past days instantly rose up to confront Drinkwater. Metcalfe's action had provided a catalyst for disaffection to become transformed into open rebellion. He was within a whisker of losing control of his ship, of having her seized and possibly handed over to the Americans, her people seeking asylum, her loss to the Royal Navy an ignominious cause of rupture between Great Britain and the United States of America.

It was imperative he acted at once and he bellowed for

silence, for the helm and braces to be trimmed and for Moncrieff to place Mr Metcalfe under immediate arrest, he was gratified, in a sweating relief, to see others, the marine officer, Sergeant Hudson, Comley the boatswain and Wyatt the master, move swiftly to divert trouble, to impose the bonds of conditioned discipline and strangle at birth the sudden surge of popular compassion and anger.

The *Stingray* had made no move to drop downstream in their wake as Drinkwater crowded on sail, as much to increase the distance between the two ships as to occupy the Patricians. Thus he had escaped into the Atlantic and set their course for home.

'If you were so certain, why did your surgeon think otherwise?' Elizabeth asked.

'Our opinions did not appear to differ at first. We confined Metcalfe to his cabin, put a guard on him and both of us agreed that insanity was the most humane explanation for his conduct, as much for himself as to avoid trouble with the people. There was, moreover, the possibility of diplomatic repercussions, though after I had discussed it with Vansittart, we concluded Captain Stewart was unlikely to have made a fuss, since it was quite clear Thurston was a deserter from *Patrician* and therefore his sheltering by Stewart could have constituted a provocative act. In the amiable circumstances then prevailing, at least according to Vansittart's account, Stewart would have embarrassed his own government and marred his already meagre chances of advancement.' Drinkwater paused, remembering the darkly handsome American. 'Stewart made a number of rather puerile threats against us if it came to war and doubtless has added the incident to his catalogue of British infamy, but I did not take him for a complete fool . . .'

'But you think, despite this trouble, it will not come to war?'

'No,' Drinkwater shook his head, 'I hope not.'

They relapsed into silence again. The gale lashed the house with a sudden flurry of rain and they both looked up, caught each other's eyes and smiled.

'It is good to have you home, my dear.'

'It is good to be home, Bess.'

He sincerely meant it, yet the gusting wind tugged at him, teasing him away from this domestic cosiness. Up and down the country men and women, even the humblest cottager, would be huddled about their fires of peat, driftwood or sea-coal. Why was it he had to suffer this perverse tugging away? In all honesty he wanted to be nowhere else on earth than here, beside his wife. Had he not blessed the severe and sudden leak that had confined *Patrician* to a graving dock in Dock Town, Plymouth, where her sprung garboard had caused the master-shipwright to scratch his head? He sighed, stared into the fire and missed the look his wife threw him.

'So what made your surgeon change his mind?'

Drinkwater wrenched his thoughts back to the present. 'A theory – a theory he was developing into a thesis. If I understood him aright, it was his contention (and Metcalfe had, apparently, furnished him with evidence over a long period) that Metcalfe was, as it were, two people. No, that ain't right: he considered Metcalfe possessed two individual personalities . . .

'Pym argued we all have a tendency to be two people, a fusion of opposites, of contrary humours. The relationship between weaknesses and strengths, likes and dislikes, the imbalance of these humours and so forth, nevertheless produces an equilibrium which inclines in favour of one or the other, making us predominantly one type of person, or another and hence forming our characters.

'He seemed to think Metcalfe's disparate parts were out of kilter in the sense that they exactly balanced, do you see? Thus, he postulated, if you conceive circumstances acting like the moon upon water, the water being these leanings, or inclinations inherent in us, our response is the vacillation of moods and humours. Because one humour predominates, we remain in character, whereas in Metcalfe's case the swings from one to another were equal, his personality was not weighted in favour of choler or sanguinity or phlegm, for instance, but swung more violently and uncontrollably from one *exclusive* humour to another.

'Therefore he became wholly one half of his complete character, before changing and becoming the other. Pym

152

dignified his hypothesis the Pendular Personality and proposed to publish a treatise about it.'

'But surely such a condition is, nevertheless, a form of madness.'

'Yes, I suppose it is. Though Pym suggested that so rational an explanation made of it a disease, madness being a condition beyond explanation. At all events it does not sit happily upon a sea-officer's shoulders.'

Poor Metcalfe. He had wept with remorse when his accusers confronted him with the enormity of murder, yet a day later, when Drinkwater had visited him again, he had screamed ingratitude, claiming to have done everything and more that his commander wished for and chastising Drinkwater for abandoning a loyal subordinate capable of great distinction. Pym had prescribed laudanum and they had brought him back dopey with the opiate.

There had been nothing more that Drinkwater could have done for Metcalfe. He waited upon the man's wife in her lodgings at Southsea and expressed his condolences. He gave her a testimonial for the Sick and Hurt Board and twenty guineas to tide her over. She had a snot-nosed brat at her side and another barely off the breast. Drinkwater had been led to believe Metcalfe came from a good family, but the appearance of his wife suggested a life of penurious scrimping and saving, of pretensions beyond means and ambitions beyond ability. The impression left by this sad meeting weighed heavily upon his own troubles as he made his way home.

Was Pym right? His theory had, as far as Drinkwater could judge, a logical attraction. He had himself proved to be two men and had behaved as such in the verdant woodlands of Virginia, so much so that he seemed now to be a different person to the man who had lain with Arabella Shaw. That careless spirit had been younger and wilder than the heat-stupefied, half-soaked, married and middle-aged sea-officer now sprawled before the fire in Gantley Hall. Had he, at least temporarily, suffered from an onset of the same dichotomous insanity which had seized so permanent a hold on Metcalfe? Was he in the grip of Pym's pendular personality?

The ridiculous humour of the alliteration escaped him.

153

One could argue he had done no more than thousands of men had done before him. He had, after all, spent most of his adult life cooped up on ship-board, estranged even from the body of his lawful wedded wife, so that the willing proximity of so enchanting, comely and passionate a woman as Arabella was irresistible. He could cite other encounters, with Doña Ana Maria Conchita Arguello de Salas and Hortense Santhonax, women whose beauty was fabled and yet with whom he had behaved with utter propriety, notwithstanding fate had thrown them together in unusual circumstances. He could *invent* no end of excuses for his momentary weakness and *invent* no end of specious proofs as to his probity. But he could think of no justification for his behaviour with Arabella.

He dared not look at his wife, lest she catch his eye and ask, in her acutely intuitive way, what troubled him. The events of that afternoon, the riot in the blood which had ended in their physical commingling, stood as a great sin in Drinkwater's mind.

Yet, God knew, he had committed greater sins. He was a murderer himself, perhaps more so than poor Metcalfe, for he had killed in cold blood, mechanically, under orders, at the behest of his Sovereign. And not once but many times.

He had shot out the brains of a Spanish seaman and hacked down a French officer long before his majority, yet had suffered no remorse, rather, he recollected, the contrary. Had the sanction of war relieved him of the trouble of a conscience over such matters? It was not logical to suppose that he suffered now merely because he loved his wife and he had threatened her with his mindless infidelity. Conscience should, if he understood it aright, prick him for every sin, not just the one that threatened his domestic security.

No, he had loved Arabella Shaw that afternoon, loved her as completely and consumingly as he had loved his wife and it was the diminution of the latter that wounded him most.

Arabella too had been driven by more than the demand of physical release, he was certain. She could have had the pick of those eager young officers, yet had chosen him, and as surely as he had recoiled after their wild fling, she had made no move to renew their passion, as if she too half-regretted it. She too harboured another love: that for her dead husband.

The moment he seized upon the thought, he doubted it.

'Could you still love me after my death?' he found himself blurting out, so introverted had his train of thought become.

Elizabeth looked up, hand poised above the circular frame, the candlelight playing upon the needle with its trail of scarlet thread.

'Why do you ask?'

He shrugged, colouring, wishing he had guarded his tongue and seized by a sudden conviction that Elizabeth knew all about his affair, that he had spoken in his sleep and had called Arabella's name in his dreams. 'A fancy I have,' he said lamely, 'a self-conceit...'

'I love you when you are not here,' she replied, 'it is as bad sometimes as being a widow.'

The phrases struck him as confirmation of his fears, yet it might be mere foolishness on his part. He felt her eyes upon him almost quizzically.

'You are exhausted with this war,' she said, watching her husband with concern, thinking him much older since he returned from America in a way she had not previously noticed.

'I am *perverted* by this war,' he wanted to say, but he nodded his weariness and thrust himself to his feet. He could not apportion blame elsewhere but within himself. 'I'll take a turn outside before we go up, Bess,' he said instead, 'to see all's well.' He bent over her head and kissed her hair. The strands of grey caught the yellow light and looked almost golden.

'Don't be long,' she said, and the catch in her voice articulated her desire. He squeezed her shoulder. Yes, he would drown his senses in the all-encompassing warmth of her body, but first he must excoriate his soul.

The soughing of the wind in the trees was like the wild hiss of the sea when it leaps high alongside a running ship. The chill of the night and the gale pained him with a

155

heartless mortification which he welcomed. The snorting and stamping from the stables told where the horses were distracted by the wild night and, as he struck the edge of the wood behind the house, he caught a glimpse of the lighthouses at Orfordness. Standing still he thought he could hear, just below the roar of the gale, the sussuration of shingle on the foreshore of Hollesley Bay. Turning his back to the wind and the sea, he headed inland.

The ruins of the old priory had seemed a fashionable embellishment to the acquisition of the hall, a Gothic fantasy within which to indulge his wife and daughter with picnics, not to mention his son to whom the ivy ruins had become a private kingdom. And while he loved the simple modernity of the house, these rambling ecclesiastical remnants had assumed an entirely different character in his mind.

This was the place he came when he was torn by the estrangement assailing all seamen, even when in the bosom of their families. Man returns always and most happily to the familiar, even when it pains him, for from there he can contemplate what he most desires in its most ideal, anticipatory state. For Drinkwater the ruined priory was the place where he came closest to the spiritual, and hence to what he conceived as God. His faith in the timeless wisdom of an omnipotent providence had been shaken by his riotous passion for Arabella. Intellectually he knew the thing to have been a temporary, if overpowering aberration, but he was rocked by its violence, by his own loss of control, by its pointlessness in a universe he imagined ordered. And then it struck him as a terrible self-delusion, this assumption. Either all was indeed vanity or all had a hidden purpose. If the former then every endeavour was destined to a redundancy comparable to the consecrated ruins about him; if the latter then every act was of unperceived, incomprehensible significance. Not only his adultery, but also Metcalfe's Parthian shot.

The enormous significance of this disarmingly simple choice rocked him to the very edge of sanity. He stood alone on the few flags that graced the roofless chancel, unconsciously spread his arms apart and howled at the magnificently merciless sky.

156

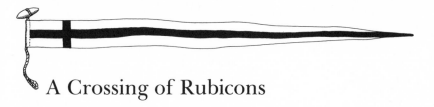

A Crossing of Rubicons

When the assassination occurred, Captain and Mrs Natha-
niel Drinkwater were in London as guests of Lord Dun-
garth, no more than a few hundred yards from the lobby of
Parliament where the Prime Minister was shot. Spencer
Perceval's policy of non-conciliation with the Americans,
maintained against a vociferous opposition led by the liberal
Whitbread and the banker Baring, also flew in the face of
Canning's advice. His calm leadership through the Regency
crisis was unappreciated in the country, where the Prince
Regent was unpopular, and by retaining his former post as
Chancellor of the Exchequer he attracted obloquy, for he
controlled the nation's purse-strings. He was widely blamed
for the economic chaos prevailing in the country. The
middle classes held him responsible for the widespread
bankruptcies among themselves, while the town labourers,
who had been driven to loom- and machine-smashing in a
spate of desperate vandalism, thought him an agent of the
devil.

The authorities ruthlessly hanged sixteen Luddite frame-
breakers, but failed to quell the widespread discontent
resulting from inflation, the depreciation of the pound
sterling, bad harvests and a consequent depression. Perceval's name was inseparable from these misfortunes. Starva-
tion, vagrancy and the ills of unemployment in the crowded
industrial wens tied down regiments of light horse, while the
drain of gold in support of the Portuguese and Spanish in
their fight against the French invader further exacerbated
the situation.

But Great Britain was not alone. France herself was in the grip of depression and the Tsar of Russia had withdrawn from Napoleon's Continental System sixteen months earlier in an attempt to repair the damage it had done to his own country's economy. Lord Dungarth had been sanguine that open hostilities between Russia and France would follow. For years the efforts of his Secret Department had been largely devoted to promoting this breach, but time had passed and although rumour rebounded, particularly from a Parisian bookseller in British pay who reported the ordering of all available books about Russia by the Tuileries, nothing concrete happened.

Closer to home Perceval was as intransigent as the Admiralty were devoid of instructions for His Britannic Majesty's frigate *Patrician*. He refused any revocation of Britain's Orders-in-Council, even to reopen trade with the United States. Although both the French and British issued special licences to beat their own embargoes by the back door, it was insufficient to relieve the general distress. On 11 May, four days after the Drinkwaters had come up to town, Perceval was shot by a Lancastrian bankrupt named Bellingham. The assassin was declared mad, a diagnosis uncomfortably close to Drinkwater's own solution of the dilemma of Metcalfe.

It was to be the first in a series of events which were to make the year 1812, already heavy with astrological portents, so memorable. Even the inactivity of his frigate seemed to the susceptible Drinkwater to be but a hiatus, a calm presaging a storm.

For Drinkwater and Elizabeth, his Lordship's invitation was a mark of both favour and condescension. Elizabeth was openly flattered but worried about her wardrobe, certain that her own homespun was quite inappropriate and that even the best efforts of the self-styled couturiers of Ipswich were equally unsuitable. She need not have worried. Dungarth was an ageing, peg-legged widower, his house in Lord North Street chilly and without a trace of feminine frippery. The bachelor establishment was, he declared on their arrival, entirely at Elizabeth's disposal and she was to consider herself its mistress. For himself, he required only two meals a day and the more or less

158

constant company of her husband.

Drinkwater was reluctant to tell his wife of their private conversations. She correctly deduced they had some bearing upon affairs of state. In any case the earl redeemed himself by his society during the evenings. Drinkwater knew the effort it cost him, but he held his peace; Elizabeth was enchanted and flattered, and blossomed under Dungarth's generous patronage. They visited a number of distinguished houses, which gratified Elizabeth's curiosity and her desire to sample society, though she continued to suffer agonies over her lack of fashionable attire. Conscience compelled Drinkwater to remedy this deficiency to some extent, but she nevertheless felt her provincial awkwardness acutely. Her ignorance of affairs of the world, by which was meant not what she read in the broadsheets (about which she was exceedingly well-informed) but the gossip and innuendo of the *ton*, provoked sufficient *faux pas* to spoil several evenings. It was an experience she soon tired of.

As for Dungarth, Drinkwater was appalled by his appearance. He had marked the earl's decline at their last meeting, but Dungarth's obesity was dropsical in its extent and his corpulent figure distressed him for its awkwardness as much as it stirred the pity of his friends.

'I am told it is fashionable,' he grumbled, putting a brave face on it, 'that the friends of Holland House all eat like hogs to put on the kind of weight borne by the Prince of Wales, imitation being the sincerest form of flattery. But, by God, I'd sell my soul to the devil if it went with a stone or two of this gross avoirdupois. Forgive me, m'dear,' he apologized to Elizabeth.

'Please, my Lord . . .' She waved aside his embarrassment, moved by the brave and gallant twinkle in his hazel eyes.

'For God's sake, call me John.' Dungarth dropped into a creaking chair and waved Drinkwater to sit. 'They tell me your ship's held up, Nat.'

'Aye, dockyard delays, a shortage of almost everything . . .'

'Including orders . . .'

'So,' Drinkwater grinned, scratching his scarred cheek, 'you *do* have a hand in her inactivity.'

Dungarth shrugged. 'Interruption of the Baltic trade

159

confounds the dockyards, I suppose, despite *our* best efforts', this with significance and a heavy emphasis on the plural pronoun, 'and the Tsar's declared intention of abandoning the dictates of Paris.'

'And lack of men, of course,' Drinkwater added, suddenly gloomy, 'always a want of them. I understand from Lieutenant Frey that every cruiser putting into the Sound poaches a handful despite my orders and those of the Port Admiral. They have even taken my coxswain.'

'Your worst enemies are always your own cloth, Nat.'

'I hope, my Lord,' put in Elizabeth, 'that that is not too enigmatic a response.'

'Ah-ha, ma'am, you're shrewd, but in this case mistaken. I have nothing to do with the felonious practices of cruiser captains.'

'Since I am so out of tune with you, then, my Lord,' Elizabeth said with mock severity, rising to draw the gentlemen after her and waving a relieved Dungarth back into his sagging chair, 'and since you are so lately come in, I shall leave you to your gossip and decanters.'

'You are cross with me, ma'am . . .'

'Incensed, my Lord . . .'

'But too gentle to tell me; you have an angel for a wife, Nathaniel.'

The men settled to their port and sat for a few moments in companionable silence.

'You're ready to go to sea again, aren't you, Nat?' Dungarth said at last.

'I've no need to argue the circumstances, my Lord . . .'

'John, for heaven's sake . . .'

'You know the tug of one thing when the other is at hand.'

'This damned war has ruined us as men, though only God alone knows what it will do to us as a nation.'

'You want me for the Baltic?'

'If and when.'

'I loathe waiting.'

'If you commanded a ship of the line, you would be doing nothing other than waiting and watching off La Rochelle, or L'Orient, or Ushant . . .'

'The reflection does not stopper off my impatience.'

Dungarth looked at his friend with a shrewd eye.

160

'Something's amiss, Nat; what the devil's eating you?'

Drinkwater met Dungarth's gaze. He had no need of pretence with so old and trusted a colleague. 'Unfinished business,' he replied.

'In the Baltic?'

'In America.'

'Not a woman like Hortense Santhonax? A temptress? No, a siren?'

'Not entirely, though I am not blameless in that quarter; more a feeling, an intuition.'

Dungarth's look changed to one of admiration and he slapped his good knee. 'My dear fellow, I *knew* you were the man for the task after I'm gone. 'Tis the *feeling* you need for the game, to be sure, and you have it in abundance. You'll suffer for it, as I warrant you already have done – are doing, by the look of you, but 'tis an indispensable ingredient for the puppet-master.'

Drinkwater shook his head at the use of this phrase, 'No, my Lord,' he said with firm formality, 'not that.'

'There is quite simply no one else,' Dungarth expostulated, waving this protest aside, 'but there is a little time. I'm not called to answer for my sins just yet.'

'You've heard news today, haven't you?' Drinkwater asked directly. 'Is it from the Baltic?'

'No, America. I've asked Moira to dinner tomorrow. He has correspondents in the southern states which in general are hostile to us but where he left a few friends. I think Vansittart's mission was, after all, a failure.'

Drinkwater went gloomily to bed. Elizabeth was reading one of Miss Austen's novels by candlelight, Drinkwater noticed, but closed it upon her finger and looked up at her husband who added his own candelabra to the one illuminating the bed. 'May one ask what you two find to talk about?'

Drinkwater knew the question to be arch, that its bluntness hid a pent-up and justifiable curiosity. Elizabeth, with her talent for divination, had sensed from the very length and earnestness of the men's deliberations that something more than mere idle male gossip about politics was in the air. He knew too, with some relief, that she had concluded his own preoccupations were bound up with

161

these almost hermetic discussions.

He took off his coat and sat on the bed to kick off his shoes.

'He knows himself to be dying, Bess, and is concerned for his life's work. Did I ever tell you he was once, when I knew him as the first lieutenant of the *Cyclops*, the most liberal of men? He was largely sympathetic with the American rebels at one time. His implacable hatred of the French derives from the mischief done to the body of his wife. She died in Florence shortly after the outbreak of the revolution. He was bringing her back through France when the revolutionaries, seeing the arms on his coach, tore the coffin open . . .'

'How awful . . .'

'You have seen Romney's portrait of her?'

'Yes, yes. She was extraordinarily beautiful.' Elizabeth paused, looked down at her book and set it aside. 'And . . . ?'

'Dungarth has become', Drinkwater said with a sigh, 'the Admiralty's chief intelligencer, the repository and digest of a thousand titbits and snippets, reports of facts and rumours; in short a puppet-master pulling strings across half Europe, even as far as the steppes of Asia . . .'

'And you are to succeed him?'

Drinkwater looked at his wife full-face. 'How the deuce . . . ?'

She shrugged. 'I guessed. You have done nothing but closet yourselves and I know he is not a man to show prejudice to a woman merely because of her sex.'

Drinkwater nodded. 'Of course, I am quite inadequate to the task,' he said earnestly, 'but it appears no one else is fitter and I am slightly acquainted with something of the business, being known to agents in France and Russia . . .'

'Spies, you mean,' Elizabeth said flatly and Drinkwater bridled at the implicit disapproval. He opened his mouth to explain, thought better of it and shifted tack.

'Anyway, Dungarth has invited Lord Moira to dinner tomorrow . . .'

'And shall I be allowed to . . . ?'

'Oh, come, Elizabeth,' Drinkwater said irritably, hooking a finger in his stock, 'I like this whole situation no better than you . . .'

Elizabeth leaned forward and placed a finger on his lips.

'Tell me who this Lord Moira is.'

'Better I tell you who he was. The Yankees knew him as Lord Rawdon, and he gave them hell through the pine-barrens of Georgia and the Carolinas in the American War. Of late his occupations have been more sedentary. He went into politics alongside Fox and the Whig party in opposition, and is an intimate of the Prince Regent, being numbered among the Holland House set . . .'

Elizabeth seemed bucked by this piece of news. 'Is he married?' she asked.

'To the Countess of Loudoun, his equal in her own right. He is also considered to be a man of singular ugliness,' he added waspishly.

'Oh,' said Elizabeth smiling, 'how fascinating.'

General Francis Rawdon Hastings, Earl of Moira, proved far from ugly, though bushy black eyebrows, a pair of sharply observant eyes and a dark complexion marked his appearance as unfashionable. He was, moreover, a man of strong opinions and frank speech. His oft-quoted opinion as to the virtue of American women expressed while a young man serving in North America had brought him a degree of wholly unmerited notoriety. His more solid achievements included distinguishing himself at the Battle of Bunker Hill and later defeating Washington's most able general, Nathaniel Greene, in the long and hard-fought campaign of the Carolinas. Such talents might have marked him out for command in the peninsula but, like Tarleton vegetating in County Cork, he was out to grass, though talked of as the next governor-general of India.

'Frank has news of a determined war-party in the Congress,' Dungarth said as he carved the beef with its oyster stuffing.

'War *hawks*, they style themselves,' Moira said, sipping the glass of burgundy Dungarth's man Williams poured for him. 'Your health, ma'am,' he added, inclining his head in Elizabeth's direction. 'We shan't bore you with our political clap-trap?'

'Mrs Drinkwater is better informed than most of your subalterns, Frank,' Dungarth said.

'That ain't difficult,' replied Moira, smiling engagingly,

'though I mean that as no slight to you, ma'am.'

'And what are the designs of these hawks, my Lord; my husband tells me the Americans have no navy to speak of.'

'Canada, ma'am, they covet Canada. They tried for it in the late rebellion and failed, they'll try for it again. As for their navy, I can't answer for it. I understand they've a deal of gunboats and such, much like the *radeaux* they had on Lake Champlain, I imagine, but as to a regular navy, well, I don't know.' Moira shrugged dismissively.

'They've some fine ships,' said Dungarth, 'but too few in commission and a fierce competition for them.'

'And some determined men to command them,' Drinkwater agreed, thinking of Captain Stewart.

'So,' said Moira, between mouthfuls, 'we may have the upper hand at sea, but with half the army marching and counter-marching in Spain', Moira paused to allow his opinion of Wellesley's generalship to pervade the atmosphere of the dining-room, 'and the other half aiding the civil power in the north, they have the advantage on land. I'm damned if I know what, begging your pardon, Mistress Drinkwater, will transpire if they do decide on war and advance on Canada.'

'Is it that much a matter of chance, then?' Drinkwater asked. 'I mean to say, will Madison blow like a weather-cock to the prevailing breeze?'

'So my correspondents in the southern states write, and they, needless to say, are opposed to this madness. Everywhere they are surrounded by men intent upon it.' This gloomy assessment laid a silence on them. 'I suppose we'll drum up sufficient ruffians to hold Canada. There are enough loyalists in New Brunswick to form a division, I daresay, and the Six Nations of Mohawks are more inclined to favour us than the perfidious Yankees. With the navy blockading the coast, I daresay things will turn out to our advantage in the end.'

'If we can afford it,' put in Elizabeth shrewdly.

'You *are* well informed, ma'am, my compliments.' Moira downed another glass of the burgundy. 'The India trade will sustain us, though I don't doubt but it'll be a close-run thing.'

'There is one matter we have not considered,' Drinkwater said, an uncomfortable thought striking him with a growing

164

foreboding. He realized that for months he had been subconsciously brooding on Stewart's last remarks. The American officer's allusion to the bluff-bowed British frigates was a criticism that had stuck in Drinkwater's craw if only for its very accuracy. The memory, thirty years old, of being prize-master aboard the Yankee privateer schooner *Algonquin* when a young midshipman had been all the evidence he needed to realize Stewart had been indiscreet; that, and the knowledge Stewart had himself commanded a schooner.

They were all looking at him expectantly.

'The Americans will use privateers, my Lords, if it comes to war; scores of 'em, schooners mostly, manned with the most energetic young officers they can muster from their mercantile and naval stock . . .'

He was gratified by the exchange of appreciative looks between Moira and Dungarth. He sensed, in a moment of self-esteem, he had divined the passing of a test.

'They will attack our trade wherever they are able, just as they did in the last war. Moreover, their success will tempt out the more active of the French commanders and corsairs who would not need to rely on the blockaded ports of Europe, but could shift their operations to American bases where there will be no dearth of support and sympathy, reviving the old alliance of '79 in the name of the twin republics . . .'

'Do you have any more horrors for us, Captain?' Moira asked mockingly.

'Do you want any more, my Lord?' Drinkwater asked seriously. 'They will ambush the India trade, attack our fishing fleets and whalers, ravage the West Indies . . .'

'And how do you know all this, Captain?' Moira asked drily.

'It is what he would do in Madison's place, ain't it, Nathaniel?'

'It is certainly what I would do if I were Secretary of Madison's navy, my Lords, and wanted to compensate for its weaknesses. When it cannot achieve something itself, the state encourages its more rapacious citizenry to do it on its behalf.'

'And will it come to this?' Elizabeth asked. 'You are all

165

talking as if the matter were a *fait accompli.*'

'If Napoleon don't invade Russia, Elizabeth,' Dungarth said with solemn intimacy, 'then he will surely not miss the opportunity to capitalize on a breach between London and Washington which he has for months now been so assiduously encouraging.' And then he snicked his fingers with such violence that the sudden noise made them jump and the candle-flames flickered, adding, as if it had just occurred to him, 'By God! It's what he has been waiting for!'

And for a moment they stared at the puffy face of the once-handsome man, transfigured as it was by realization.

And so it proved, despite a stone-walling by the so-called doves. The hawks, roaring into the Congress chamber banging cuspidors, startled a tedious orator into sitting and conceding the floor. Thus provoked, Speaker Clay put the question which was carried almost two to one in favour of war with Great Britain. Later the Senate agreed and within two days the *National Intelligencer* of Washington, the *Freeman's Journal and Mercantile Advertiser* of Philadelphia and every other broadsheet in the United States repeated the text of the Act opening hostilities. Even the news that the British had finally set aside the infamous Orders-in-Council, anxious to protect the American supplies vital to Wellington's advancing army, failed to stem the headlong dash to war. Madison's intention of issuing letters-of-marque and of general-reprisal against the goods, vessels and effects of the government and subjects of the United Kingdom of Great Britain and Ireland was quoted alongside the declaration.

'America, having obtained her independence from Great Britain, is going to engage her old enemy to prove the young eagle is ready to supersede the old lion,' Drinkwater explained later to his children as they watched in silence while he ordered the packing of his sea-chest.

Within days Napoleon's *Grande Armée* began to cross the River Nieman and invade Russia. Half a million men, French, Austrians, Prussians, Saxons, Württemburgers, Italians, Poles, marched, as Marshal Marmont was long afterwards to recall, 'surrounded by a kind of radiance'.

'Now we shall see, Nat,' said Dungarth, the warmth of final

166

achievement mixed with the excitement of a vast gamble, 'what this clash of Titans will decide.'

For Captain and Mrs Drinkwater there were less euphoric considerations. He waited upon their Lordships at the Admiralty immediately and within two days had received his orders. Indeed, the presence of Captain Drinkwater in the capital was considered 'most fortuitous'. While the focus of Dungarth's apprehensions lay to the east, Drinkwater shared Moira's concern for the outcome of events upon the Western Ocean and beyond. At the end of June the Drinkwaters returned home to Suffolk and their children. He was impatient, his heart beating at a faster pace. *Patrician* was to be hurried to sea again, her lack of men notwithstanding.

Drinkwater's last days at Gantley Hall were spent writing letters which Richard, his son, took into Woodbridge for the post. Drinkwater dismissed Richard's pleas to be rated captain's servant aboard the *Patrician*. Instead he roused Lieutenant Quilhampton from his connubial bliss, thundering upon his cottage door on a wet evening when the sun set behind yellow cloud.

'My dear sir,' said Quilhampton, stepping backwards and beckoning Drinkwater indoors. 'We heard you had gone up to town . . .'

'You've heard of the outbreak of war with America?' Drinkwater snapped, cutting short his host's pleasantries.

'Well, yes, yesterday. I meant to try for a ship . . .'

'My dear James, I have no time, forgive me . . . ma'am,' he bowed curtly to Catriona who had come into the room from the kitchen beyond, with an offer of tea, 'can you spare your husband?'

'You have a ship for me?' broke in Quilhampton, nodding to his wife and ignoring her silent protest.

'Not exactly, James. As a lieutenant I can get you a cutter or a gun-brig, but nothing more. I am, however, desperate for a first luff in *Patrician*.' He paused, watching the disappointment clear in Quilhampton's expression. 'It ain't what you want, I know, but nor is it as bad as you think, James. I am to be the senior captain of a flying squadron . . .'

'A commodore, sir?'

'Aye, but only of the second class. They will not let me have a post-captain under me, but I can promise you advancement at the first opportunity, to Master and Commander at the very least . . .'

'I'll come, sir, of course I will.' Quilhampton held out his remaining hand.

'That's handsome of you, James, damned handsome,' Drinkwater grinned, seizing the outstretched paw. 'God bless you, my friend.'

'He was mortified you sailed for America without him last autumn, Captain Drinkwater,' Catriona said quietly in her Scots accent, pouring the bohea. Drinkwater noticed her thickening waist and recalled Elizabeth telling him the Quilhamptons were expecting.

'My dear, I am an insensitive dullard, forgive me, my congratulations to you both . . .'

Catriona handed him a cup. The delicate scent of the tea filled the room, but cup and saucer chattered slightly from the shaking of her hand. She caught his eye, her own fierce and tearful beneath the mop of tawny hair. 'My child needs a father, Captain. Even a one-armed one is better than none.'

'Ma'am . . .' Drinkwater stammered, 'I am, I mean, I, er . . .'

'Take him,' she said and withdrew, retiring to her kitchen.

Drinkwater looked at Quilhampton who shrugged.

'When can you be ready?'

'Tomorrow?'

'We'll post. Time is of the essence.'

'Talking of which, I have something . . .' Quilhampton turned aside and opened the door of a long-case clock that ticked majestically in a corner. He lifted a dark, dusty bottle from its base.

'Cognac, James?' Drinkwater asked, raising an eyebrow, 'How reprehensible.' Quilhampton smiled at Drinkwater's ill-disguised expression of appreciation.

'It is usually Hollands on this coast, but I can't stand the stuff. This', he held up the bottle after lacing both their cups of tea, 'the rector of Waldringfield mysteriously acquires.'

'Here's to the confinement, James. Tell her to stay with Elizabeth when her time comes.'

'I will, and thank you. Here's to the ship.'

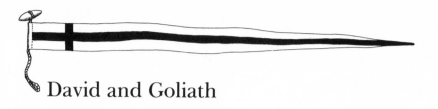

David and Goliath

'What is it, Mr Gordon?' Drinkwater emerged on to the quarterdeck and clapped his hand to his hat as a gust of wind tore at his cloak.

'*Hasty*, sir; she's just fired a gun and thrown out the signal for a sail in sight.'

'Very well. Make *Hasty*'s number and tell him to investigate.'

'Aye, aye, sir.'

Fishing for his Dollond glass Drinkwater levelled it at the small twenty-eight gun frigate bobbing on the rim of the horizon as they exchanged signals with her over the five miles of heaving grey Atlantic. Then he cast a quick look round the circumscribed circle of their visible horizon at the other ships of the squadron.

The little schooner *Sprite* clung to *Patrician* like a child to a parent, while two miles to leeward he could make out the thirty-eight gun, 18-pounder frigate *Cymbeline*, and beyond her the topsails of *Icarus*, a thirty-two, mounting 12-pounders on her gun deck.

'*Hasty* acknowledges, sir.'

Drinkwater swung back to Gordon and nodded. 'Very well. And now I think 'tis time we hoisted French colours with a gun to loo'ard, if you please, Mr Gordon.'

Midshipman Belchambers had anticipated the order, for it had long been known that they would close the American coast under an equivocal disguise. The red, white and blue bunting spilled from his arms as the assisting yeoman tugged at the halliards. Clear of the wind eddies about the deck, the tricolour snapped out clear of the bunt of the spanker and rose, stiff as a board, to the peak. The trio of officers watched the curiosity for a moment, then Drinkwater held his pocket-glass out to the midshipman.

'Up you go, Mr Belchambers. Keep me informed. We should sight land before sunset.' He hoped he sounded confident, instead of merely optimistic, for they had not obtained a single sight during the week the gale had prevailed.

The boom of the signal gun drowned Belchambers' reply, but he scampered away, tucking the precious spy-glass in his trousers and reaching for the main shrouds. Drinkwater stared at *Hasty* again as she shook out her topgallants. Captain Tyrell was very young, younger than poor Quilhampton, and he was inordinately proud of his command which, by contrast, was grown old, though of a class universally acknowledged as pretty. Drinkwater suspected a multitude of defects lurked beneath the paint, whitewash and gilded brightwork of her dandified appearance. Yet the young man in command seemed efficient enough, had understood the signals thrown out on their tedious passage across the Atlantic and handled his ship with every sign of competence. Perhaps he had a good sailing-master, Drinkwater thought, again turning his attention to the *Sprite*: they must be damnably uncomfortable aboard the schooner.

Sprite's commander was a different kettle of fish, a man of middle age whose commission as lieutenant was but two years old. Lieutenant Sundercombe had come up the hard way, pressed into the Royal Navy from a Guinea slaver whose mate he had been. He had languished on the lower deck for five years before winning recognition and being rated master's mate. There was both a resentment and a burning passion in the man, Drinkwater had concluded, which was doubtless due to his enforced service as a seaman. Maybe contact with the helpless human cargo carried on the middle passage had made him philosophical about the whims and vagaries of fate, maybe not. His most significant attribute as far as Drinkwater was concerned was his skill as a fore-and-aft sailor. His Majesty's armed schooner *Sprite* had been built in the Bahamas to an American design and attached to the squadron as a dispatch vessel.

As for the other frigates and their captains, the bluff and hearty Thorowgood of the *Cymbeline* and the stooped and consumptive Ashby of the *Icarus*, though as different as chalk from cheese in appearance, were typical of their generation. With the exception of Sundercombe and his schooner, in whose selection Drinkwater had enlisted Dungarth's influence, the histories of the younger men were unremarkable, their appointment to join his so-called 'flying squadron' uninfluenced by anything other than the Admiratlty's sudden fright at the depredations of Yankee privateers. None of them had seen action of any real kind, rising quickly through patronage or influence, and had been either cruising uneventfully in home waters or employed on convoy duties. Tyrell on the Irish coast where, in the Cove of Cork, he had been able to titivate his ship to his heart's content; and Thorowgood in the West Indies, where rum and women of colour seemed to have made a deep impression upon him. Ashby looked too frail to remain long in this world, though he possessed an admirable doggedness if his conduct in the recent gale was anything to go by, for *Icarus* had carried away her fore topmast shortly before sunset a few days earlier and had been separated from the rest of the squadron. The last that had been seen of her as she disappeared behind a grey curtain of rain was not encouraging. The violent line squall had dragged waterspouts from the surface of the sea and the wild sweep of lowering cloud had compelled them all to look to their own ships and shorten sail with alacrity. *Patrician*'s raw crew, once more decimated by idleness and filled from every available and unsuitable source, had been hard-pressed for an hour.

Captain Ashby had fired guns to disperse a spout that threatened his frigate and these had been taken for distress signals. When the weather cleared, however, there was no sign of the *Icarus*, and though the squadron reversed course until darkness and then hove-to for the night, the dawn showed the three remaining frigates and the schooner alone.

'I suppose', Drinkwater had remarked as David Gordon returned to the deck shaking his head after sweeping the

171

horizon from the masthead, '*our* still being in company is a small miracle.'

But two days later Ashby's *Icarus* had hove over the eastern horizon, her damage repaired and a cloud of canvas rashly set, proving at least that she was a fast sailer and Ashby a resourceful man with a competent ship's company. Now, as the gale blew itself out and they closed the lee of the American coast, Drinkwater chewed over their prospects of success and the risky means by which he hoped to achieve it. His orders gave him wide discretion; the problem with such latitude was that his judgement was proportionately open to criticism.

'A sail, I hear, sir,' said Quilhampton, coming on deck and touching the fore-cock of his hat at the lonely figure jammed at the foot of the weather mizen rigging.

Drinkwater stirred out of his brown study. 'Ah, James, yes; Tyrell's gone to investigate and Belchambers is aloft keeping an eye on the chase.'

'I see we've the frog ensign at the peak . . .'

'You disapprove?'

Quilhampton shrugged and cast his eyes upwards. 'I comprehend your reasoning, sir, it just feels damned odd . . .'

'Any ruse that allows us time to gather intelligence is worth adopting.'

'Has *Icarus* gone off flying the thing, sir?'

'If he obeyed orders he has, yes.'

'Deck there!' Both officers broke off to stare upwards to where Belchambers swung against the monotone grey of the overcast, his arm outstretched. 'Land, sir, four points on the starboard bow!'

'What of the chase?' Drinkwater bellowed back.

'Looks like a schooner, sir, to the sou'westward. *Hasty*'s hull down but I don't think he's gaining.'

'He won't against a Yankee schooner,' Drinkwater grumbled to his first lieutenant. 'Though Belchambers can't see it yet, she'll be tucked under the lee of the land there with a beam wind, damn it.' Drinkwater sighed, and made a hopeless gesture with his hand. 'I really don't know how best to achieve success . . .'

'I heard scores of Yankee merchantmen left New York on

172

the eve of the declaration with clearances for the Tagus,' remarked Quilhampton.

'Aye, and we'll buy their cargoes, just to keep Wellington's army in the field, and issue licences for more, I daresay.' He thought of the boasting finality he had threatened Captain Stewart with, calling up the iron ring of blockade to confound the American's airy theories of maritime war. Now the government in London showed every sign of pusillanimity in their desire not to interfere with supplies to the army in Spain. 'I wish to God the government would order a full blockade and bring the Americans to their senses quickly.'

'They misjudged the Yankee's temper,' agreed Quilhampton, 'thinking they would be content with the eventual rescinding of the Orders-in-Council.'

'Too little too late,' grumbled Drinkwater, 'and then David struck Goliath right betwixt the eyes . . .'

No further reference was necessary between the two men to conjure up in their minds the humiliations the despised Yankee navy had visited upon the proud might of the British. Before leaving Plymouth they had heard that Commodore Rodgers' squadron had sailed from New York on the outbreak of war and, though the commodore had missed the West India convoy, his ships had chased the British frigate *Belvidera* and taken seven merchantmen before returning to Boston. Furthermore the *Essex* had seized the troop transport *Alert* and ten other ships. They knew, too, that the USS *Constitution* had escaped a British squadron by kedging in a calm, and finally, a week or two later, she had brought His Britannic Majesty's frigate *Guerrière* to battle and hammered her into submission with devastating broadsides.

The latest edition of *The Times* they had brought with them from England was full of outrage and unanswered questions at this blow to Britannia's prestige. The defeat of a single British frigate was considered incomprehensible, outweighed Wellington's defeat of the French at Salamanca and obscured the news that Napoleon had entered Moscow. On their passage westward, Drinkwater had plenty of time to mull over the problems his discretionary orders had brought him. They contained a caution about single cruisers

173

engaging 'the unusually heavily armed and built frigates of the enemy', and the desirability of 'drawing them down upon a ship-of-the-line', an admission of weakness that Drinkwater found shocking, if sensible, had a ship-of-the-line been within hail. Yet he had been under no illusion that with 'so powerful a force as four frigates' great things were expected of him, and was conscious that he sailed on detached service, not under the direct command of either Sawyer at Halifax or his successor, Sir John Borlase Warren, even then proceeding westwards like themselves.

Drinkwater had been close enough to Admiralty thinking in those last weeks before he sailed, when he cast about desperately for men to make up his ship's company again and the Admiralty dithered, to know of their Lordships' concern over Commodore Rodgers. The news that Rodgers had sailed with a squadron and had not dispersed his ships, added to the rumour that he had been after the West India convoy and had sailed almost within sight of the Scillies, had caused consternation at the Admiralty. To defend so many interests, the convoy routes from the West Indies, from India and the Baltic, the coastal trades and the distant fisheries and, by far the most important, the supply route to Lisbon and Wellington's Anglo-Portuguese army, meant the deployment of a disproportionate number of ships spread over a quarter of the world's oceans. Until Warren reached Halifax and organized some offensive operations with the inadequate resources in that theatre, Captain Drinkwater's scratch squadron was the *only* force able to mount offensive operations against the Americans. With a thousand men-of-war at sea the irony of the situation was overwhelming.

Drinkwater had twice posted up to London for consultations, briefings and last-minute modifications to his orders. Suddenly the fact that he was a senior captain fortuitously on hand to combat the alarming situation was not so flattering. Imbued with a sense of urgency, the difficulties the Admiralty experienced in scraping together the exigous collection of ships they had at last dignified with the name of 'flying squadron' seemed trivial; Drinkwater was more concerned with his lack of manpower.

Now, however, after the most pressing problem had been

at least partially solved, the Admiralty's concern was understandable.

Byron of the *Belvidera* had reported well of the American squadron's abilities, though outraged he had been attacked without a warning that hostilities had commenced. His escape he had attributed to superior sailing, not knowing the true cause was the explosion of a gun in which Rodgers himself had been wounded. Drinkwater did not share the overweening assumption of superiority nursed by young bloods like Tyrell and Thorowgood. He was too old or too honest with himself not to harbour doubts. Even ship for ship, *his* squadron matched against a squadron of Yankees could, he admitted privately to himself, be bested.

If Stewart was anything to go by, the American navy did not lack men of temper and determination, young men, too, men with experience of waging war in the Mediterranean, three thousand miles from their nearest base.

'I think we should not regard the Americans with too much contempt, James,' he said, in summation of his thoughts.

But any concurrence from Quilhampton was cut short by Belchambers hailing the deck again.

'*Hasty*'s broken off the chase, sir!'

'Where away is the chase herself?' Drinkwater shouted.

'Can't see her, sir.'

'He's lost her, by God,' snapped Quilhampton.

'She's fast, James,' Drinkwater said consolingly, 'don't blame Tyrell; I tell you these damned Yankees are going to give us all a confounded headache before we're through.'

Quilhampton's sigh of resignation was audible even above the noise of the wind in the rigging, though whether it was submission to Drinkwater's argument or his excuse for Tyrell's failure, Drinkwater did not know. He felt a twinge of pity for his friend; perhaps Quilhampton himself should be in command of *Patrician*, perhaps he would make a better job of the task ahead . . .

'Well,' Quilhampton said, breaking into Drinkwater's gloom, 'at least we've got Warren taking over from that old fart Sawyer at Halifax.'

'Yes. I knew Sir John once, when I was master's mate in the cutter *Kestrel*. He had command of a flying squadron just

175

after the outbreak of war with France . . .'

Odd he made that distinction between war with France and war with the United States, when he knew it was all part of the same, interminable struggle.

'Warren had some of the finest frigates in the navy with him, the *Flora*, the *Melampus*, the *Diamond* under Sir Sydney Smith, Nagle's *Artois* and the *Arethusa* under Pellew . . .'

'And look what we've got,' grumbled Quilhampton, watching *Hasty* approach. 'Not a bloody Pellew in sight . . .'

The little sixth-rate bore down towards them. They could see the French ensign at *Hasty*'s gaff, before losing sight of it behind the bellying bunt of her topsails. As she surged past, to dodge under *Sprite*'s stern and come round again in *Patrician*'s wake, Captain Tyrell stood on her rail and raised his hat. Drinkwater acknowledged the salute and felt the wind nearly carry his own into the sea running in marbled green and white between the two frigates.

'Too fast for us, sir!' he heard Tyrell hail, 'A privateer schooner by the look of her. She ran like smoke!'

Drinkwater waved his hat in acknowledgement. It was no more, nor anything less than he had expected.

'The problem is, where to start,' Drinkwater said, leaning over the chart. 'It would be a simple matter if my orders were to blockade the Chesapeake . . .'

'I'm damned if I know why they aren't, sir,' Quilhampton fizzed.

'It isn't government policy, James, at least not yet. Warren has a damnably difficult job, but he *must* maintain American supplies to the Tagus. Such a policy may, if we are lucky, promote sentiments of opposition to President Madison who has to maintain at least the illusion of not coming in on the French side in the peninsula. Warren will do his best to foment this discord by appealing to American mercantile avarice and issuing licences.'

'I see,' said Quilhampton, looking at his commander and thinking him unusually well-informed and then remembering the summonses, post-haste, to London from Plymouth. 'On the other hand Yankee avarice will be fired by the vision of plundering our trade,' protested Quilhampton, coming to terms with the enormous complexities Madison's declara-

176

tion of war had caused. 'And we know the Americans have skilful seamen aplenty, men trained in the mercantile marine . . .?'

'Who know exactly where to intercept our trade.' Drinkwater overrode Quilhampton's exposition. 'And our task is to sweep – an apt verb for a copying clerk to apply, if impossible to obey in practice – to sweep the seas for American privateers . . .'

'With a handful of elderly frigates that can't catch a cold in a squall of rain, let alone a Baltimore schooner on or off the wind.' Quilhampton's protesting asides were meant to be signals of sympathy; they only served to irritate Drinkwater. Or was he annoyed because, all unbidden, his eyes were drawn to the legend *Potomac* on the chart. He fell silent and, watching his face, Quilhampton knew from experience that his expression presaged an idea which, in its turn, would father a plan. He shifted tack, moved to noises of positive encouragement.

'Of course with good visibility we can form a line abreast to cover fifty miles of sea and if we conduct such a sweep, at a focal point of trade, a point at which these smart Yankee skippers will reason they can best intercept a homeward convoy . . .'

'Yes, but which homeward convoy, James?' Drinkwater snapped, his voice suddenly vibrant with determination.

'Well, the West India trade, sir,' Quilhampton said, riffling through the other charts on the table and drawing out a second one. 'Now the hurricane season is over, I suggest – here.' He stabbed his finger at the northern end of the Florida Strait, where the Gulf Stream favoured homeward ships, but where the channel between the coast and the Great Bahama Banks narrowed to less than sixty miles. 'With the *Sprite* to increase our scouting front,' went on Quilhampton, 'we could almost completely cover the strait.' He paused, then added, 'Though I suppose we need her in the centre of the line to let slip like a hound and tie down any privateers until we can come up in the frigates.' Pleased with himself, he looked up at Drinkwater.

The captain's face was clouded and he was not looking at the chart of the Florida Strait. Instead he seemed abstracted, as though he had not been listening, obsessed with the chart of the Chesapeake. Quilhampton coughed discreetly, drawing attention to his presence, if not his expressed opinion. Drinkwater looked up.

'Er... yes. Yes. I applaud your tactics, James, but not your strategy.'

'Oh,' Quilhampton bridled, puzzled.

'No offence, but what would *you* do?'

'As I say, the Florida Strait...'

'No, no, forgive me, I haven't made myself clear. Suppose, well perhaps for you it is not so much a supposition, for you may sympathize with my hypothesis, but suppose you are a bold, resolute American officer – an ambitious man, but not one who gained distinction in the quasi-war with France, or the Tripolitan adventure and, as a result, out of favour, denied a naval ship but, being still a man of influence, one who could command a letter-of-marque, perhaps a small squadron of them...'

'It would make no difference...'

'Bear with me, James,' Drinkwater said tolerantly. 'Now you know perfectly well that every other privateer commander will make his station either the Florida Strait, or the Windward Passage, or some other focal point to intercept the West India ships...'

'Yes, but there'll be rich enough pickings for all,' insisted Quilhampton, knowing the way Drinkwater thought, 'and it'll rouse the sugar lobby, bring pressure to bear in Parliament and win the successful privateersman a reputation quicker perhaps than command of a Yankee frigate.'

'D'you rest your case?' Drinkwater asked drily.

Quilhampton blushed, aware that he had presumed on friendship at the cost of respect for rank.

'I beg your pardon, sir.'

'There's no need for that; you're my first lieutenant, such considerations must be encouraged, but think bigger, James. You're *very* ambitious, ambitious enough to attempt the single-handed destruction of the British government at a stroke, not merely stirring up an opposition lobby.' Quilhampton looked blank. 'Come on; you know how parlous a state our country's in...' Drinkwater paused, expectant. 'No?'

'I'm afraid not, sir...'

178

'Look; we need American wheat to supply Wellington; with what do we pay for it?'

'Gold, sir.'

'Or maybe a trifling amount of manufactures, to be sure, but principally gold. It is what the American masters want to take home with them. We need a Portuguese army in the field; with what do we pay them? And what do we pay the Spaniards with for fighting to free their own country?'

'Gold again . . .'

'And our troops do not live off the land but pay the Spaniards for their provisions in . . .?'

'Gold.'

'Quite so. A privateersman could stop the advance of Wellington for six weeks if he took a cargo of boots, or greatcoats, or cartridges. But there's precious little profit in a prize containing anything so prosaic. So the death-or-glory Yankee skipper will go for the source of our wealth, James . . .'

'You mean the India fleet, sir?'

'Exactly,' Drinkwater said triumphantly, 'the East Indiamen. They'll be leaving the factories now, catching the north-east monsoon down through the Indian seas, a convoy of 'em. Richer pickings than their West India cousins, by far.'

'So where would you intercept them, sir, St Helena?' Drinkwater could tell by Quilhampton's tone that he was sceptical, suggesting the British outpost as some remote, almost ridiculous area.

'I think so,' he said with perfect gravity, amused by the sharp look Quilhampton threw him. 'But first we'll blockade the Chesapeake, show our noses to the enemy. Let it be known there are detached flying squadrons at sea, it may deter them a little. I'll shift to the *Sprite* for a day or two.' Drinkwater grinned at the look of surprise spreading on Quilhampton's face. 'You'll be in command, James.'

'But why, sir? I mean, why shift to the *Sprite*?'

'Because I intend paying a visit to the Potomac. There is something I wish to know.'

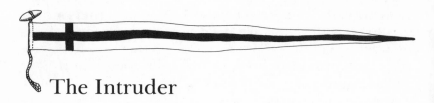

The Intruder

'Do we have much further to go, sir?' Sundercombe asked, looming out of the darkness. 'The wind is dying.'

'Bring her to an anchor, Mr Sundercombe, then haul the cutter alongside and I'll continue by boat. You'll be all right lying hereabouts and I'll be back by dawn. If I'm not, keep the American colours hoisted and lie quiet.'

'If I'm attacked, sir, or challenged?'

'Get out to sea.'

Drinkwater sensed the relief in Sundercombe's voice. They were seventy miles from the Atlantic, though only sixty from *Hasty*, ordered inside the Virginia capes to flaunt French colours in an attempt to keep inquisitive Americans guessing. They had left *Hasty* before noon, ignored the merchant ships anchored in Mockjack Bay and the James and York rivers, and headed north, exchanging innocent waves with passing fishing boats and coasters. Sundercombe's was an unenviable task, and Drinkwater had given him no opportunity to ask questions, nor offered him an explanation. The fewer people who knew what he was doing, the better. If he was wrong in his hunch, the sooner they got out to sea the better, though their presence under either French or British colours would confuse the enemy. If he had guessed correctly, confirmation would give him the confidence he needed, though he could not deny a powerful ulterior motive: the chance of seeing Arabella Shaw again swelled a bubble of anticipation in his belly. Either way, if he lost

Hasty or the schooner in the Chesapeake, he would be hard put to offer an explanation. Assuming he survived any such engagement, of course. He thrust such megrim-ish thoughts roughly aside.

'Pass word for Caldecott.'

Drinkwater's new coxswain rolled aft, a small, wiry figure, even in the darkness.

'I'm going on in the cutter, Caldecott. I have to make a rendezvous, with an informer,' he added, lest the man thought otherwise. 'I want perfect silence in the boat, particularly when and where I tell you to beach her. You must then stand by the place until I return. The slightest noise will raise the alarm and if any of your bullies think of desertin', dissuade them. They might have got away with it a twelve-month ago, but no one loves an Englishman hereabouts now. D'you understand me?'

'Aye, sir. No one'll desert, an' I'll swing if a single noise escapes their bleedin' mouths.' The raw Cockney accent cut the night.

'Good. There'll be a bottle or two for good conduct when we get back.'

'Beg pardon, sir . . .'

'What is it?'

''Ow long'll you be?'

'An hour or two at the most. Now make ready. It's almost midnight.'

'Aye, aye, sir.'

Moonrise was at about two, but they were two days after the new moon and the thin sliver of the distant satellite would scarcely betray them. Besides, it was clouding over.

The *Sprite's* gaffs came down, the mast hoops rattling in their descent, and from forward came the splash of the anchor and the low rumble of cable. The schooner's crew moved in disciplined silence about the deck and Drinkwater marked the fact, reminding himself to advance Sundercombe, if it came into his power.

'Your cutter's alongside, sir. I've had a barricoe of water and a bag of biscuit put in it,' Sundercombe paused, as if weighing up his superior. 'I did not think it would be appropriate to add any liquor though . . .' His voice tailed off, inviting praise or condemnation.

181

'You acted quite properly, Mr Sundercombe. We can enjoy a glass later, when this business is over.' Drinkwater had explained to Caldecott, he ought at the very least to confide now in Mr Sundercombe. 'I intend to meet an informer, d'you see, Mr Sundercombe?'

'You have a rendezvous arranged, sir?' The question was shrewd.

'No, but I know the person's house.' Drinkwater made a move, a signal the confidence was over. 'I shall be back by dawn.'

'Good fortune, sir.'

Sundercombe watched as Drinkwater threw his leg over the schooner's rail and clambered down into the waiting boat. A few moments later it pulled into the darkness, the dim, pale splashes of the oar blades gradually fading with the soft noise of their movement.

'What's he up to?' A man in the plain blue of master's mate asked Sundercombe after reporting the *Sprite* brought to her anchor.

'Damned if I know,' growled the lieutenant.

Caldecott's men pulled silently upstream for an hour before Drinkwater began to recognize features in the landscape that betokened the confluence of the Potomac with the Chesapeake. He ordered the tiller over and they inclined their course more to the westward, entering the Potomac itself, a grey swathe between the darker shadows of the wooded banks up which they worked their way.

'Inshore now,' he murmured at last, and Caldecott swung the boat's head. 'Easy now, lads.'

The men no longer pulled, merely dipped their oar blades in the rhythm which had become almost hypnotic while the cutter carried her way. A roosting heron rose, startled, with a heavy flapping of its large wings. Drinkwater caught sight of the outline of Castle Point against the sky.

'Here's the place,' whispered Drinkwater.

'Oars,' hissed Caldecot. 'Toss oars. Boat your oars.' The knock and rumble of the oars as they were stowed were terminated in the sharp crunch and lurch as the boat

182

grounded. Drinkwater stood up. He could see the eastern wing of the house clearly now, pale in the darkness, the surrounding trees gathered like protective wood spirits guarding it against incursions like his own. Before him the lawns came to the water's edge. He bent towards Caldecott's ear.

'Remember what I said.'

'No fear of forgettin', sir.'

'Keep quiet, you men,' he said in a low voice as he stepped from thwart to thwart. A moment later his boots landed on the gravel and he was ashore on enemy territory. He pulled his cloak closely round him and checked the seaman's knife lodged in its sheath in the small of his back. Taking a backward glance at the boat, he began to walk boldly up towards the house.

'Where's 'e gone, Bill?' someone asked.

'For a fuck, I shouldn't wonder, lucky bastard.'

'Stow it,' growled Caldecott, 'or it'll be you that's fucked.'

Immediately upon leaving the boat Drinkwater knew he had allowed himself insufficient time. The information he wanted had seemed vital in the security of *Patrician*'s cabin, vital to the scenario he had conjured out of Dungarth's intelligence reports, Moira's correspondence, the Admiralty's fears and his own peculiar brand of intuition, guesswork and faith in providence. Others would call it luck, no doubt, but to Drinkwater it was the hunch upon which he gambled his reputation.

Within minutes he reached the trees surrounding the stables forming the eastern wing of the house. He tried to recall where old Zebulon Shaw kept his hounds and thanked heaven for a windless night. He paused to catch his breath, looking back and seeing no sign of the boat or her crew tucked under the low river-bank. Noises came from the kitchen wing, a few bars of a song and the clatter of dishes, suggesting the servants were about late. He moved off, round the front of the house, traversing it in the shelter of the battlemented terrace until he reached the steps. Below the balustrade where he and Arabella had first traded the repartee which had had such fateful consequences, he stepped back and looked up at the façade.

There were lights still burning behind the heavy, brocade curtains. He tried to recall the plan of the house, located the withdrawing room and moved cautiously on to the terrace. An attack of nerves made him look down at the deserted lawns and the glimmer of the Potomac, empty now, where once, an age ago it seemed, the *Patrician* and the *Stingray* had lain uneasily together.

A fissure in the curtains revealed Shaw seated at an escritoire, his wig abandoned, the candlelight shining on his bald pate and a pen in his hand. A variety of papers were scattered on the small area of boards visible to Drinkwater.

With a thumping heart he stepped back and looked up again at the black windows whose glazed panes stared out indifferently at the night. Her bedroom was on the first floor, one of the rooms he had seen lit the evening before he had dined at Castle Point. A drain-pipe led directly up beside the shallow balcony upon which tall casements opened. Throwing back his cloak Drinkwater drew a deep breath and began to climb.

It was fortunate the house was not old, nor that the drain-pipe's fastenings had been skimped, for he struggled manfully in his effort to be silent. The climb was no more than fifteen feet, yet it took all his strength to claw his way up the wall and get his footing on the balcony's stone rail.

He stopped to catch his breath again, ruminating on the ruinous effects of age and short-windedness, aware that *here*, this close to her, he could not stop the terrible pounding of his heart. He strained his ears, but could hear nothing beyond the curtains. Putting his hand behind his back he drew the seaman's sheath knife, inserting the steel blade between the edges of the windows. With infinite care he located the latch and increased the pressure. To his relief it gave way easily, but he could afford no further delay, not knowing the noise its release had made within. He thrust aside the drapery and stepped inside the bedroom.

She was not alone, but sitting before a mirror, bathed in golden candlelight while her maid brushed out her hair. The unexpected presence of another person surprised him, instantly putting him on his guard, and drove the carefully prepared speech from his head. The unexpected, however, made him cautious not reckless. He drew the door to behind him and faced the astonished pair.

Both women had turned as he burst in. The maid, a white woman of uncertain years and not the negress Drinkwater might have thought likely had he anticipated her being there, dropped the hairbrush and squealed, putting her hands to her face as she backed away. Arabella, deathly pale, her face like wax, her eyes fixed upon the cloaked figure of the intruder, put out a hand to silence the frightened woman.

'There is no cause for alarm,' he said, a catch in his voice.

With a slow majesty Arabella rose to her feet and confronted the intruder. Her recently removed dress lay across her bed and she wore a fine silk negligée over her chemise. Her disarray twisted Drinkwater's gut with a tortuous spasm of desire and she caught this flickering regard of herself, sensed her mastery of his passion at the instant of knowing she might as easily lose it if he meditated rape.

'You! What is it you want?' Her voice trembled with emotion and the maid, pressed back against the wall, watched in terrified fascination, aware of a tension existing in the room extending beyond the mere fact of the stranger's burglarous entry. She too recognized the man, though he did not know her.

Drinkwater suppressed the goading of desire, aware she had divined the effect of her *déshabillé*, and annoyed by it. The reflection steadied him again, reminded him of his purpose, of the enormity of his gamble.

'Only a word, ma'am. I shall not detain you long, nor do I offer you any harm.' He shot a look at the maid. 'Will she hold her tongue?'

Arabella looked round at the quailing yet immobile figure. 'Tell me something of your purpose,' she said, addressing Drinkwater again.

'To speak with you,' he said simply, with a lover's implication, gratified that she lowered her eyes, momentarily confused. She remained silent, struggling with his dramatic and violent appearance. Again she turned to her maid and, in a low voice, murmured something. Drinkwater recognized the language and his words arrested the woman's trembling retreat towards the door.

'She is French?' he asked, his voice suddenly harsh.

Arabella nodded. 'Yes, but she can be trusted. She will say nothing about your being here.'

Drinkwater fixed the woman with his most balefully intimidating glare. He was not unduly worried. He had *Patrician*'s red cutter's crew of nine men within hail, men who would delight in rescuing him if it meant they might also make free with the contents of Castle Point while they were about it.

'I am not alone,' he warned, 'there are others outside.'

His stare made the poor woman cringe, her hand desperately reaching for the door-knob.

'She understands, Nathaniel,' Arabella insisted, lowering the tension between the three of them.

'Very well.'

Arabella nodded, the maid fled and they were alone in the perfumed intimacy of her boudoir.

'Why have you come back?' she whispered, her face contorted with anguish as she sat back upon the chair and her right hand drew the silk wrap defensively about her breast.

'Are you in health, Arabella?' he asked, keeping his distance, hardening his painfully thumping heart at her plight.

'Yes,' she nodded, seizing the proprieties he offered, ignoring the incongruity of their situation, 'and you?'

'Yes,' he paused and she saw the struggle in his own face.

'You have nothing to fear,' she said more firmly, looking at him, 'I miscarried in the second month.'

She had conceived! The shock of it struck Drinkwater like a whiplash. It brought him no goatish pleasure, only an appalling regret and a piteous compassion which was out of kilter with his present purpose. 'My dear . . .' he made a move towards her, then stopped at the precise moment she held up her hand to arrest him.

'No! It is over, and it is for the best!'

He avoided her eyes. 'Yes,' he mumbled, 'the war . . .'

'I did not mean the war, Nathaniel, though that too is an impediment now.' She paused, then added, 'You found your wife well?'

'Arabella,' he protested, utterly confused, desperately hanging on to the reason for his unceremonious arrival. In his heart he had no real wish to revive their liaison and her continuing assumption piqued him.

'No blame attaches to you,' she said, sensing his mood, 'but why have you come back?'

He sighed, ashamed of himself now the moment of truth had come. 'I need some information, Arabella, information I thought our former intimacy might entitle me at least to ask of you.'

'You wish me to turn traitor?' she enquired, that lilting, bantering tone on which they had first established their friendship back in her voice, 'just as I once turned whore.'

'No,' he replied levelly, pleased he had at least anticipated *this* question. 'I merely wish to know if the *Stingray* is at sea under your brother's command. Such a question may easily be discovered from other sources; it is rumoured that a Yankee comes cheaper than Judas Iscariot.'

She opened her mouth to protest and then a curiously reticent look crossed her face. Her eyes searched his for some clue, as though he had said something implicit and she was gauging the extent of his knowledge. Then, as soon as the expression appeared it had faded and he was mystified, almost uncertain whether or not he had read it aright, merely left staring at her singular beauty.

'Why should you wish to know this? And why come all the way from England and up the Chesapeake if it may be bought from some fisherman for a few dollars?'

'Because I wished for an excuse to see you,' he replied, voicing a gallant half-truth, 'and because it might stop your brother and I from trying to kill each other,' he lied. He watched the words sink in, hoping she might recall the respective attitudes he and Stewart had professed when

187

the possibility of war between their two countries had been discussed. He hoped, too, she might not begin to guess how large was the ocean and how unlikely they were to meet. Unless . . .

'The *Stingray*, Captain Drinkwater, is undergoing repairs at the Washington Navy Yard,' she said with a cool and dismissive air. 'My brother is unemployed by the Navy Department . . . out of your reach . . .'

He admired her quick intelligence, her guessing of his dissimulation, and was now only mildly offended at her assumption of motive.

'Madam,' he said with a wry smile that savaged her with its attractiveness, 'I do not meditate any revenge, I assure you.'

The formality had evaporated the passion between them. He was no longer a slave to their concupiscence; his imagination ran in a contrary direction.

'He is at sea, though, ma'am, is he not?'

She inclined her head. 'Perhaps.'

'In a Baltimore clipper schooner . . .' He flattened his tone, kept the interrogative out of his voice, made of the question a statement of fact and watched like a falcon the tiny reactive muscles about her lovely eyes.

'You knew,' she said before perceiving his trap and clenching her fist in her anger. 'You . . . you . . .' She stammered her outrage and he stepped forward and put a hand upon her shoulder. The white silk was warmed by the soft flesh beneath.

'Arabella . . .' She looked up, her eyes bright with fury. 'I truly mean no harm to either of you, but I have my obligations as you have yours. Please do not be angry with me. The web we find ourselves caught in is not of our making.'

She put her hand on his and it felt like a talon as it clawed at him. 'Why do you help weave it, then? You men are all the same! Why, you knew all along,' she whispered. Her fingers dug into the back of his hand, bearing it down upon her own shoulder as though she wanted to mutilate herself for her treachery. As he bent to kiss her hair the door was flung open with a crash of the handle upon the plaster.

188

Drinkwater looked round. Zebulon Shaw stood in the doorway with a scatter gun levelled at Drinkwater's belly. Behind him, the dull gleam of a musket barrel in his hands, was the dark presence of the negro groom and the pale face of the maid.

'Take your hands off!' Shaw roared.

Shaw's misreading of the situation in thinking the moment of anguished intimacy one of imminent violence, moved Drinkwater to fury. Arabella, too, reacted.

'Father...' she expostulated, but Drinkwater seized her shoulders, drew her to her feet, jerked her round and pulled her to him. Whipping the knife from his belt he held it to her neck, hissing a reassurance in her ear.

He had no idea to what extent and in what detail the French maid had betrayed her mistress; he hoped she had acted protectively with some discretion, concerned only for Arabella's safety in the presence of a man who, once her lover, was now at the very least an enemy. Whatever the niceties, he could, he realized, avoid compromising Arabella further while at the same time facilitating his escape. Zebulon Shaw's next remark gave him grounds for thinking he had guessed right.

'Drinkwater? Is it you? What in hell's name d'you mean by...?'

'I wished to know the whereabouts of the USS *Stingray*, Mr Shaw, and if you'll stand aside, I'll trouble your home no further. I have armed men outside and I have no need to remind you we are at war.'

Shaw's tongue flicked out over dry lips and his face lost its resolute expression. Drinkwater pressed his advantage.

'I apologize for my method,' he went on, sensing Shaw's indecision, 'and it would distress me even more if I had to add mutilation or murder to a trifling burglary.' As he spoke he moved the knife menacingly across Arabella's white throat.

'Damn you!' Shaw growled, drawing back.

'Very well, Mrs Shaw,' Drinkwater said with a calm insolence, 'precede me and no harm will come to you.' He pressed her gently forward, passed into the passage and ran the gauntlet of Shaw and the negro, glaring at the maid as she held up a wildly flickering candelabra in a

189

shaking hand. 'No tricks, sir . . .'

They were convinced by his show of bravado in which Arabella played her part submissively.

'Go, sir,' Shaw called after them, 'go and be damned to you if this is how you treat our hospitality . . .'

'Needs must, sir, when the devil drives,' Drinkwater flung over his shoulder as they reached the head of the staircase. 'Careful, m'dear,' he muttered to Arabella as they descended to the darkened hall.

Shaw and the negro covered their descent and Drinkwater was aware of open doors closing on their approach as inquisitive servants, roused by noises on the floor above, retreated before the sight of the cloaked intruder with their mistress a hostage. He paused at the main door and turned.

'Remain here, Shaw. I shall take your daughter-in-law a pistol shot from the house and release her. I trust you to wait here.'

'Be damned, Captain . . .'

'Do you agree?'

Shaw grunted. 'Under protest, yes, I agree.'

'I bid you farewell, Mr Shaw, and I repeat my apologies that the harsh necessities of war compel me to this action. Perhaps in happier times . . .'

He had the door open and thrust Arabella through, followed her and pulled the door to behind them, then seized her hand.

'Beyond the trees,' he ordered, walking quickly down the wide steps and across the gravel. 'And hurry, I pray you. I do not want you to catch a fever. I am sorry for what has happened. No blame attaches to you and if your maid was at least loyal to *you*, then I think no great harm can have been done. Tell your father-in-law you confessed only that your brother no longer had command of the *Stingray*'.

They reached the trees as he finished this monologue and he let go her wrist. She turned and faced him.

'I am sorry we must part like this,' he ran on, 'as sorry as I was by the manner of our last parting.'

'Sir,' she said, drawing her breath with difficulty, 'I

190

should hate you for this humiliation, but I cannot pretend
. . . no, it is no matter. It was guilt the last time, guilt and
shame and the confusion of love, but it was better than
this!' She almost spat the last word at him. 'God,' her voice
rose, exasperation and hurt charging it with a desperate
vehemence, 'had I not . . . damn you! Go, for God's sake,
go quickly.'

'God bless you, Arabella.'

'Go!'

He turned and ran, not hearing her poor, strangled cry,
wondering why on earth he had invoked the Deity. A
moment later he cannoned into Caldecott.

'Damn you, Caldecott – is the boat ready?'

'Beg pardon. Aye, sir.'

Drinkwater looked back. There was a brief flash of pale
silk and then only the trees and their shadows stood
between him and Castle Point.

'Everything all right, sir?'

In answer to Caldecott's query the wild barking of dogs,
the gleam of lanterns and shouts of men filled the night.
Then came the sharp crack of a musket.

'Not exactly. Come on, let's go.'

Cry Havoc...

'What d'you make of her, Mr Sundercombe?'

'I'm not sure, sir, beyond the fact she's a native and determined to pass close.'

Sundercombe handed Drinkwater his telescope. The American brig had trimmed her yards and laid a course to intercept the *Sprite* as the schooner ran south to pass the Virginia capes and reach the open Atlantic. It was mid-morning and Drinkwater was bleary-eyed from insufficient sleep. He had trouble focusing and passed the glass back to Sundercombe.

'Send your gun's crews quietly to their stations, load canister on ball, but don't run 'em out. Tell them when they get word, to aim high and cut up her riggin'. You handle the ship, I'll give the order to open fire.' Drinkwater looked up at the stars and bars rippling at the main peak. 'Better pass word for my coxswain.'

'I'm 'ere, sir, an' I've got some coffee.'

'Obliged, Caldecott...' Drinkwater took the hot mug.

Sundercombe was already issuing orders, turning up the watch below and giving instructions quietly to his gunners. The *Sprite* mounted six 6-pounders a side, enough to startle the stranger if Drinkwater timed his bird-scaring broadside correctly. He sipped gratefully at the scalding coffee which tasted of acorns.

'Caldecott,' he said, 'I want you to stand by the ensign halliards with one of our cutter's crew. The moment I give you the word, that ensign aloft must come down and our own be hoisted, d'you understand? 'Tis a matter of extreme punctilio.'

'Punctilio – aye, aye, sir.'

Drinkwater grinned after the retreating seaman. He seemed suitably imbued with *gravitas*. Quilhampton had discovered him and sent him aft for approval, concerned that Drinkwater had himself found no substitute for old Tregembo. 'You must have a cox'n, sir. I can't spare a midshipman every time you want a boat,' Quilhampton had protested.

'Can't, or won't?' Drinkwater had enquired.

'You *must* have a cox'n,' Quilhampton repeated doggedly, the flat assertion brooking no protest.

'Oh, very well,' Drinkwater relented, 'have you someone in mind?' Half an hour later the stunted form of Caldecott stood before him. 'Have you acted in a personal capacity before, Caldecott?' Drinkwater had asked, watching the man's eyes darting about the cabin and revealing a bright and curious interest.

'I 'ave, sir, to Captings Dawson and Peachey, sir, an' I was bargeman to Lord Collin'wood in the old *Ocean*, sir, an' 'ad lots of occasions to be 'andling 'is Lordship's personal an' diplomatic effects, sir.'

'Matter of punctilio,' Drinkwater now heard Caldecott repeat to his oarsman and, still grinning, he watched the Yankee brig bear down upon them.

The sight combined with the coffee and the invigorating chill of the morning breeze to cheer him, making him forget his fatigue. His brief nap had laid a period of time between this forenoon and the events of the previous night. They might have occurred to a different man. He was filled with a sudden happiness such as he had not felt for many, many months, the inspiriting renewal discovered by the penitent sinner.

Was that why he had called upon God to bless Arabella last night? Did he detect the finger of the Deity or providence in that last encounter; or in the fortuitous natural abortion of the child their helpless lust had made?

It was, he realized, much, much more than that. Certainly their odd, mutual avoidance had been in some strange way a holding back in anticipation of the final

193

parting which had now occurred. They were, he reflected without bitterness, not young, and though their affair had not lacked heat it had not been conducted without a little wisdom. Moreover, she had loved him as he had loved her, with the self-wounding passion of hopeless intensity. Such things happened, rocked the boats of otherwise loyal lives and sent their ripples out to slap the planking of other such boats, God help them all.

But there was also the timely confirmation of his hunch. The drunk and incautious Stewart had opened his mind and had put Drinkwater in possession of a key, not to the strategic planning of Madison and his colleagues, but to the freebooting aspirations of his commercial warriors, the privateersmen and their backers. Drinkwater was as certain of this as of the breeze itself.

Sundercombe approached and stood beside him. The brig was two miles away, a merchant ship by the look of her.

'There's a brace of sail hull down to the s'uthard,' Sundercombe volunteered.

'*Hasty?*'

'One of 'em perhaps, sir.'

The old sensation of excitement and anxiety wormed in Drinkwater's gut. They had nothing much to fear from the brig, he thought, any more than the brig had to fear from the schooner she was so trustingly running down towards. Unmistakably Yankee in design, the American ensign at her peak and approaching from the direction of Baltimore, the *Sprite* could be nothing other than a privateer putting to sea. He looked along the waist. The gunners crouched at their pieces, waiting.

'We've forgotten something,' Drinkwater said sharply. 'Have your men drop the fore topm'st stays'l. Contrive to have it hang over the starboard rail and cover our trail boards. Have the men fuss about up there, as though dissatisfied with something. Those men yonder may smell a rat if they know there's no *Sprite* out of Baltimore or the Chesapeake.'

With a sharp intake of breath, Sundercombe hurried off. He had large yellow teeth, like an old horse, thought Drinkwater. He suddenly craved the catharsis of action,

194

knowing that in a few moments he would open fire on the defenceless ship. What else was there for him to do? He was a King's officer, bound by his duty. They were all shackled, one way or another, making a nonsense of notions of liberty.

How could a man be free? He was tied to a trade, to a master, to his family, to his land, to his throne if one chased the argument to its summit. Even poor Thurston, exponent of freedom though he was, had been chained to his beliefs, governed to excess by his obsession with democracy. Everything everywhere was either passive in equilibrium, or else active in collision, in the process of transition ending in balance and inertia. In that state of grace men called natural order, equilibrium reigned; the affairs of men were otherwise and ran, for the most part, contrary to natural order. Shocking though it had been at the hand of a maniac, Thurston's murder was comprehensible if seen as a drawing upon himself, the libertarian extremist, the pistol ball of an extreme agent of repression.

In such a world what was a reasonable man to do? What he was doing now, Drinkwater concluded as he watched an officer mount the brig's quarter rail, clinging to the larboard gaff vang. He must hasten the end of this long, wearisome war. Duty ruled his existence and providence decided the outcome of his acts.

And what of Christian charity? What of compassion, his conscience whispered? He provided for his family; he was not unkind to his friends; he had done his best in those circumstances where his decisions impinged upon the lives of others; he had taken in those lame ducks whose existence depended upon his charity . . .

'Schooner, 'hoy!'

There was a flurry of activity on the deck of the brig as she drew rapidly closer. Sundercombe came aft again, wandering with a studied casualness and impressing Drinkwater with his coolness. Forward, the staysail flapped over the *Sprite*'s name.

'Schooner 'hoy? What ship?'

Drinkwater drew himself up, doffed his hat and waved. 'Tender to the United States ship *Stingray*, out of the

Washington Navy Yard,' he hailed.

The brig was a cable distant, trimming her yards as she braced round to run parallel with the schooner.

'Have you had word? There's a British frigate cruising off the capes.'

'Must be *Hasty*,' a perplexed Sundercombe murmured.

'No,' Drinkwater called back. What the devil had induced Tyrell to douse French colours? 'When was she last sighted?'

'Day before yesterday. He took a Norfolk ship prize.'

'The hell he did!' Drinkwater shouted back with unfeigned surprise. 'He can't have seen those two sails to the south,' he muttered in an aside to Sundercombe.

'He's too big for you to take on, Cap'n,' the American continued as the two vessels surged alongside, their crews staring at one another, the *Sprite*'s gunners still crouching out of sight.

'Where are you bound?' Drinkwater pressed.

'The Delaware.'

'I could give you an escort. We could divert the Britisher, hold him off while you got out. I heard there were some French ships in the offing,' Drinkwater drawled.

Drinkwater watched the American officer throw a remark behind him then he nodded. 'I calculate you're correct, Cap'n, and we'd be mightily obliged.'

'I'll take station on your starboard quarter then. Can you make a little more sail?'

'Sure, and thanks.'

'My pleasure.' Drinkwater turned his attention inboard. 'I think we've hooked him, Mr Sundercombe. Keep your gunners well down. Let him draw ahead and then have us range up on his weather side.'

'Ease the foresheet, there,' Sundercombe growled, clearly not trusting himself to imitate an American accent like Drinkwater. The big gaff sail flogged and the schooner lost some way as the brig's crew raced aloft to impress the navy men and shook out their royals. Sundercombe went aft and lent his weight to the helmsman. *Sprite* luffed under the brig's stern and then, with the foresheet retrimmed, slowly overhauled her victim on her starboard side.

'Get your larboard guns ready,' Drinkwater said, aware

the Americans could not hear him but anxious lest they might realize they had been deceived.

He thought he detected some such appreciation, someone pointing at them and drawing the attention of the officer he had seen on the brig's rail to something. He realized with a spurt of irritation that he had forgotten their name exposed on the larboard bow.

The *Sprite* was fast overhauling the brig and Drinkwater knew he dared delay no longer if, as the inconvenient discomfort of his conscience prompted, he was to avoid excessive bloodshed.

'Ensign, Caldecott! Run out your guns, Mr Sundercombe!'

They could not fail to see now. The jerky lowering of the American colours and the hand-over-hand ascent of the white ensign brought a howl of rage from the brig, a howl quite audible above the trundle of the 6-pounder carriages over the *Sprite*'s pine decks.

'Strike, sir, or I'll open fire!' Drinkwater hailed.

'God damn you to hell!' came a defiant roar and Drinkwater nodded. The three 6-pounders barked in a ragged broadside. It was point-blank range; even at the maximum elevation originally intended to cripple the brig's rigging and with the schooner heeling to the breeze, the trajectories of the shot could not avoid hitting the brig's rail. What appeared like a burst of lethal splinters exploded over the brig's deck. A moment later, as the gun-captains' hands went up in signal of their readiness to fire again, the American flag came down.

An hour later the brig *Louise* of Norfolk, Virginia, Captain Samuel Bethnal, Master, had been fired. Bethnal and his people hoisted the lugsail of the red cutter lately belonging to His Britannic Majesty's frigate *Patrician* and miserably set course to the south-west and the coast of Virginia. To the east the horizon was broken only by the grey smudges of a pair of British frigates, and the twin jags of a schooner's sails as she slipped over the rim of the world and left the coast of America astern.

'I don't see the sense in it myself,' said Wyatt, burying his nose in a tankard and bracing himself as the *Patrician*

197

shouldered her way through a swell. 'It ain't logical,' he added, surfacing briefly to deliver his final opinion on Captain Drinkwater's conduct in the dank haven of the wardroom.

'I suppose the Commodore has his reasons,' offered Pym with a detached and largely disinterested loyalty.

'I'm sure he has,' Simpson, the chaplain, said cautiously, then affirming, 'of course he has,' with an air of conviction, before destroying the effect by appending in a far from certain tone of voice: 'in fact I'm certain of it.'

Slowly Wyatt raised his face from the tankard. Rum ran from his slack mouth, adding gloss to an already greasy complexion. 'You don't know what you're talking about,' he mouthed with utter contempt.

'Nevertheless, Mr Wyatt,' the hitherto silent Frey piped up, 'I agree with Simpson and the surgeon.'

Wyatt turned his red eyes on the junior lieutenant. 'An' you know bugger all,' he said offensively.

Frey was about to leap to his feet when he felt Simpson's restraining hand on his sleeve. 'Hold hard, young man, he doesn't know what he's saying.'

'Don't know what I'm saying, d'you say? Is that what you said, you God-bothering bastard?' Wyatt rose unsteadily to his feet, instinctively bracing himself against *Patrician*'s motion. 'With hundreds of bloody privateers shipping out of every creek and runnel on the coast of North America, we, we,' Wyatt slammed his now empty tankard on the table top with a dull, emphatic thud, 'we go waltzing off into the wide Atlantic with the strongest frigate squadron south of Halifax . . .'

'We're going to rendezvous with the homeward Indiamen . . .' Frey began, but was choked in mid-sentence.

'Indiamen be buggered. If we were going to do that why did we go all the way to America?'

'Why *did* we go to America then, Wyatt?' Pym asked provocatively.

Wyatt swung a pitying look on Pym. 'So he', Wyatt gestured a thumb at the deck above, 'could lay with his lady love again.'

'Mr Wyatt, hold your tongue!' Frey snapped, leaping to his feet and this time avoiding Simpson's tardy hand.

'Ah, be buggered,' Wyatt sneered, 'Caldecott saw the woman; half naked she was, in her shift . . .'

'Are you drunk again, Mr Wyatt?'

Quilhampton stood just inside the doorway, his one hand grasping a stanchion. The creaking of the ship and the gloom of the day had allowed him to enter unobserved. Wyatt swung ponderously on his accuser as the other officers heaved a sigh of collective relief. As the frigate lurched and rolled to leeward, the master lost his already unsteady balance and reached for the back of his chair which he only succeeded in knocking over. The motion of the frigate accelerated their fall and Wyatt stretched full length on the deck. He made no move to recover himself and for a long, expectant moment no one in the wardroom moved. Then a snore broke what passed for silence between decks.

'I see you are,' said Quilhampton drily. Looking round the table, he continued, 'Let us avoid complete dishonour, gentlemen, and get the old soak into his cot without the benefit of the messman.'

They rallied round the one-armed lieutenant and, shuffling awkwardly with the dead weight of the big man between them, squeezed into his cabin and manhandled Wyatt into his swinging cot.

Catching their breath they regarded their late burden for a moment.

'Sad when you see drink consume an otherwise able man, ain't it?' Quilhampton asked in a general way. 'I presume he was running the Captain down again.'

'Yes,' Frey said, 'like Metcalfe used to, and in a particularly personal manner, too.'

'It was disgraceful,' said Simpson.

'This story about the woman again, was it?' asked Quilhampton.

'Indeed it was, Mr Q,' said Simpson.

'Well, gentlemen, let me tell you something,' Quilhampton said, herding them back into the common area of the wardroom where they resumed their places at the battered table. 'I have been acquainted with Captain Drinkwater for many years and in that time I have not known him to act improperly. Moreover, I do know him to have the confidence of government, and that if he claims this mysterious woman was an agent, or a spy, then that is very likely what she was. Now I think we can cease speculatin' on the matter and assume the Captain knows what he is doin', eh?' Quilhampton looked round the table as Moncrieff came in.

'Don't you think, Mr Q,' Simpson said, his neat, rosebud mouth pursed primly, 'that you should properly refer to Drinkwater as the Commodore?'

'I daresay I should, Mr Simpson,' Quilhampton said laconically, helping himself to a biscuit, 'what is it, Moncrieff?'

'I am a messenger, James. The Captain, I beg your pardon, Mr Simpson, the Commodore,' Moncrieff said, with ironic emphasis, desires a word with you.'

Quilhampton brushed his coat, rose and bowed to the company. 'Gentlemen, excuse me . . .'

'I suppose they think I'm mad in the wardroom?' Drinkwater said flatly, not expecting contradiction. He remained bent over the chart as Quilhampton replied, 'Something like that, sir.'

Drinkwater looked up at his first lieutenant. 'You're damnably cheerful.'

'The weather's to my taste, sir.'

'You're perverse, James.'

'My wife says something similar, sir.' They grinned at each other.

'What is it they say?' Drinkwater asked, now he had Quilhampton's full attention. He saw Quilhampton drop his eyes, saw the evasive, non-committal shrug and listened to the half-truth.

'Oh, that damned fool Wyatt thinks we should stay on the American coast. I've tried to explain, but . . .'

Again the shrug and then Quilhampton looked up and caught a bleak look of utter loneliness on Drinkwater's face, a look which vanished as Drinkwater recovered himself, cast adrift his abstracted train of thought and fixed his eyes upon his friend.

'I'll admit to it being a long shot, James; perhaps a *very* long shot, and certainly a risky one. I appreciate too, that

200

twenty-two days out of the Chesapeake with nothing to our account beyond a fired brig don't amount to much but . . .'

Quilhampton watched now, saw the inward glance take ignition from the conviction lurking somewhere inside this man he respected and loved, but could never understand.

'You have explained to me, sir, at least in part, but may I presume?'

'Of course.'

'We are on the defensive now. Even our blockading squadrons keep watch and ward off the French ports as the first line of defence against invasion. To some extent I share Wyatt's misgivings. We are a long way from home. Our present passage to the South Atlantic exposes our rear when every ship should be sealing home waters against the enemy. That is where, I have heard you yourself say, American privateers struck hardest during the last war. I fear, sir, for what may happen if you have miscalculated . . .'

Drinkwater gave a short bark of a laugh. 'So do I, James,' he interrupted.

'How *are* you so sure?'

'Because if I were in the same position this is what I would do.'

'And you really think it is him? This man Stewart?'

'Yes.'

'How?'

'I don't really know . . .'

'Then how can you be sure of his mind?'

'I can't be entirely sure of it, James . . .'

'But,' Quilhampton expostulated vainly, frustrated at Drinkwater's failure to see where the decision to sail south might lead them, 'a month ago you were in doubt as to how to proceed . . .'

'But we reasoned here, in this very cabin, the interception of the East India fleet was the most likely thing,' Drinkwater paused. 'Come, James, have faith; stick like a limpet to your decision.' There was a vehemence, a wildness in Drinkwater's voice, almost a passion that disturbed Quilhampton. It just then occurred to him with a vivid awfulness that Drinkwater might indeed be on the verge of madness. He stared at his friend and tried again: 'But how . . . ?'

'By the prickin' of my thumbs,' Drinkwater said, looking down at the chart again, and Quilhampton withdrew, a cold and chilling sensation laying siege to his heart.

'What do you think, damn it?' Quilhampton asked Pym as the surgeon, spectacles perched on the end of his nose, looked up from the candlelit pages that he held before him against the roll of the ship. 'They're your confounded theories, ain't they? All this bloody obsession and conviction and what-not. Damn it, Pym, I've known the man since I was a boy. He's brilliant, but dogged like so many of us with never quite bein' in the right place at the right time. He got me out of Hamburg in terrible circumstances, all the way down the Elbe in the winter in a blasted duck-punt . . .'

'Yes, I heard about that.'

'D'you think the ordeal might have turned his mind?'

Pym shrugged. 'This', he tapped the notes he had abandoned when Quilhampton sought him out, 'is no more than a theory, based on a single case, that of your predecessor. I don't know about Drinkwater . . . You say he's changed?'

The use of Drinkwater's unqualified surname shocked Quilhampton. It almost smacked of mutiny, as if Pym, in his detached, objectively professional way, had actually committed a preliminary act by divesting Drinkwater of his rank. Quilhampton shied away from committing himself.

'Certainly,' Pym rumbled on, 'there are signs of obsession in his conduct, but I have to say we are not party to his orders and, as you yourself suggested, these may be of a clandestine nature. Wasn't he in Hamburg on some such mission?'

'Yes,' Quilhampton agreed, worried at the direction the conversation was taking.

'Perhaps,' Pym suggested with an air of slyness, removing his spectacles and leaning back in his chair to clean them on his neck-cloth, 'there is something else the matter.'

'What the deuce d'you mean?' Quilhampton asked sharply.

'You've heard the stories of the woman. Perhaps it isn't obsession he suffers from, but remorse . . .'

'Preposterous!' snapped Quilhampton dismissively, starting to his feet and looking down at the surgeon.

'If you say so, Mr Q.' Pym replaced the spectacles and picked up his pen.

'I most emphatically do say so, Mr Pym.' Quilhampton turned the handle on the surgeon's cabin door, then paused in his exit. 'This conversation, Mr Pym, must be regarded as confidential.'

'We can regard it as never having happened if you wish, Mr Q.'

Quilhampton expelled his breath. 'It would be best, I think.'

'I think so too.'

'Obliged. Good-night, Mr Pym.'

Pym bent to his manuscript and picked up his pen. The ship's motion was easier now and the lantern gyrated less, so he was able to write without the flying shadows distracting his failing sight.

It seems to me from a long observation of commanders in His Majesty's navy, that unopposed command may distort the reasoning powers of a clever man, that the balance of his rational, thinking mind may be warped by lack of good counter-argument and his imagination seized by obsession.

Pym paused, tapping his pen on the broken teeth of his lower jaw. 'The trouble is,' he puzzled to himself, 'this is quite the reverse of a man vacillating between two distinct manners of thought. And if I am to identify the one, I needs must also consider the other.'

A warm glow of ambitious satisfaction welled in his stomach. Perhaps, unlike his subjects, he *was* in the right place at the right time. He dipped his pen and bent to his task.

The Whaler

'The rendezvous, gentlemen.' Drinkwater tapped the
spread chart with the closed points of the dividers and
watched as they leaned forward to study the tiny, isolated
archipelago a few miles north of the Equator and already
far astern of them as they ran down the latitude of
Ascension Island. 'St Paul's Rocks, as likely a spot for the
Americans to use too, so ensure you approach them with
caution, should you become detached, and that you use
the private signals . . .'

He looked round at them. Ashby was still studying the
chart but Thorowgood's florid face, evidence, Drinkwater
suspected, of a self-indulgent Christmas, hung on his
every word, while Sundercombe, a mere lieutenant in the
company of four post-captains, regarded him thoughtfully from the rear.

'Now as for our cruising station, you will observe the
rhumb-line from Ascension to St Helena as being exactly
contrary to the south-east trade wind . . .'

They would, he explained, sweep in extended line
abreast, the frigates just in sight of one another, tacking at
dawn and dusk, in the hope of intercepting the East India
convoy before any American privateers.

'We know the Indiamen will have at least one frigate as
escort, but Yankee clipper-schooners will have no trouble
outmanoeuvring her and cutting out the choicest victims
at their will. News of hostilities with America will have
reached the Cape by now and it may be that a second

cruiser will have been attached; not that that will make very much difference. However, four additional frigates plus a schooner to match Yankee nimbleness', he paused and smiled at Sundercombe, 'should bring the convoy home safely. Any questions?'

'Sir,' said Ashby, 'may I enquire whether your orders were to escort the East Indiamen, or remain on the American coast? I mean no criticism, but had we proceeded directly to the Cape we would have met with the India fleet for a certainty.'

A groundswell of concurrence rose from the other post-captains. Drinkwater had no way of knowing that the news of the silk petticoat had spread round the squadron by that mysterious telegraphy which exists among ships in company. *Sprite*'s tendering and message-bearing had much to do with it, and the breath of intrigue had engendered a note of misgiving into the minds of Drinkwater's young and ambitious juniors.

For himself, his own sense of guilt had been superseded by the conviction that he had picked up a vital trail at Castle Point, and he saw in Ashby's mildly impertinent question, full of the criticism he denied, the arrogance of young bucks seeking the downfall of an old bull. He lacked in their eyes, he knew, the bold dash expected of a frigate captain, and was, moreover, a tarpaulin officer of an older school than they cared to associate with. He knew, too, they had objected to his burning of the *Louise*. Tyrell, by being in sight in *Hasty*, would have had a legitimate claim to the prize money her sale might have realized, while the general principle of burning valuable prizes appealed to none of them. Ashby's question invited a snub; he decided to administer a lecture. Signalling Mullender to offer wine and sweet-treacle biscuits to his guests, he stared out of the stern windows. Only the lightest of breezes ruffled the sea and *Patrician* ghosted along, the other frigates' boats towing in the slight ripples of her wake. He knew from the silence, broken only by the soft chink of decanter on glass, that they waited for his reply. He swung on them with a sudden, unexpected ferocity.

'You cannot *buy* yourself into the sea-service, gentlemen, as you can into the army. A ship-of-the-line is not to be had like a regiment or a whore. Oh, to be sure, interest, be it parliamentary or petticoat, sees many a fool up the quarterdeck ladder. But that does not *prevent* an able man getting there, though it stops many. Fortunately for the sea-service that peculiarly snobbish genius of the English, that of giving the greater glory to what costs 'em most, is absent in principle from naval promotion.'

He paused, glaring at them, gratified to see in their eyes the expressions of the midshipmen they once had been.

'Nevertheless, a deal of useless articles have arrived on quarterdecks. Since Lord Nelson's apotheosis at Trafalgar, the Royal Navy has appealed to the second of England's vices after snobbery: that of fashion. How a service which accepts boys to be sodomized or killed at twelve or thirteen, poxed at eighteen and shot or knighted by their majority should become fashionable, is a matter for philosophers more objective than myself. All I know is that those of us who remember the last war with the Americans, if we aren't rotting ashore, dead, or been promoted to flags or dockyards, have been consigned to the living entombment of blockade, whilst injudiciously *fashionable* young men command our cruisers and risk destruction at the hands of the Americans . . .'

'Excuse me, sir.'

'What the devil d'you want?' Drinkwater broke off his diatribe, aware that Belchambers had been hovering by the door for some time. 'Excuse me a moment, gentlemen,' Drinkwater said, secretly delighted that Thorowgood was nearly purple with fury and Ashby's eyes glittered dangerously. Tyrell was studying his nails.

'The wind's freshening a trifle, sir, and Mr Quilhampton says there's a strange sail coming up from the south-'ard. She's carrying a wind and looks to be a whaler.'

The news transformed the gathering, the whiff of a prize, a Yankee whaler, affected them all, with the exception of their commodore.

'Shall we go on deck, gentlemen, and see what we make of this newcomer before you return to your ships?'

The notion of waiting aboard *Patrician* while the whaler closed the squadron obviously irritated them still further.

Coolly Drinkwater led the way past the ramrod figure of the marine sentry and up the quarterdeck ladder.

'British colours, sir.'

Quilhampton, who had the deck, lowered his glass and offered it to Drinkwater. Behind them the knot of frustrated frigate commanders and Lieutenant Sundercombe, who stood slightly apart and gravitated towards Mr Wyatt beside the binnacle, drew pocket-glasses from their tail pockets. With irritable snaps the telescopes were raised.

'Maybe a ruse,' growled Thorowgood in a stage whisper.

'Indeed it might,' Ashby added archly.

The whaler, her low rig extended laterally by studding sails, came up from the south with a bone in her teeth. Gradually her sails fell slack as she closed the British frigates and her way fell off.

'I think not, gentlemen, she's losing the wind and lowering a boat.'

They watched as the whaleboat danced over the wavelets towards *Patrician*, the most advanced of the squadron.

'He's pulling pell-mell. Ain't he afraid we might press such active fellows?' Drinkwater asked in an aside to Quilhampton.

'D'you want me to, sir?'

'I think we should see what he has to say, Mr Q,' Drinkwater replied.

The whaleboat swung parallel to the *Patrician*'s side, half a pistol-shot to starboard.

'Good-day, sir,' Drinkwater called, standing conspicuously beside the hance. 'You seem in a damned hurry.'

'Aye, sir, I've news, damnable news. Do I have to shout it out, or may I come aboard with the promise that you won't molest my men?'

'Come aboard. You have my word on the matter of your men.' Drinkwater's heart was suddenly thumping excitedly in his breast. A sense of anticipation filled him, a sense of luck and providence conspiring to bring him at last the news he so desired.

The whaling master clambered over the rail. He was a

big, bluff, elderly man, dressed in an old-fashioned brown coat with grey breeches and red woollen stockings, despite the warmth of the day. He drew off his hat and revealed a bald pate and a fringe of long, lank hair.

'I'm Cap'n Hugh Orwig, master of the whaling barque *Altair* homeward bound towards Milford,' the man said in a rush, waving aside any introductions Drinkwater might have felt propriety compelled him to offer, 'you'll be after news of the Yankee frigate.'

'What Yankee frigate?' Drinkwater asked sharply.

'You ain't chasing a Yankee frigate?'

'Not specifically, but if you've news of one at large . . .'

'News, Cap'n? Bloody hell, I've news for you, aye, all of you,' he nodded at the semi-circle of gold epaulettes that caught the sunshine as they drew closer.

'I heard yesterday, from a Portuguese brig, that a big Yankee frigate has taken the *Java*, British frigate . . .'

'Stap me . . .' An explosion of incredulity behind him caused Drinkwater to turn and glare at his subordinates.

'The *Java*, you say . . . ?' He could not place the ship.

'A former Frenchman, sir,' Ashby said smoothly, 'formerly the *Renommée*, taken off Madagascar in May, the year before last, by Captain Schomberg's squadron. I believe Lambert to have been in command.'

'Thank you, Captain Ashby.' Drinkwater returned to Orwig. 'D'you know the name of the American frigate?'

'No, sir, but I don't think she was the same as took the *Macedonian*.'

'What's that you say? The *Macedonian*'s been taken too?'

'Aye, Cap'n, didn't you know? I fell in with another Milford ship, the *Martha*, Cap'n Raynes; cruising for Sperm we were, off Martin Vaz, and he told me the *Macedonian* had been knocked to pieces by the *United States*, said the alarm had gone out there was a Yankee squadron at large . . .'

'God's bones!'

The sense of having been caught out laid its cold fingers round Drinkwater's heart. The American ships must have left from New York or Boston; they could have slipped past within a few miles of his own vessels! It was quite possible the Americans would attempt to combine their heavy frigates with a swarm of privateers, privateers with trained but surplus naval officers like Stewart and, perhaps, Lieutenant Tucker, to command them. It struck him that if such a thing occurred, the United States navy might quadruple itself at a stroke, greatly reducing the assumed superiority of the Royal Navy! The thought made his blood run cold and about him it had precipitated a buzz of angry reaction.

'When did this happen?' he heard Ashby asking Orwig.

'Sometime in October, I think. Off the Canaries, Raynes said,' Orwig replied, adding in a surprised tone, 'I thought you gennelmen would have knowed.'

'No, sir, we did not know.' Ashby's tone was icily accusatory, levelled at Drinkwater as though, in condemning his superior officer for glaring into one crystal ball, he had failed to divine the truth in another, and taking Drinkwater's silence for bewilderment.

'Well, we know now,' Drinkwater said, rounding on them, 'and the India fleet is all the more in need of our protection.' Quilhampton caught his attention; the first lieutenant's face was twisted with anxiety and apprehension.

'You'll be seekin' convoy, Captain Orwig?' Drinkwater enquired.

Orwig nodded, then shook his head. 'You'll not be able to spare it, Cap'n, not if the Yankees are as good as they seem and you've the India fleet to consider. Leadenhall Street will not forgive you if you lose them their annual profit.'

Drinkwater had no need to contemplate the consequences of the displeasure of the Court of Directors of the Honourable East India Company. 'And you, Captain,' he said, warming to the elderly man's consideration, 'how long did it take *you* to fill your barrels?'

'Three years, sir, an' in all three oceans.'

'Then you shall have convoy, sir, and my hand upon it. I would not have you or your company end a three-year voyage in American hands. Captain Tyrell . . .'

'Sir?' Tyrell stepped forward.

'I will write you out orders in a few moments, the sense of which will be to take Captain Orwig, and such other

209

British merchantmen as you may sight, under your protection and convoy them to Milford Haven and then Plymouth. You will take also my dispatches and there await the instructions of their Lordships. Please take this opportunity to discuss details with Captain Orwig.' Drinkwater ignored the astonished look on Tyrell's face and addressed Ashby, Thorowgood and Sundercombe. 'Return to your ships, if you please, gentlemen. We will proceed as we agreed the moment I have written Captain Tyrell's orders. Your servant, gentlemen; Captain Orwig, a safe passage; Captain Tyrell, I'd be obliged if you'd wait upon me when you have concluded your business with Orwig.'

In his cabin Drinkwater drew pen, ink and paper towards him and wrote furiously for twenty minutes. He first addressed a brief report of proceedings to the Admiralty, stating he had reason to believe a force of privateers was loose in the South Atlantic. That much, insubstantial as it was in fact, yet justified the detachment of *Hasty*. Next he wrote to his wife, enclosing the missive with his private letter to Lord Dungarth to whom he gave vent to his concern over an American frigate squadron supported by private auxiliaries operating on the British trade routes. He was completing this last when Tyrell knocked and came in.

'Sit down, Tyrell, help yourself to another glass, I shall be with you directly.'

'Captain Drinkwater, I don't wish to appear importunate...'

'Then don't, my dear fellow,' said Drinkwater, looking up as he sanded the last sheet and stifling Tyrell's protest. 'Now listen, I want you to deliver this letter to Lord Dungarth when you call on the Admiralty. It is for his hand only, and if you fail to find his Lordship at the Admiralty, you are to wait upon him at his residence in Lord North Street; d'you understand?'

'Yes.'

'Good.' Drinkwater rose, handed over the papers and extended his right hand. 'Good luck, and don't get yourself taken if you can help it.'

Drinkwater saw, from the sudden widening of Tyrell's

eyes, that he had not, until that moment, considered the possibility.

'Well, Wyatt, what d'you make of the news?' Frey asked as the officers sat over their wine and the *Patrician* heeled to the gathering south-easterly breeze which promised to be the long-sought trade wind.

'The American ships were lucky. I expect their gunners were British deserters. It wouldn't have happened ten years ago . . .'

'I don't mean the American victories, Wyatt, I mean the effect their being at sea has on the safety of the East Indiamen, something you were prepared to regard as . . .'

'Don't resurrect old arguments, Mr Frey,' Simpson cautioned. 'Let sleeping dogs lie.'

'Oh ye of little faith,' Frey said, throwing the remark at the master, who buried his nose in his slopping tankard.

On the deck above Drinkwater dozed in his cot. Orwig's news was worrying. He had felt as though someone had punched him in the belly earlier, such was its impact. The latitude allowed in discretionary orders could hang an officer if he made the wrong decision more certainly than it could bring him success. There were so many options open, but only one which could be taken up. He dulled his anxiety with half a bottle of blackstrap and then settled to think the matter over. Yet the more he worried at the problem, the more convinced he was of the rightness of his decision, despite its unorthodox roots.

The logic of the thing was inescapable; as he had said to Quilhampton and repeated in substance to Dungarth, it was not only what he would have done himself had he been in Stewart's shoes, but what he would do if given President Madison's choices. Over and over he turned the thing until he dozed off in his chair. After some fifteen minutes the empty wine glass slipped from his fingers and the crash of its breaking woke him with a start.

The sudden shock made his heart pound, the wine made his head ache and his mouth felt foul. He rubbed his face, grinding his knuckles into his eyes. Bright scarlet and yellow flashes danced before him.

'God's bones!' he exlaimed, leaping to his feet and striking his head a numbing blow on the deck beams above. He sank back into his chair, his hands over his skull, feeling the bruise rising. 'God damn and blast it,' he muttered through clenched teeth, 'was I dreaming, or not?'

Mullender looked in from the pantry and smartly withdrew. Captain Drinkwater's antics seemed scarcely normal, but Mullender knew personal survival for men in his station largely depended on feigned indifference.

'I *was* dreaming,' Drinkwater continued to himself, 'but it wasn't a phantasm.' He sat up, dropping his hands from his head and staring straight before him, seeing not the bulkhead, but a glimpse of a room through a gap in heavy brocaded curtains and a litter of papers spread about an escritoire.

Had Mullender chosen this moment to enquire after the well-being of his master, he would have thought him stark, staring mad; but Captain Nathaniel Drinkwater had never been saner in his life.

PART THREE

A Furious Aside

'O miserable advocates! In the name of God, what was done with this immense superiority of force?'

'Oh, what a charm is hereby dissolved! What hopes, will be excited in the breasts of our enemies!'

The Times,
London,
27 and 29 December 1812

Lord Dungarth set down the stained paper he had been reading and rose from the desk, heaving himself on to the crutch which bent under his weight. The reflection of his gross figure in the uncurtained window disgusted him momentarily, until he was close enough to the glass to peer through.

Below, the carriage lights in Whitehall threw their glimmering illumination on streaks of sleeting rain that threatened to turn to snow before the night had ended. He raised his eyes above the roof-tops and gazed at the night sky. Dark clouds streaked across, permitting the occasional glimpse of a pair of stars.

The vision of his long-dead wife's face formed itself around the distant stars, then cloud obscured her image and he saw only the pale hemisphere of his own bald and reflected head. The onset of the pain overwhelmed him; the attacks were more frequent now, more intense, like the pains of labour as the moment of crisis approached. He seemed to shrink on his crutch, diminished in size as death sapped at his very being.

The pain ebbed and ceased to be an overwhelming preoccupation; he was aware of the stink of his own fearful sweat. Slowly he turned and began the long haul back to his desk. He slumped into his creaking chair and, with a shaking hand, reached for the decanter. He had given up hiding the laudanum and, with a carelessly shaking hand, added half a dozen drops to the *oporto*.

Sipping the concoction, he half-closed his eyes, trying to recapture the vision of his countess, but instead there came before his mind's eye a picture of gunfire and dismasted ships: the *Guerrière*, the *Macedonian*, with more to follow, he felt certain, the imminence of death and the opiate lending him prescience, an awareness of approaching bad tidings.

And yet . . .

His hand reached out tremulously, seeking the travel-stained dispatch in its curious, runic cipher. He had thought, too, that disaster and defeat were inevitable from that quarter after the news of the Russians' abandonment of Moscow following the battle at Borodino.

But now . . .

He frowned with the effort of focusing on the piece of paper. He was so used to the cryptography, he needed no key to decode it, but read the words as if they headlined a broadsheet: *French army have abandoned Moscow. Line of retreat dictated by Russian pursuit. Attacks to be mounted at their crossing of the Beresina* . . .

Lord Dungarth looked up at the dark window. The sleet had turned to snow. The secret dispatch was already a month old.

'At last,' he whispered as the pain gathered itself again and he drained the glass.

The Dogs of War

It was high summer in the southern hemisphere, day after day of blue skies dusted with fair-weather cumulus. Sunlight sparkled off the sapphire seas and the wavecaps broke into rainbows as they tumbled. For a week the squadron tacked wearily to windward. Gulls, petrels and frigate birds rode the invisible air currents disturbed by their passage, amusing the bored lookouts who saw nothing beyond the topgallants of the ships on either flank, though the visibility was as far as the eye could see. A sense of futility was borne in upon them all with their growing comprehension of the vastness of the ocean.

In the wardroom, grumbling and criticism accompanied every meal and even the inhabitants of the lower deck, whose burden was at its lightest in such prime sailing conditions, were permeated by a gloom begun by the news of the three British frigate defeats, and daily worsened with their frustration at discovering no sail upon the broad bosom of the South Atlantic.

As for Drinkwater himself, he endured the loneliness and isolation of his position by withdrawing into himself. Even Quilhampton's diligent and loyal support seemed less enthusiastic, a remnant of past friendship, rather than the whole-hearted support of the present. Quilhampton was friendly with Frey, Drinkwater noted, supposing them both to be presuming on long acquaintanceship and discussing his own descent into madness.

Perhaps he was going mad. The thought occurred to

him repeatedly. Loneliness and guilt combined to make his mood vacillate so that he might, had Pym known it, be set fair to become a subject for the worthy surgeon's treatise on the pendular personality. On the one hand his metaphysical preoccupations saw the quest he had set the squadron upon as a cogent consequence of all that had occurred at Castle Point. On the other loomed the awful spectre of a mighty misjudgement, a spectre made more terrible by the ominous threat explicit in the wording of his commission: *you may fail as you will answer at your peril.*

He became unable to sleep properly, his cabin a prison, so that he preferred to doze on deck, wrapped in his cloak and jammed in the familiar place by the weather mizen rigging. As the watches changed, the officers merely nodded at the solitary figure whose very presence betrayed his anxiety and further amplified the depression of their own spirits.

And yet they knew, for all its interminable nature, that such a state of affairs could not go on for ever. One morning, an hour after dawn when the squadron had tacked, reversed the consequent echelon of its advance, and sent the lookouts aloft, the hail from the masthead swept aside the prevailing mood:

'Deck there! *Icarus*'s let fly her t'garn sheets!'

'A fleet in sight!' Frey said with unnatural loudness, rounding on the figure standing by the larboard mizen pinrail. 'The India fleet?'

'Pray to God it is,' someone muttered.

'Mr Belchambers,' Frey said curtly, 'get a long glass aloft. Mr Davies, rouse the watch, stand by the main t'gallant sheets and let 'em fly, and Mr Belchambers . . .'

The midshipman paused in the lower rigging. 'Sir?'

'Make sure *Cymbeline* has seen and acknowledged our repetition.'

'Aye, aye, sir,' Belchambers acknowledged, his reply verging on the irritated, as though weary of being told how to suck eggs. Frey ignored the insubordinate tone and approached Drinkwater, who had detached himself from support and, dopey with fatigue, his face grey, stubbled and red-eyed, stumbled before the circulation returned properly to his legs.

'Thorowgood may have trouble seeing us, sir, in this light.'

'You have a talent for stating the obvious this morning,' snapped Drinkwater testily, 'let us see what Ashby does.'

Frey bit his lip and raised his speaking trumpet. 'Mr Belchambers!' he roared at the midshipman who paused, hanging down at the main upper futtocks. 'Get a move on, boy!'

As the morning advanced ship after ship hove over the southern horizon, the unmistakable sight of laden India-men running before the favourable trade wind. Far ahead of them they watched as Ashby's *Icarus* beat up towards a small, brig-rigged sloop-of-war, which was crowding on sail to intercept and identify the first of what must have seemed to her commander to be a naval squadron of potentially overwhelming force.

From aloft Belchambers passed a running commentary to the quarterdeck. 'Eighteen sail, sir ... The escort's a brig-sloop, sir ... looks to have a jury main topmast. No other escort in sight, but I can see *Sprite* coming up from the south-west, sir ...'

'What of *Cymbeline*?' Frey roared.

They saw Belchambers swivel round. 'She's coming up fast, sir, stun's'ls set alow and aloft!'

'I can see her from the deck, Mr Frey,' Drinkwater remarked.

After the private signals had been exchanged, the *Icarus* wore round in the brig's wake and the two men-of-war ran alongside each other. The brig then veered away from the thirty-two and the men now crowding *Patrician*'s deck saw her run down towards them.

'Heave to, if you please, Mr Frey,' Drinkwater ordered, rubbing his chin. 'I'm going below for a shave.'

'Aye, aye, sir,' Frey replied, grinning at the captain's retreating back. The sight of the East Indiamen, splendid symbols of their country's maritime might, transformed the morale of the *Patrician*. Idlers and men of the watch below had turned out to see the marvellous panorama; Frey could forgive the cross-patch Drinkwater, even provoke a grudging acknowledgement of his misjudgement from Mr Wyatt.

'Told you so, Wyatt,' Frey muttered, reaching for the speaking trumpet beside the master.

'You're right – for once.'

Frey grinned and raised the megaphone: 'Stand by the chess trees and catheads! Clew garnets and buntlines there! Rise tacks and sheets!'

'Three ships, you say, Lieutenant?' Drinkwater handed a glass to the young officer from the brig-of-war *Sparrowhawk*.

'Aye, sir, in two attacks . . .'

'And the last when?'

'The day before yesterday, sir. If the wind had been lighter we would have lost more, sir. As it was the India Johnnies gave a good account of themselves. We did our best but . . .' The young officer gestured hopelessly.

'You were outsailed by Yankee schooners.'

'Exactly so. Beg pardon, but how did you know, sir?'

'Intuition, Lieutenant . . .'

'Wykeham, sir.'

'Well, Lieutenant Wykeham, return to Captain Sudbury and tell him we shall do our best to assist you. Your ship is wounded?'

'Aye, sir, we lost the main topmast. One of those confounded Americans had a long gun, barbette-mounted amidships on a traversing carriage. She shot the stick clean out of us and hulled us badly. We lost four men with that one shot alone.'

'How many of them, enemy schooners, I mean?' Drinkwater wiped a hand across his face as if to remove his weariness.

'Six, sir,'

'Any sign of a frigate?'

'An American frigate? No, sir.'

Drinkwater grunted. 'Does Captain Sudbury anticipate another attack?'

'I don't think so, sir. We gave them a bloody nose last time. One of them was definitely hulled and with her rigging knocked about.'

'It doesn't occur to you that the hiatus may be due solely to their effecting repairs to that schooner?'

It had clearly not occurred to either Lieutenant Wykeham or his young commander, Sudbury.

'Young men are too often optimists, Mr Wykeham.' Drinkwater paused, letting this piece of homespun wisdom sink in. 'I have already given my squadron written orders as to their dispositions upon meeting with you. I think you had better cover the van of the convoy. Tell Captain Sudbury to act as he sees fit in the event of another attack, to throw out his routine convoy signals as has been his practice to date. My squadron will act according to their orders. However, I shall not condemn him if he gets his ship into action with one of these fellows. Tell him to aim high, langridge and bar shot, I think, if you have it, otherwise the galley pots and the carpenter's best nails, cripple' em, clip their confounded wings, Lieutenant, for they are better flyers then we.'

'Very well, sir.'

'By-the-by, in which direction did they retire?'

'To the east, sir, that is why we were . . .'

'To the east of the convoy, yes, yes, I understand. You had better return to your ship. Tell Captain Sudbury he is under my orders now and I relieve him of the chief responsibility, but I expect him to carry on as normal, entirely as normal, d'you see? Perhaps we may deceive the enemy, if he returns, into not noticing *our* presence until it is too late. D'you understand me?'

'Very well, sir.'

After the young man had gone, Drinkwater turned and stared astern. The sea, so lately empty of anything but his own squadron, was crowded with the black hulls and towering white sails of the Honourable East India Company's ships. Craning round, he could just see *Cymbeline* making her way to the windward station. Ashby should be doing the same on the other wing. Once Wykeham's boat had gone, *Patrician* must take up her own position.

There was no American frigate; not yet, anyway, Drinkwater mused. On the other hand, Wykeham had informed him that the last ship to be lost was the Indiaman

Kenilworth Castle and she had been carrying a fortune in specie.

It cost Drinkwater no great effort to imagine Captain Sudbury's mortification at losing three such valuable ships to the enemy; he had once been in the same position himself.*

In the right circumstances Indiamen could, and had, given the enemy a thrashing. An unescorted convoy of them under Commodore Nathaniel Dance had manoeuvred like men-of-war and driven off a marauding squadron of French ships under Admiral Linois eight years earlier. Their batteries of cannon were effective enough, if well handled, but they could not outmanoeuvre swift gaff-schooners stuffed with men spoiling to tweak the lion's tail and seize rich prizes to boot. During the following day Drinkwater pored over his charts, trying to divine what Stewart intended, for he was convinced Stewart commanded this aggressive group of letters-of-marque.

Stewart would come back, that much was certain, like a pack of hounds baying for more meat once the smell of blood was in their nostrils, but with one of his vessels damaged and three rich prizes to shepherd to safety.

Drinkwater considered the alternatives open to the enemy. Manning the prizes would not prove a problem. The privateers would have a surplus of men, indeed they signed on extra hands for the purpose, engaging prizemasters in anticipation of a profitable cruise. In all likelihood Stewart would gamble on another attack, cut out what he could, and then return triumphantly to the Chesapeake.

Drinkwater could recapture the *Kenilworth Castle* off the Virginia capes, but to act on that assumption would be dangerous. Now that he had encountered the convoy he could not so easily abandon it. Yet he was prepared to wager that if another attack was mounted it would argue cogently in favour of his theory; and if events fell out in

*See *A Private Revenge*.

this fashion a spirited pursuit had a good chance of recovering the lost ships.

It was true Baltimore clippers could outsail a heavy frigate, but the same frigate could outsail a laden India-man, and even a two-day start would make little difference.

'Sentry!' The marine's head peered round the door. 'Pass word for the midshipman of the watch.'

When Porter's red face appeared, Drinkwater said, 'Make *Sprite*'s number and have her close us.'

'Messages, sir?'

'Just so, Mr Porter.'

'Aye, aye, sir.'

Drawing pen, paper and ink towards him he began to draft new orders to his squadron.

Drinkwater's judgement proved uncannily accurate. Five jagged pairs of sails broke the eastern horizon two hours before sunset, an hour and a half after *Sprite* had delivered the last packet to *Cymbeline*. Thorowgood threw out the alarm signal without firing a warning gun, which proved he had digested his orders on receipt. *Patrician* had not yet made the acknowledgement before her marine drummer was beating to quarters and she was edging out of line, skittering laterally across the rear of the convoy, as, far ahead, Sudbury's little *Sparrowhawk* fired a warning gun and signalled the convoy to turn away from the threat. With luck, Drinkwater calculated, he could close the distance between himself and the point of attack as he had outlined to Wykeham. If he could trap any of the privateers within the convoy, hamper their manoeuvrability, he might . . .

He felt his heart thump uncomfortably in his chest. Already the sun was westering. He hoped the Americans could not see too well against the brilliant path it laid upon the sea . . .

'Steady, steady as you go,' Wyatt intoned, standing beside the men at the wheel, gauging distances as they lifted to a scending sea and threatened to overrun the plodding Indiaman, the *Indus*, upon whose quarter they sought to hide until the privateers singled out their quarry and struck. Two officers on the Indiaman's quarterdeck were regarding them, their attention clearly divided between the following frigate and the predatory Americans on their opposite bow. Wyatt turned to Drinkwater: 'We're overhauling, sir . . .'

'Let fly a weather sheet, or two. I want to cross under this fellow's stern in a moment, not across his bow.'

'Aye, aye, sir. Ease the fore an' main tops'l sheets there!'

'And start the foresheet . . .'

'Aye, aye, sir.'

It took a few moments for the adjustments to take effect, then *Patrician* slowed appreciably.

'What's Thorowgood doing, James, can you see him?'

Quilhampton was up on the rail, telescope levelled and braced against a shroud. 'Aye, sir. He's tucked in behind the *Lord Mornington* . . .' With his one hand Quilhampton deftly swivelled his glass at the schooners. 'They don't suspect a damned thing yet.'

'Perhaps they can't count.' Drinkwater looked at the setting sun. The privateers' strategy of attacking from the east allowed them to escape into the darkness, and silhouetted their victims against the sunset, but it made precise identification tricky. He hoped his frigates might be lost amid the convoy and thus steal a march upon the brash predators. The sooner they were occupied by the business of capture, the sooner he could attack.

From somewhere ahead a ragged broadside rumbled out.

'Deck there,' Belchambers hailed from his action station in the main-top, 'Indiaman has opened fire.'

'Can you see the *Sparrowhawk?*' Drinkwater called, levelling his own glass at the mass of sails ahead of them. Sudbury's little brig must be five or six miles away.

'Yes, sir, she's on the wind, starboard tack, just ahead of the eastern column.'

It was this column which was under attack and Sudbury was doing what was expected of him, attempting to cover his flank. His puny aggression was, however, being ignored by the Americans. The two leading schooners, the stars and bars streaming from their main peaks, huge

224

pennants bearing the words *Free trade and sailors' rights* flying from their mastheads, were coming down fast upon the third ship in the column, the *Lady Lennox.*

All the Indiamen in the eastern column were firing now, filling the air with dense clouds of powder smoke which trailed along with the ships, driven, like them, by the following wind. The approaching schooners shortened the range with the rapidity of swooping falcons, leaving alongside their respective wakes an impotent colonnade of water-plumes from plunging shot.

'Down helm, Mr Wyatt, let us try to keep those fellows in sight.'

In obedience to Drinkwater's order *Patrician*'s head swung slowly to starboard. From the quarterdeck the end of her jib boom seemed to rake the taffrail of the *Indus* as the heavy frigate edged out from the column of Indiamen.

'Haul aft those sheets,' Wyatt was calling. 'Steady there, steady . . .'

'Set stuns'ls, if you please, Mr Wyatt, and bring us back to the convoy's course,' Drinkwater ordered, keeping his voice measured, fighting the rising tension within.

With all her sails drawing again, *Patrician* increased her speed and began to overhaul the *Indus* on a parallel heading. Beyond the Indiamen and taking his cue from Drinkwater, Captain Thorowgood followed suit. *Cymbeline* made sail past the *Lord Mornington*, which ceased her own fire, and both frigates, in line ahead, the *Cymbeline* leading, bore down upon the enemy schooners, partially hidden in the pall of smoke drifting in dense wraiths about the convoy.

This smoke, which half-concealed their approach, also masked their quarry from them. The last glimpse Drinkwater had caught of the privateers had revealed the most advanced of the pair slipping under their chosen victim's stern preparatory to ranging up on the *Lady Lennox*'s port side, while her confederate did the same on the starboard beam.

The boom of a heavy gun floated over the water and Drinkwater recalled Wykeham's report of a traversing cannon mounted amidships in one of the schooners. The moment to press his carefully planned counter-attack had arrived.

He swung around. The remaining three corsairs were in the clear air to windward and astern of them, working round to the southward of the convoy.

'Where's *Sprite?*' he asked Quilhampton.

'There, sir!' Quilhampton pointed. In a gap between two Indiamen Drinkwater caught a glimpse of the British schooner beating up to place herself between three ships and the convoy. Sundercombe carried his little vessel into action with an apparent contempt for the odds against him.

'And there's *Icarus!*' Ashby's frigate was in silhouette. Only her foreshortening against the sunset as she swung identified her as a warship. Even as Drinkwater watched, the bulk of the *Lord Mornington* interposed itself as they swept past. He would have to depend upon Ashby's steadiness in support of Sundercombe to guard the convoy's rear.

'*Cymbeline*'s coming up alongside the outboard schooner, sir!' Quilhampton reported, his voice shrill with excitement, and Drinkwater whirled round.

They had dropped the *Lord Mornington* astern and were almost up with the *Windsor*, the East India Company ship next ahead of her and directly astern of the *Lady Lennox*. The *Windsor* was hauling her yards, a row of white-shirted lascars straining at the braces clearly visible, as she pulled to port to avoid the fracas erupting under her bow. She was also still firing her guns and these presented a greater threat to the overtaking *Patrician* than to the low, rakish schooners grappling her sister-ship ahead.

'Cease fire, damn you!' Drinkwater roared at the offending Company officers who turned in astonishment at the apparition looming out of the smoke astern. They must have been aware of *Cymbeline* overtaking them, but had clearly not seen *Patrician* coming up hand over fist in her wake.

'God damn, we've got 'em!' shouted Quilhampton jubilantly, dancing a jig on the rail and bringing a laugh from the men at the wheel and the quarterdeck guns whose comprehension of events was as confused as that of the officers of the *Windsor*. Drinkwater drew himself up in the mizen rigging to get a better view. The pall of smoke rolled slowly along with them, lifting like fog, but at sea-level it was clear and he could see the hull of yet another Indiaman, her name blazoned in gold letters across her stern below the windows of the great cabin which reflected the glory of the sunset: *Lady Lennox*. A schooner was fast to either of her sides like hounds on a stag's flanks, except that the privateer on the Indiaman's starboard beam was crushed between *Cymbeline*'s hull, and boarders were pouring down the frigate's tumblehome like a human torrent, the air full of their shouts and the spitfire flashes of small arms.

Even as Thorowgood's men scrambled down the side of their frigate to board the schooner, men from the second schooner to port were boarding the Indiaman.

'Mr Moncrieff!'

'Sir?'

'Your men to open fire on those boarders.'

'Aye, aye, sir!'

'What is it?' Drinkwater addressed Midshipman Porter, redder than usual from his run up from below.

'Mr Frey says the guns won't depress enough to hit the enemy, sir.'

'Boarders, Mr Porter, through the gun ports as soon as we're alongside.'

Beside him Moncrieff's marines jostled, levelling their muskets on the hammocks in the nettings, drawing back the hammers and flicking the frizzens. The air crackled with the vicious sputter of musketry and the solider boom of cannon as somewhere forward, in defiance of the laws of ballistics, several guns were fired. Amid the smoke and racket, Wyatt, Quilhampton, Moncrieff and Drinkwater bawled their orders as *Patrician* ranged up alongside her quarry.

'Douse the stuns'ls . . . rig in the booms and look lively there!'

'Steady, steady as you go . . .'

'Another point to starboard, Mr Wyatt, if you please. Crush 'em, damn it, and don't overrun her!'

'Aye, aye, sir!'

Drinkwater looked up, gauging the diminishing distance, before *Patrician*'s bulk sandwiched the Yankee schooner against the *Lady Lennox*. At the Indiaman's stern an American officer was hacking at the ensign halliards, the last rays of the sun flashing on the sword blade. He looked up, suddenly aware the ship bearing down on them from astern was not another Indiaman, as he had supposed, but a second British frigate. Drinkwater could clearly see him turn and bellow something, he even thought he caught the noise of his order above the shouts and screams and clash of steel. Moncrieff had seen the man too.

'Marine!' he bellowed, his face distorted by excitement, 'Hit that bastard beside the ensign halliards!'

'Yessir!'

There was a crash which sent a tremor through the *Patrician* as the big frigate's starboard bow drove into the larboard quarter of the American schooner and she ground her way past. The ebb and flow of men upon the *Lady Lennox* where American, Briton, lascar and Chinaman contended for the deck in a dozen desperate fights, seemed to freeze for a brief moment as the impact of the *Patrician*'s arrival made them stagger.

Into this mêlée Moncrieff's marines poured a withering fire. Drinkwater saw the man at the Indiaman's ensign halliards drop his sword, spin round and fall from sight. Men began sliding down the *Lady Lennox*'s side, Americans, Drinkwater guessed, trying to regain their own ship. Beyond the *Lady Lennox*'s farther rail, the bulk of the *Cymbeline* dominated the second schooner, invisible to Drinkwater's summary gaze. He looked down. The deck of the crushed schooner lay exposed, the caulking worming from her sprung deck planking, the long gun on its traversing mounting jammed as its crew fought to swing it round at the *Patrician*. With a thunderous crash the main and fore chain-whales gave way under the compression of the *Patrician*'s hull and the schooner's masts came down, a mass of spars, sails and cordage which obscured the marines' targets and hid the unfortunate Americans from their vengeful enemies.

From the gun ports below, like imps of hell intent on

228

some terrible harvest, dark shapes in the gathering shadows, the gun-crews squeezed through, dropping on to the schooner's decks. They rooted under the canvas with their pikes, savagely pitch forking at every movement in a wild catharsis of relief after weeks of fruitless cruising, venting pent-up emotions and repressed urges in an orgy of licensed butchery so that the schooner's deck assumed the bloody aspect of an ampitheatre of death.

The sight revolted Drinkwater and he picked up a speaking trumpet.

'D'you strike, there?' he shouted, 'Strike, sir, and put an end to this madness!'

A man, an officer by his torn blue coat and brass buttons that gleamed dully in the fading light, fought his way clear of the encumbering bunt of the huge mainsail and waved his hand. It was covered with blood which fell upon the canvas beside him. Drinkwater recognized him as the man who had, a few moments earlier, been on the point of hauling down the *Lady Lennox*'s ensign. Somehow he had regained his own deck under Moncrieff's murderous fire.

'Hold your fire, Moncrieff. Cease fire there, cease fire!'

The officer on the deck below him staggered and Drinkwater realized the schooner was sinking beneath his feet.

'Mr Q,' he called, 'have a boat lowered. Mr Davies is to take the survivors off, and pass word to the surgeon to expect some badly wounded. Mr Porter, recall your gunners before they lose their heads completely.' He raised the speaking trumpet again. '*Lady Lennox* 'hoy!'

An officer in the panoply of the Honourable East India Company appeared at the rail. 'Have you suffered much?' Drinkwater enquired.

'A score or so killed and twice as many wounded, mostly lascars and coolies, sir,' the officer said dismissively. 'We took round shot through the hull, but we can plug the holes.' Drinkwater recalled the heavy traversing cannon now hidden under the wrecked top-hamper of the schooner.

'What's the news from the starboard side?' Drinkwater called.

'Much the same. Your frigate's hauling off with the

enemy secured alongside. My commander, Captain Barnard, presents his compliments and his deepest sense of obligation to you, sir, and desires to know your name.'

'My respects to Captain Barnard, sir,' Drinkwater replied. 'My name is Drinkwater, Nathaniel Drinkwater, and I am glad to be of service.'

'You have saved the Company a fortune, Captain Drinkwater.'

'I am glad to hear it . . .'

'I know that man,' Moncrieff's voice suddenly announced, cutting through the calm that followed the surrender and the exchange between Drinkwater and the *Lady Lennox*'s officer. 'That fellow staring up at us; he was in the Potomac.'

Distracted, Drinkwater looked down again. The officer with the shattered hand was swaying, the stain of blood on the canvas beside him spreading darkly.

'God's bones,' Drinkwater blasphemed, 'get him aboard at once. It's Tucker!'

The Flying Squadron

'Who commands you?' Drinkwater asked. Ashen-faced, Lieutenant Tucker lolled in the chair, eyes closed, panting with pain. His roughly bandaged hand with a tourniquet above the wrist lay across his breast. Quilhampton stood anxiously at his shoulder.

It was growing dark in the cabin and other matters clamoured for attention as night fell. 'Come, sir, answer. You may see the surgeon the moment you have told me what I want to know. Who commands you?'

Eyes closed, Tucker shook his head. Drinkwater and Quilhampton exchanged glances. 'It's Stewart , isn't it, eh? Captain Stewart?' Drinkwater raised his voice, cutting through the fog of agony clouding Tucker's consciousness, 'late of the *Stingray*.'

Tucker's eyes flickered open; the small affirmative was enough for Drinkwater. 'Is there a frigate with you?'

There was no doubt, even in his befuddled state, of Tucker's surprise. 'Frigate . . .' he murmured, adding a second word that Drinkwater failed to catch.

'What did he say?'

'Didn't hear, sir, answered Quilhampton, bending over the prisoner.

'Come, sir, you're a damned pirate. You ain't a naval officer and can't expect exchange in a cartel. Answer me and I'll do my best to see you aren't thrown into Dartmoor Gaol. In the meantime you need the services of my surgeon. Is there a frigate in the offing? An American frigate?'

Something like comprehension passed a shadow over Tucker's face, he moved on the chair, tried to draw himself upright, shook his head and muttered, 'Not an American . . .'

'He said, "Not an American . . ."'

'I heard him, James . . . A *French* frigate, then? Is that it? There's a French frigate to the eastward?'

Tucker's face crumpled, he closed his eyes tightly, and sank into the chair. The bandages wrapped around his stump were sodden with blood.

'Good God!' Drinkwater ran a hand through his hair, ''Tis worse than I thought . . .' He looked up at Quilhampton. 'James, I'll stake my hat the lost Indiamen and a French frigate are to the eastward . . . I'll have to explain later. Be a good fellow and see to Tucker here.'

'I'll get him below, sir . . .'

'No, he's a brave fellow, we'll spare him the indignity of Pym's cockpit. Have Pym operate on him here.'

Drinkwater stood for a moment beside the wounded American and put a hand on his shoulder. 'You've betrayed nothing, Mr Tucker, I assure you, merely confirmed my suspicions. Mr Quilhampton will attend to you, he knows what it's like to lose a hand. Give him some laudanum, James, I fear I've used him barbarously.'

Running on deck Drinkwater cast a quick look about him. Night was upon them. The convoy was to the north-north-west, etched black against the last gleam of twilight. Both *Patrician* and *Cymbeline* had detached themselves from the convoy and lay hove-to in its wake. All that remained of the schooner *Patrician* had crushed was some wreckage, dark debris on the grey surface of the ocean. Thorowgood was busy putting a prize-crew aboard the other which, a master's mate in one of *Cymbeline*'s boats was just then reporting to Lieutenant Gordon, had proved to be the *Shark* of Baltimore.

'Tell Captain Thorowgood to rejoin the convoy with *Sprite* and his prize,' Drinkwater called down to the boat, 'I'm going in pursuit.'

Ashby and Sundercombe had ably covered the convoy's

rear. Discovering the force against them, the remaining privateers had not pressed their attack. They were making off in the darkness to windward as fast as they could with *Icarus* in lagging pursuit and *Sprite* hard on their heels, white blurs in the gathering night. Drinkwater waved the boat off and rounded on Wyatt.

'Set the stuns'ls, Mr Wyatt, and lay me a course to the eastward.'

'The eastward, sir?' Wyatt stared at the dull gleam of *Icarus*'s battle lantern to the southward.

'Yes, damn you, the *eastward*. Mr Gordon, make to *Icarus* and *Sprite*: discontinue the chase. The night signal, if you please.'

'Aye, aye, sir.'

Quilhampton hauled himself wearily up the quarter-deck ladder. He was aware he had misjudged Drinkwater.

'Well, James,' Drinkwater said briskly, 'I'm setting the kites.'

'You're going in pursuit, sir?' Quilhampton threw a bewildered look at the disparate heading of the schooners and *Patrician*. Wyatt gave a mighty shrug. Drinkwater laughed. His spirits were soaring. 'I'm after bigger fish than those minnows, James . . .'

'Tucker's frigate?'

'Tucker's frigate.'

'You're certain of her being there?'

'As certain of anything in this perilous life, James.'

'Sometime, sir, you might oblige me with an explanation.'

Drinkwater laughed again. 'The moment I'm proved right.' Tiredness and then the exhilaration of the last hours had raised Drinkwater's morale to a pitch of almost unbearable anticipation. 'Is Tucker being attended to?' he asked, in an attempt to recapture the dignity consonant with his rank.

'He's under Pym's knife at the moment, sir.'

'Pym's a good surgeon and Tucker looked to have the constitution of an ox.'

'Very well.'

The formal, non-commital response might have described them all. They had done very well. He was

233

ridiculously pleased he had harangued his captains. It was perhaps fortunate that their gunnery had not been tested, that they had confronted nothing more than privateers, but they had manoeuvred like veterans and he must remember to say so in his report to their Lordships. The escaping schooners were unlikely to return to harry the convoy; they had been thoroughly frightened. Guile and skilful ship-handling had brought the British a local ascendancy. Now, Drinkwater mused, they must hold the advantage surprise had conferred.

'Mr Wyatt!' Drinkwater beckoned to the master and he crossed the deck, expecting a rebuke. 'You did very well, Mr Wyatt. The ship was handled with perfect precision.'

'Thank you, sir,' Wyatt said smugly.

'I may need your skill again before dawn, Mr Wyatt. I am in quest of a frigate . . .'

'A frigate . . . ?' Wyatt's tone was incredulous in the dark.

'Not an American frigate, you'll be pleased to hear,' Drinkwater said ironically, 'at least, I hope not . . .' He was interrupted by a hail from the maintop:

'Deck there! I can see fire, fire on the larboard bow!'

'Ah,' sighed Drinkwater, 'ease the helm a half-point, Mr Wyatt. James, pipe up spirits, and then send the men back to their stations.'

An hour later they were approaching the source of the fire with every man at his station, and under fighting sails.

'Ease the helm another point, Mr Wyatt. Let us drop a little to loo'ard and cut off their retreat.' The dull glow of the fire opened on the starboard bow, allowing a better view from the quarterdeck. Their approach, concealed by darkness, was slow enough for Drinkwater, studying the dispositions of a number of vessels clustered about and illuminated by the burning Indiaman, to deduce the gist of what was happening.

'They have very likely spent the day transhipping what they wanted out of the Indiaman they have fired,' he explained to Quilhampton, as both men stood side by side, their telescopes braced against the mizen rigging. 'You can see the schooner which was mauled by *Sparrow-hawk* . . .'

'She's lying alongside another East India Company ship,' observed Quilhampton.

'It looks as though they used her mainyard as mast-sheers, they've got what looks like two handy spars back in that schooner already,' he said admiringly.

'There's another ship, looks like an Indiaman, though she could be your frigate, just to the left; d'you see?'

Drinkwater shifted his glass. 'Yes. They're waiting for the schooners to come back with another prize, I think. One of those two will be the *Kenilworth Castle*. She's carrying specie.'

'Didn't that Company Johnnie indicate the *Lennox* was similarly loaded?' Quilhampton asked, catching something of his commander's excitement.

'Indeed he did,' Drinkwater said with a sudden, tense deliberation which made Quilhampton lower his glass, look at Drinkwater and then smartly raise it again.

There was no mistaking the ship that now came into view. Hidden from them at first by the glow of the burning Indiaman, her lower hull was concealed, her tall masts indistinguishable behind the mass of the Indiaman's top-hamper up which the flames were now racing as the fire took a hold. The sudden flaring of the gigantic torch lit up all within its illuminating circle.

Quilhampton gave a low whistle. 'There's your French frigate, sir.'

Patrician was directly downwind of the group now, and a wave of warm air drifted towards them. A dull crackling roar could be heard, borne on the trade wind. The French frigate was hove to, like the Indiamen, under a backed main topsail, drifting slowly past the burning ship from which a cloud of sparks suddenly shot upwards. Concealed from the American and French allies busy at their mid-ocean rendezvous by the utter darkness beyond the range of their bonfire, *Patrician* slipped past unobserved, a mile to the north of them.

'I'm going about in a moment or two, gentlemen,' Drinkwater announced to the officers assembled on the quarterdeck. 'When I have done so we will engage the Frenchman from windward. Starboard battery to open fire. We shall have to watch that burning Indiaman, but

235

his windage is being fast consumed and the others are making greater leeway, increasing the distance between them. I will then attempt to rake . . .'

'Sir!' Gordon was pointing; a moment later the concussion of cannon-fire rolled over the water.

'They've seen us . . .' someone said.

'No they haven't,' shouted Moncrieff, 'they're firing away from us . . .'

'What the devil . . . ?'

'It isn't them firing, it's *Icarus*!'

'Hands to tack ship!' Drinkwater roared, 'By God we've got 'em! Take post, gentlemen, upon the instant if you please!'

There was a bustling aboard the *Patrician*, as the officers dispersed to their stations. The men, watching the conflagration in ordered silence, suddenly tensed. They were no longer observers, now they were to participate.

'Mainsail haul!' Wyatt shouted, 'Leggo and haul . . . haul aft the lee sheets, stretch those bowlines forrard now! Keep your eyes inboard and attend to your business!'

'*Icarus* must have mistaken your signal, sir.'

'Aye, we never thought to look astern in our conceit, did we?'

'I doubt we'd have seen her . . . there she is . . . she's got *Sprite* under her lee bow. Ashby must have assumed he was to follow us.'

'Perhaps it was no bad assumption and, damn it, I bet it fooled the buggers – the two of 'em look like a Yankee clipper and a captured Indiaman!'

Icarus could be seen clearly now looming on the edge of the firelit circle, hauling up her fore and mainsail, shortening down to fighting sail as she came up with less caution than Drinkwater's *Patrician*. A broadside rippled along her side, the brilliance of the gun's discharges bright points in the night, though they could see nothing of the fall of the shot.

'Bring her round a little more to starboard, Mr Wyatt. Let us see if we can add to the confusion.'

Slowly *Patrician* swung and gathered way as she came off the wind. With the burning Indiaman, now almost reduced to a hulk, the other ships were drifting away fast.

At any moment *Patrician* herself would come between them and the blaze, revealing her presence.

Midshipman Porter bobbed close to Drinkwater, his red face ruddier in the glow. 'Mr Gordon's compliments and the starboard chase guns will bear.'

'Very well, Mr Porter, you may tell Mr Gordon to fire at will, but to have every gun-captain lay his piece carefully. I want no noisy, ineffectual broadsides.'

'Aye, aye, sir.'

'The frog's making sail, sir.' They were too late for complete surprise. Someone aboard the French frigate had seen *Patrician* and she was hauling her backed main yards and letting fall her lower canvas. Just then the first of Gordon's 24-pounders roared, followed by a second and a third. A cheer went up from the waist and Quilhampton bellowed for silence.

'He's going to rake Ashby, by God!' Moncrieff called, but Drinkwater had already seen Ashby's dilemma and watched as he threw his helm over, attempting to swing round on to a parallel course to the Frenchman and trade broadside for broadside.

'He's no fool,' Drinkwater muttered admiringly of the French commander. The broadside itself was hidden from them, but they saw the impact clearly on the *Icarus*, even in the dark, for she rolled in the swell as she turned and the pale rectangle of her fore topsail became first a triangle, then ceased to exist as her foremast crashed to the deck.

'Firing high, by God, he's goin' to run!'

Bright pin-points, like two blinking cat's eyes, sparked from the Frenchman's stern. A column of water rose up close to *Patrician*'s starboard bow and a crash from forward, followed by the murderous whirr of flying splinters, told where a shot had struck home.

'He's firing his stern chasers, sir.'

'I can see that, Mr Q. Mr Wyatt, lay me a course to pass close to *Icarus*, I wish to speak to Ashby and it will at least give us a chance to get a broadside in at that fellow.'

The blazing Indiaman was broad on their larboard beam and dropping astern. The French frigate was making off to the north, leaving the remaining Indiaman and the schooner to their fate. *Sprite* had worn round under *Icarus*'s stern and was engaging the jury-rigged schooner.

'Good man, Sundercombe,' Drinkwater muttered, seizing the speaking trumpet as they bore down on the *Icarus*. Men were swarming on her forecastle and he could see the glimmer of lanterns as they sought to clear away the tangle of fallen gear. Drinkwater leapt up on the rail, clasping the mizen rigging with one hand and the speaking trumpet with the other.

'*Icarus* ahoy Captain Ashby . . .'

'Sir?'

'Secure what you can here. Those are two captured Indiamen, by the way, with prize-crews aboard. Then rejoin the convoy. Keep *Sprite* under your orders. I'm going in pursuit of that frigate.'

'He's a Frenchman, Captain Drinkwater, did you know?'

'Yes. Are you manageable?'

'Aye, I've a forecourse, I think . . .'

'Good luck.'

'And you.'

They waved, their ships rolling in the swell, and Wyatt brought *Patrician* on to a course parallel with the retiring French frigate. She was ahead and to starboard of the British ship and both had the fresh trade wind blowing on their starboard quarters.

'It's going to be a long night, James,' Drinkwater remarked.

'It's already nearly ten,' Quilhampton said after consulting his watch.

'Moonrise in three hours.'

They set every stitch of canvas the spars could stand, started the mast wedges and ran preventer stays up to the topmast caps, setting them up with luff tackles. Never had the *Patrician*'s crew been so hard driven since, those who remembered it afterwards claimed, they had been in the Pacific. There was, Drinkwater knew, little doubt of the outcome if the masts and spars and canvas and cordage stood the strain. The French frigate was a fast ship, but slightly smaller than the British, of a lighter build and, though well handled, unable to match the hardiness of her pursuer. *Patrician* was a *razée*, a cut-down sixty-four gun line-of-battle ship, heavy, but able to stand punishment and, in a strengthening wind, in her element with a quartering sea. Moonrise found the distance between the two ships significantly lessened. Patches of cloud came and went across the face of the full moon, adding to the drama and excitement of the night, and periodically Lieutenant Gordon, pointing the guns himself, tried a shot at the enemy's top-hamper, seeking to cripple him as he fled.

And periodically too, the enemy fired back, though both commanders knew the issue would not be so easily settled, that their scudding ships, heeling and scending under their press of sail, were uncertain gun-platforms, that the angle between them was too fine for more than a lucky shot to tell, and that either luck on the part of one, or disaster for the other, would bring the matter to a conclusion before daylight.

Luck, it seemed, first favoured the French. A shot from a quarter gun struck *Patrician*'s waist, felling an entire gun's crew with a burst of lacerating splinters, sending men screaming like lunatics in antic dances of pain and killing three men outright. A second shot struck *Patrician* just below the starboard fore chains, carrying away a stay-rod. But for the preventer rigged an hour earlier, the shroud above might have parted and the entire foremast gone by the board. As it was the carpenter was able to effect repairs of a kind. Half an hour later a third shot hulled the pursuing British frigate and she began taking water. Once again the carpenter and his mates were summoned. They plugged the shot hole and the pumps were manned, but it shook the Patricians' confidence and the men murmured at their inability to hit back.

'I wonder if Metcalfe would have managed anything?' Moncrieff superciliously asked no one in particular. 'He *was* a damned good shot . . .'

The remark provoked in Drinkwater's mind's eye an image of Thurston falling from the rigging, which was so vivid he started and became aware he had been half-asleep on his feet. 'Metcalfe . . . ?' he said, stupidly and shaken, 'Oh, yes, he was, wasn't he . . .'

'He's done it!' Quilhampton's cry was echoed round the ship. Gordon had fired his foremost gun, loaded with bar shot, as the *Patrician*'s stern had fallen into a trough. The rising bow had thrown the shot high, almost too high. But the crazy, eccentric hemispheres had, with the aid of centrifugal force, extended the sliding bars and the spinning projectile had struck the enemy's fore topgallant mast. For a moment the pallid oblongs of its two sails leaned, suspended in a web of rigging, flogging as the wind caught their underbellies, and then they sagged slowly downwards.

Patrician closed on her quarry; after hours of seeming inactivity her quarterdeck was again seething with officers bawling orders.

'Lay her alongside, Mr Wyatt, and shorten sail. Don't overshoot.'

They were too late for such precise niceties of manoeuvring, the night had grown too wild and they were too tired for fine judgement. *Patrician* overran the French ship, loosing off a rolling broadside and receiving fire in return. The British gunners, so long inactive, with news of the fallen topgallant to cheer them, poured more fire into the enemy. On board the Frenchman, the gunners served their cannon gallantly, but the chaos of fallen spars which just then broke free of the restraints of the upper rigging and crashed down through the boat booms, caused their rate of response to slacken as they confronted blazing gun-muzzles forty yards from their ports.

'Let fly sheets! Let her head fall to starboard! Stand by, boarders!'

The two ships closed, the *Patrician* slightly ahead. Between them the water ran black and silver where the moonlight caught it. The slop and hiss as the outward curling bow waves met and intermingled threw spray upwards to reflect the stabbing glare of the gunfire. The night was full of noise, of wind in rigging, of rushing water, of the cheers and shrieks and shouts of four hundred men, the concussions of their brutal cannon and the stutter of Moncrieff's marines as their muskets cleared the way for the mustering boarders.

'He shows no inclination to edge away,' Quilhampton

240

called, drawing his sword, and then the night was split by a
man's voice, a bull-roar of defiance:

'What ship is that?'

'That's no frog . . .' Quilhampton began.

'No, I know,' Drinkwater moved to the rail and leaned
over the hammock netting.

'His Britannic Majesty's frigate *Patrician*, Nathaniel
Drinkwater commanding. Is that you, Captain Stewart?'

'Aye . . . how in hell's name . . . ?'

Stewart's voice was drowned in the discharge of Gordon's starboard battery. 'Fate,' Drinkwater muttered as he
turned. 'Pass word to Frey to have his larbowlines ready to
board. Now, Mr Wyatt, lay us alongside.'

'Aye, aye, sir!'

'Come, James, death or glory, eh?' Drinkwater said,
sensing the puzzlement in Quilhampton by the odd stance
of the one-armed officer. He drew his sword. The gap
between the two ships closed and then they collided.
Drinkwater clambered up on the rail, fighting to get his
legs over the hammock nettings and gauge when to leap.
He dropped into the mizen chains. Below him the bulging
topsides of the ships ground together, their rails separated only by the extent of the rounded tumblehome. A
quarterdeck 18-pounder went off beside him. He was
deafened and the heat seared his stockings. He remembered he had forgotten to change his clothes before going
into action, as was customary. If he was wounded, his dirty
linen might infect him.

The two ships rolled inwards, the gap narrowed and he
flung himself across. A hemp shroud struck him, he
grabbed it with his left hand, felt his right foot land on
something solid and he steadied. Momentarily he paused,
balancing, then gathered himself and leapt down on to the
enemy's deck. Off balance he stumbled, a lunging pike
missed him and he recovered his footing in time to parry a
cutlass slash. He seemed surrounded by figures menacing
him in a terrible surreal silence. The moonlight gleamed
on naked steel, a pistol flashed noiselessly, then another
and he was surrounded by struggling men. Slowly his
hearing returned as he hacked and slithered, hardly
knowing friend from foe. A sword blade struck his right

241

epaulette and sent half a dozen heavy gold threads past his ear. He cut savagely at his assailant and felt his sword blade bite. A cry, distinct now, struck his ears. He heard again shouts and whoops, the bitter supplications of the dying and the raving of men engaged in murder. He felt the weight of his anonymous attacker roll against his legs. In a split-second of detachment he thought: 'Christ, this is a sin mightier than lying with Mistress Shaw,' and then he heard the bull-roar again.

'Captain Drinkwater. Where in the devil's name are you?'

'Here, damn you! Here!'

Why had he not held his tongue? Why had he identified himself so that, it seemed to him, even in the confusion the contending parties drew apart, exposing him to Stewart?

But Stewart had seen Drinkwater jump aboard and had kicked or thrust aside those of his friends obstructing his passage. He bore a cavalry sabre and whirled it down in a slashing cut. Drinkwater drew back and lunged over the top of Stewart's extended arm. The tip of his hanger caught the American's right bicep, though it failed to penetrate. Stewart recovered and sought to riposte, but the darkness and the confusion helped neither man. Drinkwater was jostled aside. A small, wiry man advanced on Stewart. He was inside the American officer's guard in a second, his tomahawk raised. The weapon caught the moonlight as it fell.

'No!' Drinkwater roared, but he was too late. The sabre fell to the deck and Stewart stood swaying, the dark blood gushing from his neck. 'Caldecott,' Drinkwater cried in recognition, and his coxswain turned. Just then the moon came clear of the clouds and illuminated the baleful scene. Caldecott's face was a mask of hatred. His teeth were drawn back in a snarl, his eyes glittered with a feral madness as he sought another victim. Appalled, Drinkwater stepped aside, let him pass, and then with a groan Stewart fell against him. Drinkwater let go his hanger and it dangled from its martingale. He grabbed the falling Stewart, felt the dead weight of him as his head lolled back, the mouth agape.

242

Drinkwater stood in the moonlight and held Stewart in his arms as the American died. His mind was filled with the thoughts of the likeness Stewart bore to his sister, and he was sickened to his soul. Mercifully a cloud obscured the moon and the noise of fighting drowned the howl of his anguish.

'How are you, sir?'

'Oh, well enough, James. It was only a scratch or two, you know.'

'Pym said you were lucky ...'

'Pym talks a lot of nonsense. How's Tucker?'

'The fever broke last night. He's weak, but will mend.'

'For God's sake, tell Pym not to bleed the poor devil.'

'I doubt he'll take my advice ...'

'Pour yourself a glass and sit down. I'll have one too, if you please.'

Drinkwater swung round and stared astern. The convoy was in good order, the recaptured Indiamen in their places, the prizes secure in the centre of the mass of ships. He had left a brace of Yankee schooners at large in the South Atlantic, but, under the circumstances, he did not think they would pose a great threat now the East India convoy was safe. He took the glass Quilhampton handed him. 'I believe I owe you an explanation ...' Drinkwater smiled over the rim of his glass.

'I confess to still being a little mystified, particularly about *Sybille* and this fellow Stewart you mentioned ...'

'I didn't *know* about *Sybille*, James, I guessed. Oh, I had some clues, some evidence to suppose, were I in the same position, I would do the same thing ...'

'I understand about the privateers seeking to waylay the East India fleet. The French have done it before, it is an obvious move, but there was something else, wasn't there?'

'You may have heard stories, James, about my excursion in *Sprite* to the Potomac. I went to contact a woman, a potential source of intelligence. Ah, I see by your face you have heard ...'

'Well, there *were* some rumours, sir.'

'There are always rumours aboard ship,' Drinkwater went on, unaware of Quilhampton's relief at learning his friend's liaison with the American lady had so rational an explanation after the innuendoes he had heard. 'She was able to give me certain information about Captain Stewart which confirmed what I had already guessed and deduced from information I had gleaned from Stewart and what I had been told in London.

'There was something about Stewart, whom I had met earlier, when *Patrician* was in the Potomac, before you joined us. I had a feeling about him; he practically challenged me, an odd notion unless one nursed a secret in which one had a great deal of confidence. Then luck threw something my way, quite by chance and so circumstantial that I did not know what it was until I recalled the matter much later. The woman dwelt in her father-in-law's house. His name was Shaw. When I first met him, Shaw was a veritable cooing dove, opposed to war. A day later, when we met in different circumstances and I needed his help, he seemed to have cooled. When I left you and shipped in the *Sprite*, I returned as you now know to contact the woman, Captain Stewart's sister and Shaw's daughter-in-law. I saw old Shaw working on some papers. I was at the time apprehensive at the prospect of shinning up a drain pipe at my time of life and chiefly concerned with avoiding detection. I think, having been rebuffed by Shaw, I was instinctively suspicious of him. I didn't take much notice at the time and it was only weeks afterwards that I remembered what I had seen through a crack in the curtains . . .'

'Well, sir?'

'One draught of a sheer-plan, one chart and three or four sheets of paper that looked like accounts. I was quite unaware that Shaw had an intimate knowledge of nautical matters and it suddenly struck me the chart was of Brest.'

Quilhampton was frowning, then he shrugged and waited for Drinkwater to supply the explanation.

'You see, James, the Americans have plenty of men, trained naval officers like Stewart and Tucker plus their own considerable mercantile marine to draw from. Their problem is insufficient naval vessels. I stumbled on the first part of their strategy after we encountered the whaler, *Altair*. The news her master, Orwig, brought of an

244

American frigate at large made me realize the Americans could increase the size of their fleet at a stroke by operating their own flying squadrons of a heavy frigate and a swarm of Baltimore schooners, d'you see?'

'Aye, by heaven, I do . . .'

'Then, when we interrogated Tucker, he mentioned a *French* frigate in the offing and I began to consider the implications of a revival of the old alliance, a combination of American seamen manning French-built ships. You may not be aware, James, but the French and their allies, in every suitable port between the Baltic and the Mediterranean, have been building men-o'-war of every class, including ships-of-the-line. If such ships ever got to sea and combined with additional flying squadrons of these damnable frigates and schooners . . .'

'They would have had us by the throat,' Quilhampton said in a tone of appalled wonder and growing comprehension. 'And was this all to be paid for by John Company's profits from India and China?'

Drinkwater nodded, 'I believe so . . .'

'It's a diabolically clever notion,' Quilhampton said appreciatively, then frowned. 'What was Shaw's part in all this?'

'No more than a hook upon which my suspicions were obstinately pegged. Like Stewart, I couldn't get rid of the notion of the fellow. Shaw was obviously tied up with American diplomacy and foreign policy by his very solicitude for Vansittart and the fact that Stewart had us anchor in the Potomac. Then there were those papers and so forth. Finally . . .' Drinkwater tapped a sheaf of documents lying on the table behind him, 'there was Stewart aboard a French frigate in the South Atlantic after a mid-ocean rendezvous, with this bundle weighted about his waist. No wonder the poor fellow succumbed to Caldecott's tomahawk.'

'The papers implicate Shaw?'

'Yes, he was, as it were, the broker between the French and the Americans. In concert with the French invasion of Russia the consequences of the success of this joint venture are not to be contemplated.'

'It would have compelled us to raise the blockade of

Europe and let the French fleet out . . .'

'It really doesn't do to think of such an eventuality,' said Drinkwater, suppressing a shudder. 'Come, fill your glass again.'

He had not told Quilhampton the whole story, but enough of it to make sense. Besides, how could he tell his friend of what he had learned from Arabella in her boudoir, another Parisian dress discarded on her bed, that curious moment of reticence followed by her wholesale condemnation of men and their scheming? Was that why providence had made them lovers, so he might divine these things? He threw aside the thought, discarded it with the sense of relief flooding through him. He smiled at Quilhampton.

'I make you a toast, James: to the ladies.'

'God bless 'em!'

'Johnnie? Can you hear me?'

Lord Moira bent over the man in the sick-bed. The grossness had fallen away, leaving a face that seemed twenty years younger but for the yellow pallor of approaching death.

'Frank, is that you?' Lord Dungarth opened his eyes.

'Yes. How are you today?'

'As you see, failing fast . . .'

'Come, you mustn't give up hope.'

'Damn it, Frank, don't cozen me. The quacks will kill me with their nostrums and leeches quicker than this damned distemper. I'm as good as dead.' Dungarth paused, catching his breath. 'Listen, there's something I want you to do for me.' He raised a trembling hand to his throat. The skin was translucent, the blood vessels below, ribbed and dark, writhing over the stretched tendons. Parting his nightshirt, Lord Dungarth withdrew a key, suspended from his neck by a thin black ribbon. 'Help . . . me.' He gasped with the effort.

Moira assisted Dungarth to raise his head and eased the ribbon over the bald skull.

'It is the key to my desk at the Admiralty. You are to make sure Captain Drinkwater receives it. Upon your word of honour, d'you understand?'

'Upon my word, Johnnie, I promise.'

Dungarth sighed and sank back on to his pillow. 'What news of the French?'

'The Russians are approaching the Rhine and Wellington the Pyrenees.'

'And from America?'

'Not so good . . .'

'Is there news of Drinkwater yet?' Dungarth broke in
feebly.

'We shall learn something in a few days,' Moira disem-
bled.

'I shan't last a few days, but he's the man, Frank. He has
the ability . . . the *nous*.'

Despite himself, Moira smiled at the use of the Greek
word, then wondered if the man Drinkwater, in whom
Dungarth had such faith, really had the intuition his
friend thought. A diseased man was, in Moira's experience, no very reliable judge.

'Tell him about the bookseller in the Rue de'laaah . . .'
Pain distorted Dungarth's face. Moira reached for the
bottle beside the bed and poured the neat laudanum
drops into a tumbler of water.

'Here, old fellow,' he said, putting an arm about Dungarth and lifting his shoulders. With his other hand he
held the glass to his friend's lips.

'You still pull strings, then?' Moira said admiringly.

'To the end, *mon ami*, to the end the puppet-master.
Don't forget Drinkwater . . .' Dungarth whispered as his
eyes closed. 'Your word upon it, Frank, your word . . .'

Author's Note

The depredations of privateers are largely unrecorded in purely naval histories, but 'letters-of-marque and reprisal' were issued in copious numbers by both the French and American governments at this time. Indeed, most American merchant ships carried them, so the distinction between the dedicated privateer and the opportunist cargo-carrier is somewhat blurred. However, the astonishing successes of the corsairs in the war against British trade were far from insignificant and the most interesting of the vessels used by the Americans was the Baltimore clipper schooner which possessed a revolutionary new hull form, with hollow entry and run, the antithesis of the frigates and sloops sent against them. Nevertheless, many were captured and, like the fast French frigates before them, adopted and copied by the Royal Navy.

The lengths to which the British went to keep Wellington's army in the Iberian peninsula supplied were often devious. American traders were quite happy to supply both sides, no matter their government was at war with one of them. Much of the investment available for the later expansion of nineteenth-century America originally came from this source.

Napoleon assiduously worked on an American rupture with Great Britain, seeking to embroil his implacable enemy with an opponent who had designs on Canada and posed a very real threat at sea.

Henry Vansittart is my own invention, though a King's

messenger was sent to Washington at the time Drinkwater first arrived in the Potomac. The surplus of American naval officers is also a fact; many brilliant young men were unable to find employment in naval vessels and were driven, like Stewart, to find other ways of demonstrating the fervour of their patriotism.

The value of the frigate actions between the Royal and United States navies was much exaggerated and had little real effect. In America they provided the foundation for a tradition of glory; in Britain they were taken as a sign that the Royal Navy was in decline. The Americans assumed that, like schoolboys with a triumphant conker, the victor accrued to itself the triumphs of its victim. This was plainly nonsense. The value of a navy rests on its strategic power and the fate of its individual parts is only significant if it materially affects this. The Royal Navy suffered such damage in the early years of the Second World War, not between 1812 and 1814. The defeat of a handful of British cruisers did not diminish the great and wearying achievement of continental blockade and when this was extended to America, the balance swung back in favour of the British. Nevertheless, it rattled the British public at the time, and was thought to be of greater importance than the destruction of the Grand Army in the cold of a Russian winter.